Sala

at the

Bad Café

Helene Parry

ISBN: 978-1-326-11829-7

PublishNation, London
www.publishnation.co.uk

To Graham Clinton
who died June 11th 2014.

And to Richard Nye,
who thought this should be published.
All complaints to him, please.

1.

Keeping Up With Half The Valleys Phone Book

"To take with me:

Tea bags. Screwdriver. Pyjamas.

Luchwen for making Welsh cakes, also for brandishing at people who snigger if They beat Us at the Millennium Stadium next March.

Adaptor.

Dictionary (until my French gets fluent)."

I looked up, but I might have been speaking that fluent French for all the interest they showed. The three of them were sitting there, listless. Despite my list.

"Suitcase," I added.

The back page of the *South Wales Echo* rippled with indignation. "There's no need for silliness," came Dad's voice from behind it. "And there's no need for you to go abroad at all. Young girls, roaming about the countries…" His disapproving tone made it plain he considered foreign travel by females under retirement age to be the root cause of most of society's ills.

Griff, my brother, rolled his eyes. "How do you expect Holly to get her degree if she doesn't do her year abroad?" He glared at the *Echo*, which remained impervious where a lesser paper would have crumpled. "Where's she going to learn to speak French in this town? At the Co-op, reading the labels on the bags of croissants?"

"The Cwarp hasn't got any cross ants in, at the moment," said Mam, helpfully. "I had a look, this morning."

Griff looked almost as cross as the ants. Before he could bite back, Mam turned to me: "And you've started packing a bit smart. The college haven't even told you where they'm sending you yet."

"The college doesn't know," I recited. "The college has sent my application to the people who organise these exchanges. Everyone in

1

my class had to apply. It's the exchange people who decide which part of France you're sent to, and which school you'll be teaching in."

I was beginning to sound like one of our university language lab tapes. We'd been over this a dozen times since I'd first broken the news that I was going to have to spend a year in France, working as an English language assistant, as the third year of my degree course. But Mam and Dad still couldn't cope with it. They'd been proud enough when I'd been accepted at university - Dad had had visions of me drilling the Valley schoolchildren in their three times table, or one day, making deputy supervisor in Pontycynon steelworks' typing pool. But when they'd found out the course included a year abroad, they'd decided Higher Education was the route of all evil.

I think if Dad had realised that the French lessons I'd started aged eleven would lead to such depravity, he'd have had the school bus clamped. He didn't like the thought of me crossing the Bristol Channel, let alone the English one.

"Not much shape on that college." This was Dad's well-honed critique of the university's administrative system. "They ought to have wrote to you by now with the name of the school. Then we could have found you some people to stay with, nearby."

Griff's voice could have drawn blood. "Why would the college need you to arrange this one?" He paused, then delivered what Mam would have called the *Cwarp de grâce*. "You've never even been to France."

"Neither have Holly," pointed out Mam. The familiar crease appeared in her forehead. "And how are you going to teach English to French schoolchildren? You've never taught a class in your life."

It was a question I'd been asking myself, but I wasn't going to admit that. "How hard can it be?" I asked. "There are websites with lesson plans, and film clips to play in class."

Mam sniffed. "But the school will have a French computer. As well as them squat toilets. I bet a pound you'll be home by Christmas."

I was stung. How dare she assume I wouldn't last three months abroad? "Actually, I'm planning to stay in France for the whole year," I announced. "I'd like to spend Christmas and Easter over there." I remembered flicking through library copies of *Paris-Match*. "They have oysters for Christmas dinner, not turkey. And they have their big meal on Christmas Eve - it's called the *réveillon*. It lasts for about eight courses."

Mam snickered. "You'll be taking up two seats on the Eurostar."

I bridled. Mam had a knack of going below the belt. As did most of the meals I ate between snacks. Instinctively, I pulled my T-shirt down to hide my stomach.

"I wouldn't blame you if you stayed in France for Christmas, Holly," remarked Griff. "More fun than being here with these two, listening to Dad's chesty cough. Although you'd miss the street's annual blackout when he plugs the tree lights in."

"Don't be so whass'name," grumbled Mam. "And we're not getting a tree this Christmas. Last year, I asked you to fetch one from over town, and you made out you'd strained your elbow at the office party. It was me that had to carry the bucket up Watkins the builder's, and hoik it home, full of sand." She looked suitably wounded at the memory.

"Oh, no tree this year, is it?" jeered Griff. "That's a new one. It used to be: 'You two'll get a lump of coal in your Christmas stockings.'"

"I wish I'd done it," grumbled Mam. "You might have more respect for your mother."

Griff raised his eyebrows. "I'd certainly respect someone who'd climbed down a closed shaft to excavate two lumps from an empty seam."

The *Echo* rustled menacingly. I got up. "Let's have a cuppa. Griff?" To my relief, Griff not only rose and followed me, he didn't even slam the kitchen door behind us.

"They haven't got a clue," grumbled Griff, twisting an innocent teacloth to within an inch of its life. "But don't let them get to you. You've got a chance to go somewhere, do something. I'd go for it."

I hid a smile. One of my childhood memories starred Griff, stamping on the Ker-Plunk box in frustration at the death rattle of marbles cascading into his tray. Still, I was touched. He'd gone straight from school into his clerical job, no further than a bus ride from home. Now he was watching his little sister packing for reckless adventure on the Continent. In a surge of affection, I filled his Newport County mug first.

By the time we brought the tea in, Mam and Dad were cackling. "I've got a bone to pick with you," Dad told me, holding up a hardback book. "Just found this behind my cushion. Dug into my back, it did. I thought it was your mother's lump of coal."

I took the book. Its title stared up at me. *Improve Your Memory*.

"Memory be blowed," chuckled Dad. "It was due back yesterday."

I checked the flyleaf. "Oh, no. I'd better get up the Tower."

"But they'll be closed," said Mam. "That Mrs Whipple's always out on the stroke of five. And late opening, in the mornings, 'cos she do stop at the bakery first. She've had all the ice slices by the time I get there. And then your father creates" - she frowned at him - "when we have Welsh cakes for tea instead."

Dad hadn't looked so pained since the time he'd got his big toe stuck in the fireguard. "I told you, I don't see a lot in them old Welsh cakes," he defended himself.

"Yes," shot back Mam. "After we'd been married thirty years." She turned to me. "It's ridiculous, isn't it? Stuffing yourself with sweet things, then saying you've got to watch your figure."

I looked at Dad, surprised. I'd never heard him fret about his weight, whatever Mam served for afters. Mind, that was probably because he usually had his mouth full at the time.

Mam warmed to her theme. "Parading about, dressed like a teenager. Coming out, like that, when you're over fifty."

Griff and I exchanged horrified glances. Coming out? Were there other, darker secrets Dad had closeted from us for the whole of his married life?

"Mam?" I hesitated. "How do you mean - Dad - coming out?"

"Not *him*." Mam was scornful. "That Mrs Whipple. She's in her sixties and she still dresses like Cher. Can't leave her house without showing her knickers."

Relief flooded me. Now we wouldn't be a shattered family, crushed beneath the debris of our broken home.

Mam's cup clattered into her saucer. "And she keeps you waiting at the counter while she's fiddling with her bangles."

"I don't see you wearing that chain I bought you in Twickenham," said Dad, unexpectedly. "I had to queue half-hour in the shop to get it. Nearly missed kick-off."

Mam flared up. "What do I want to wear jewellery for? When do we ever go anywhere?" She pointed a suitably underdressed finger at Dad. "I haven't forgotten the birthday you bought me a mousetrap."

"And we've never seen you wearing that, either," said Griff.

I suppressed a giggle. Mam was saddling up her high horse. I decided to make my escape before she brought up the Great Fridge Defrosting Nastiness of 1983. I reached for my jacket. "Doesn't matter if the library's shut. Lin will let me in."

Mam was intrigued. "What will she be doing there, if they'm closed?"

I leaned over her and hissed: "Opening a bottle of gin. They keep one behind the Maeve Binchy hardbacks."

"Oh, go on with you." Mam pushed me away, clearly tickled at the thought of a secret cache of liquor behind the Binchies. "Drinking in the library. The council will be having you."

"Oh, the gin's not for drinking," said Griff. "It's for cleaning Mrs Whipple's tongue stud."

I closed our front gate behind me. A pity Mam and Dad kept creating about my going to France. That was going to spoil my last few weeks at home, when normally, we all got on like a torched holiday cottage. I turned and headed uphill, my breath becoming shorter. Like in all small Valleys towns, you couldn't walk ten steps in Pontycynon without meeting someone who knew all your -

"Hello, Holly!" screeched Mrs Flook, from her doorstep. "When are you off to France, then?" She leaned on her broom expectantly.

I returned the greeting, maintaining a careful distance from the broom. Mrs Flook was rarely seen in public without it. Griff used to say that if the roof fell off her house she'd have swept the rubble into next door's yard before the fire brigade arrived.

"There's lovely, going abroad," enthused Mrs Flook. "Hello, Sylvia. Holly's going to France, did you know?"

I turned to see Mrs Stockley, another neighbour, approaching us. I just had time to smile before Mrs Flook rushed on: "Going all that way. There's brave. And all that studying for college."

Suddenly I was starring in a remake of *The Corn is Green*. I wondered if I should offer to give up my university place and marry the village trollop, just to keep in character.

You could tell Mrs Stockley was a relative newcomer to Pontycynon. She missed her cue to interrogate me about my trip, my studies and whether or not I was Courting Strong. Instead she smiled and told me: "Come and say *au revoir* to us before you go."

I liked Mrs Stockley. She and her husband had emigrated here from Surrey ("up England way" © Mam 1998) a few years ago. They'd needed time to adapt, though. At first they'd thought Dad was Welsh-speaking, until he'd put his teeth in.

"Our Georgia's doing well in school, and all," said Mrs Flook. "She passed her dancing certificate last week."

I nodded and excused myself. By and large, Pontycynon wasn't used to students. Half the town thought their grandson should have made the national news for passing GCSE History, while the other half was practising smirking for when you failed your Finals.

I turned the corner, relieved to be on a flat road. After more than twenty years of walking up hills, I still moved with the effortless grace of a bread pudding. In the High Street, the only sign of life was the flickering light from Derek Pugh The Bookie's window. Derek must have been calculating that week's dividends from his equine investment plan, a popular scheme tailored to supplementing the individual's weekly State benefit. (Our town wasn't nicknamed Ponty Sign-On for nothing.)

The Tower loomed at the top of the High Street. Once a tavern, it had reformed and become the town library a few years ago. The ground floor was now Pontycynon Computer Centre, equipped with four trestle tables, four computers and a worn but optimistic Welsh alphabet teacloth. Not many of the locals were keen to sign up for courses, though. Most of them had graduated to the town's other hostelry, The Nelson Arm.

"You've caught me with my files open," joked Lin, opening the door. "Only chance I get to work in peace. Mrs Whipple's been chopsing to me all week about Owen's summer project."

Owen, Mrs Whipple's son, was at art college. He lacked his mother's flamboyance, being something of a wet mac to her fuschia sarong. He'd sighed after Lin for years, although she hadn't the heart to tell him that his designs on her were never going to get beyond the pencil and paper stage.

"This is Owen's project," explained Lin, handing me a scroll of paper. The look on my face as I unrolled it sent her into a fit of giggles.

I put the poster down. "Lin, he can't hold a fashion show in a library. What will the models wear, dust jackets?"

Lin laughed. "He couldn't find anywhere else at short notice, so his Mam said he could have it here. Next Friday. You will come, won't you? I'm afraid to go on my own, less Owen ropes me in as a model." She giggled. "He might try to get me into his reversible hipsters."

"You'd better watch he doesn't squeeze you into a figure-hugging nightie." I spoke lightly to hide the ache inside. At least Lin had an admirer, even if he was a bit of a hopeless case. Nobody wanted to hug my figure.

I shook my head. "There's some goings-on in this library. It's ever since they took on that school-leaver."

It had been two years since our A-levels, but I still remembered the moment when Lin had set her glass of champagne down on our kitchen table and told me she'd turned down a place at college in favour of a job at the library. I'd sprayed a mouthful of Tesco's finest over Mam's Harlech Castle placemats. Rather than venture beyond the valley, Lin had chosen to surround herself with testy pensioners and Dick Francis. Still, she was earning her living, and not faced with repaying a massive student loan. In my circumstances, I couldn't afford to bring my library books back late.

"Mr Wheeler's going to take photos, at the fashion show," said Lin. "You know Mr Wheeler Upper Waun Street? He does photography. And he's going to work the projector on the night of the Mauvoisins slide show." Lin looked at me. "Are you sure...? You won't...?"

I was, and I wouldn't.

"Lin, I'm not wasting an evening listening to that Twinning Committee bragging about how they spent a whole week out there without speaking a word of French."

Pontycynon had been twinned with Mauvoisins, a town in west France roughly equal in size and ineptitude at rugby, fifteen years ago. Since then, a small, but self-important band of Pontycynon folk had organised trips there twice a year, returning to regale the stay-at-homes with tales of how they'd made the Frogs cook them bacon and eggs, none of that Garlic muck. Whatever else was uncertain about my year in France, I knew one thing for sure. I wasn't going anywhere near that town. I was going to explore France for myself, not follow the path trodden by half of Pontycynon.

"Oh, there's a pity." Lin had a twinkle in her eye. "Guess who was in here today, telling me he's writing up the evening for his newspaper?"

I felt my face grow hot. "Kim was here?" I'd had a crush on Kim Meredith for years. Kim was a few years older than us, but I sometimes saw him around the town, and pored over the articles he wrote for the Valley newspaper, *Y Llais*. It was unusual to find a Ponty boy who used his head for something other than butting another Ponty boy through a plate-glass window. But, like Owen's, my feelings were strictly one-way traffic. I'd hardly ever been close enough to Kim to stammer hello.

No-one but Lin knew my secret, although Griff sometimes remarked on how it took me forever to read *Y Llais*, these days. Griff hadn't had much time for the local paper since it had ruined his tenth birthday by erroneously naming him as bronze, not silver, medallist in the school sports day Potato and Spoon (no grass omelettes - our headmaster wasn't daft). Griff, outraged, had promptly nicknamed *Y Llais* "The Lies", an epithet that had softened, over the years, to the more affectionate "The Fibs".

"The slide show's on Tuesday at eight, in case you still don't want to come." Lin's remark interrupted my *rêverie* as I glanced at the bookshelves to check that Kipling's *Kim* was in its usual place. "Kim could interview you about your trip to France."

"Don't be daft," I said. "Hey, he didn't borrow a book called *How To Meet A Fat, Plain Languages Student*, did he?"

"I can't remember," said Lin, turning back to her files. "And you're not plain, Hol."

I gritted my ears at my best friend's honesty. I'd jog all the way home, to burn off some of my fat. No, better not. People would be slowing down their cars to laugh.

I turned the corner into our back alley. I'd slip into our house through the back gate and nip upstairs for a wash. I reached the gate and fumbled with the catch.

"Holly?" said a voice. I turned to see Mam, holding our black plastic dustbin in her arms. Behind her was a grey-haired lady of commanding height who looked oddly familiar.

"Well, open the gate for me," said Mam. "Don't you know Mrs Hathaway? Taught you in the Juniors?"

The memories came flooding back. That prison-door smile. The screams of fury if you forgot your daps for P.E. Your knees trembling in case she selected you for that day's humiliation in front of the class.

"Hello, Mrs Hathaway," I said weakly. "Nice to see you, after all these years."

Mrs Hathaway stared at me. I felt the impulse to wet myself, thought better of it, and stood quietly, WITHOUT fidgeting, instead.

"Holly." It was a statement, not a greeting. "Your mother says you're going to France."

I nodded.

Mrs Hathaway smiled. "Angeline often travels with her job - France, Germany. She speaks French fluently."

I remembered Angeline, Mrs Hathaway's niece, from junior school. She never used to share her Smarties, declaring, with her mouth full, that she didn't have enough to go round. I had a feeling that, grown up, Angeline was running the loans department of a High Street bank.

"Holly's university is arranging her year abroad." I recognised Mam's bay-window voice.

"Angeline thinks of France as a second home," stated Mrs Hathaway. "She's been going there every summer since she was twelve, with school exchange trips."

I'd never been on a school exchange trip. We'd gone on summer holidays to Mam's cousins in Tenby, when we'd gone at all.

"Holly will be teaching in a French school," said Mam airily. "We think it's a wonderful opportunity."

I nearly gasped. Not even pausing to blush, Mam took aim again. "Didn't Angeline once apply to do teacher training?"

Mrs Hathaway's smile stayed in place. "She feels more suited to being a personal assistant. She's been to quite a few company dinners, where she can use her French *and her German*."

Mam and I exchanged glances. Mrs Hathaway wished me a safe journey, pointed out that Angeline's company always paid for her trips abroad, then took her leave. Dismissed, Mam and I headed indoors.

"Hear her brag," snorted Mam, banging the kitchen door behind us. "That Angeline never got in to university. She haven't done half as well as Maggie Hathaway makes out."

"What is she doing, then?" I hadn't seen Angeline since I was eight. One day, she'd run up to Lin and me in the playground to tell us that her parents were having her transferred to a better school, and the next she'd gone.

"Secretary with some firm in Cardiff," grumbled Mam. "Typing letters."

"In French *and German*," I sneered. Knowing Angeline, she'd only learned the imperatives. Bossy? She dictated the book.

"Maggie Hathaway always tiptoed around Angeline," scoffed Mam. "'Course, she never had kids of her own. Remember when Angeline pushed your tennis racket down the drain? Maggie Hathaway never even told her off."

I sighed.

Mam tried to get her nose level with the curtain rail. "Angeline, dear," she brayed. "Remember that Gethin child who used to beat you in the spelling tests? I met her and her mother and their dustbin.

I'm glad you don't have to mix with such common people now you're Wales' top businesswoman, with your own briefcase."

I yawned. "Not now, Aunt Maggie. I've got to go to tonight's company dinner." I grabbed the tablecloth and swathed it around my shoulders, a checked evening wrap. "And if they ask me to pass the salt, I'll tell them I haven't got enough to go round."

"That Holly Gethin is going to France," sniffed Mam, mincing back and forth on invisible red Axminster.

"Well," I replied, adjusting my pashmina, "if I catch her on the Eurostar platform, I'll push her ticket down a drain."

The kitchen door opened behind me. I swung round to make a particularly snide face at Dad or Griff. The tablecloth, caught up in its role, swept around me and nearly wiped the nose of our neighbour, Mrs Price Opposite.

"Oh, excuse us, Mrs Price." Mam was quick to recover herself. "Just some silly joke of Holly's."

"Bullfighting, is it, Holly?" asked Mrs Price Opposite. I shook my head, darting an indignant look at Mam. Trust her to put the fault on me.

"I thought it was France you were going to, not Spain," continued our visitor, apparently unperturbed. "I just popped round to ask could someone help me put my bin out. The ashman do create, if you do leave it in the yard. Our Mansel would have done it, only he's gone to keep it real in Barry Island." Mrs Price Opposite's son, Mansel, was a part-time DJ and full-time rock obsessive.

"Leave it to me," said Mam. "Griff!" she scraked. "Go and help Mrs Price! And Holly, the phone went, for you. My memory's getting as good as yours."

Griff appeared, his sleeves rolled up for bin management. "A lady from your college phoned," he explained. "Olwen."

"Olwen's the secretary of our French department," I reminded Mam.

"Olwen said the professor wants you to come in for a chat on Monday." Griff said. "She said there was a problem with your year abroad. They thought they had a school for you, but apparently it's fallen through. You haven't got a place."

2.

Situation Vacances

"Cheer up, love," barked the bus driver, slamming into first gear. "Been listening to the Manic Street Preachers?"

I smiled wryly. All day Sunday the words had been turning over in my head. *"There's been a mistake. You haven't got a place."*

They'd got it wrong, I told myself, settling into a seat. Olwen had misunderstood Professor Havard's notes. (Easily done, with his handwriting.) Or Griff had got the message back to front. (Understandable, with Mam and Dad chopsing in the background while he was on the phone.)

The chopsy pair had barely concealed their delight. "It don't matter if you don't go to France now," Mam had consoled me. "Perhaps you can go after you've got your degree."

"There's no need for you to go at all," Dad had reminded me on the hour, every hour. "They've got French teachers in that college. Can't they teach you how to speak French?"

It was true that several of our lecturers were French nationals, but the thought of extra tuition with Monsieur Durieux was considerably less appealing than a year of foreign adventure. Monsieur Furieux, as he was known, was starchier than a baguette. Those of us who had sat through his analyses of Volumes 1 and 7 of Proust's masterpiece had never found out what happened in Volumes 2-6, and, by now, were past caring.

Only Griff had been supportive. "They've been organising these exchanges for years," he'd reassured me. "They must have sorted out mistakes like this before."

He had a point, I told myself. Perhaps Professor Havard had already contacted the organisers, who were now frantically searching for my application down the back of their settee. I held on tight to my seat as we jolted down the valley to the city.

I remembered the day I'd enrolled at the university. I'd been overwhelmed by the maze of streets and the traffic. For the first two weeks, finding my way around had been a full-time job. I'd spent the first two days scanning Dixons' window for news of local births, marriages and deaths.

Today I hardly noticed the people swarming around the bus station. I made a humble vow that if Professor Havard could sort out my French placement, I would be his best student from now on. Never again would I slump in the back row nibbling peanuts in his *dictée*.

The Arts Faculty door swung to behind me, the only sound in the building the squeak of my trainers along the corridor. Upstairs, in the French Department, I was met by the reassuring sight of the dog-eared poster for that old student production of "Le Mariage de Fig". Pushing the door open, I heard someone moving around in the library. I smiled. I wasn't the only living creature in the building after all.

My smile faded when I opened the library door and saw Martin Waite. Martin was in my class, its prize student, assuming they gave prizes for the number of hours spent memorising textbook chapters. The only things about him bursting with sheer animal vitality were his pimples.

"Hello, Martin. Busy?" I asked.

Martin was clearly intent on enjoying his summer holiday. He only had four books open. "I'll be leaving for Avignon in five weeks' time," he told me. "I shall find it invaluable to research the history of the town."

In an attempt to hi-jack his intellectual plane, I nodded sagely. "Living in France will be the only way to learn French properly." Smiling, I confided: "My oral French is useless. Remember when we read those extracts from *Madame Bovary* aloud in class? Everyone was laughing at me."

"I wasn't laughing at you," said Martin. "The person next to me was," he added.

I gave up. No fun talking to Martin, even if he was smarter than the average bore. I bid him a swift *adieu* and rushed off before he could criticise my pronunciation.

Professor Havard was in the corridor near Olwen's office. Normally a smiley bulldog, today he seemed preoccupied.

"Holly," he greeted me.

"Olwen rang and said you wanted to see me," I gabbled. "She said there was a problem with my year abroad. I can still go, can't I?"

For a man who routinely discussed salary terms with junior lecturers, Professor Havard seemed ill at ease with displays of naked emotion. He ushered me across the corridor to his own room. Panic gripped me as I saw the angular frame of Mr Horton, the department's senior lecturer, folded into the guest chair. This was serious if it needed two of them to tell me what was going on.

Professor Havard turned to close the door. The panic went straight to my knees.

"Sit down, Holly," urged Professor Havard, indicating his second-best guest chair. My knees didn't need to be asked twice.

"A week ago," said Professor Havard, "we received the names of the schools our students had been assigned to. Your name was missing from the list. We got in touch with the centre straight away. But they told us you weren't among the successful applicants."

My face burned. I wasn't top of the class, but I hadn't thought I was that dull. How come all the others had got schools? I couldn't help it if my French wasn't as good as theirs. Lucy had been to that French school in London, and Cerys spent every summer in Brittany. If ever I'd told Mam and Dad that I was off to hitch-hike around the Dordogne, I'd have spent the next three months eating my meals through a grille in our cellar door.

"It's nothing to do with your course work, Holly," Professor Havard assured me. "There must have been a computer error, because they have no record of your application."

"So we looked into finding you a university course," cut in Mr Horton. I leaned back in my chair. Good old Mr Horton. This department needed more men of action. I beamed at Mr Horton, silently squeezing him into a vacant slot in my heart, just below Kim

Meredith, and next to Neil Morgan, lead guitarist with The Whinberries.

"Only it's too late for you to register now," continued my new hero. "So you can't enrol at a French university either."

Another door slammed in my face. Mr Horton added: "We've never had this happen before, Holly."

Even the prospect of seeing my name in the record books wasn't going to make up for losing my chance. I blinked hard, swallowed and managed to growl: "So I can't go to France."

"It looks like that." The kindness in Professor Havard's voice was more than I could bear. "But you'll go straight into the fourth year, take your Finals next June, and graduate a year ahead of the rest of your class." He made it sound as if *they'd* missed out on the chance of *their* lifetime.

"It's not compulsory for language students to spend a year abroad, you know," he said. "Some institutions have found that intensive oral work in a language laboratory can ensure a similar standard of fluency."

There's no need for you to go abroad at all. Any minute now he was going to pick up the *Times Higher Education Supplement* and talk at me from behind it.

"Monsieur Durieux is willing to give you extra conversation lessons," broke in Mr Horton. "He's got a splendid collection of cassettes on Proust you could borrow."

Well, there was lovely. I'd be drafted into the steelworks twelve months earlier, prodded along by the French Stick. I looked from the professor to Mr Horton. "Can't I go anyway? Get a job, instead?"

Professor Havard was silent for a moment. "We're not trying to discourage you, Holly," he said. "But you'd have trouble finding work for the full nine months, at this late stage."

"I could look," I argued. "I could be an au pair girl." Since neither lecturer had seen the state of my bedroom, they weren't to know I'd never have scraped through GCSE Housework.

"Or I could do fruit-picking." At least there I wasn't without experience, having ambled through the brambles with Griff and a couple of jam-jars every summer since we were little.

My lecturers exchanged glances. I fidgeted. If only I'd had the sense to take Advanced Shelf Stacking instead of The Seventeenth-Century Psychological Novel as my second-year option.

"Autumn term starts on October 8th, Holly," said Mr Horton. "Registration from 10am." He handed me a typewritten list. "These are the final-year course books."

Professor Havard stood up. "Thank you for coming in, Holly. I'm sorry this has happened. But, who knows, it may turn out to be to your advantage after all. We'll see you in October." He opened the door. I got to my feet and trudged out into the corridor.

I gazed at the corkboards lining the walls of the corridor. The exam results were still up there, listing those fourth-year students who had just graduated, two with first-class degrees and the rest with upper seconds. I'd be going to lectures with a crowd of third-year sophisticates just back from their year in France. And they'd spend every other minute reminiscing about it.

"Every weekend we'd go to Paris. You could find amazing bargains in the *Marché des Puces*."

"The old town was stunning, all cobbled streets and low doorways. After the tourists had gone, we'd walk around the city walls at dusk. The *son et lumière* shows were magical."

What could I contribute? "If you spend five pounds in one go at Polly Half-Bad's, you get a pink sticker. Save up ten of those and you get a free hand of bananas."

What sort of performance could I produce in the Finals, compared to the others? I'd be lucky to get a third-class degree. And it would be branded on my academic record for the rest of my life.

Someone was speaking. I turned to see Martin and his briefcase.

"I said, are you all right?" he asked. "You look pale."

"I'm fine," I responded automatically.

"I saw you with the professor," persisted Martin. "What did he say to you?"

"Nothing," I said, but Martin had grasped a suspicious thread and was bent on unravelling the truth.

"Was it about the year abroad?" he demanded.

Inside me, something snapped. "Yes," I said. "I was telling Professor Havard I'd made my own arrangements, so I won't be going to the school they'd lined up for me. Someone else can have my place." I smiled, moved by my own generosity.

Martin was curious. "Do you have a job, then? Whereabouts in France?"

Martin wasn't a local. He wouldn't know Pontycynon's twin town from a laundry basket. "I'm going to Mauvoisins," I told him. "In the west, near the Atlantic coast. I'll go to the beach on my days off."

"So you do have a job?" said Martin. "It must be a good one if you've refused a teaching post. What kind of work?"

"Grape-minding," I said. "Er, child-picking. While I raise the grapes. Got to go, Martin, or I'll miss my bus." I hoisted my bag and sped off, calling over my shoulder: "*Bon voyage.*" That was one phrase I was pretty confident of.

It was one thing to pull my homespun yarn over Martin's eyes, I reflected as I walked through the city centre, but I wasn't going to be able to keep up this charade with everyone. I was going to have to find a real job in France. I sighed. This was going to prove tricky.

"Well, that's that. You don't need to go anywhere." Dad settled into his chair and reached for his slippers. I hadn't seen him so relieved since the time we'd pulled back from 9-8 with three minutes to go, to clinch the 2005 Six Nations decider.

"Dad's right. It would be better if you stayed here," Mam said. "What if something happened to you, abroad?"

"Better for *you*," I grumbled. "And they do have hospitals in France."

"Going off on your own is not the solution," declared Mam.

The doorbell rang. Satisfied she had made her point, Mam went to answer its summons. Dad looked at me. "Your mother would worry herself to death," he said.

I couldn't speak. In my selfish desire to get a qualification, I'd signed my mother's death warrant.

"Come in, love," chirped the condemned woman, ushering Lin into the living room. "There's cold it is, out."

"Yes, quite nippy," agreed Lin, squashing on to the settee beside me. "All right, Hol? How did it go at college?"

I ran through the story. Mam and Dad would come round to the au pair idea when they saw that Lin approved of it.

"Au pair? Oh, I wouldn't do that, Hol," said Lin. "Fiona Brankley did it in Amsterdam and she's on blood-pressure tablets now."

With a flourish of his teacup, Dad followed Mam out to the kitchen, presumably to discuss how Lin's parents had managed to produce a much more sensible daughter than either they or Mr and Mrs Brankley had.

"Lin!" I hissed. "Did you have to say that? They'll do anything to stop me seeing the world and having fun."

"Oh, sorry, Hol," said Lin. "But anyway, I came to ask you a favour. Will you help me serve the tea at the twin town slide show? Mrs Whipple's off to salsa that night, so I need a hand."

I thought about it. I'd get to see Kim. "OK, I'll help."

"We could ask if anyone knows a family that needs an au pair," suggested Lin. "Some of them have been to Mauvoisins. They'll know people."

It wasn't a bad idea. In spite of my reservations about the twin town, it might be worth trying.

"By the way, Lin," I asked. "Is Mr Llewellyn still chairman of the twinning committee?"

"No, he's stood down this long time," said Lin. "He wants to concentrate on his *Z Cars* website."

"Who's running it now?" I asked.

Lin looked at me. "Stand by your desks. It's Mrs Hathaway."

3.

I Flirted Through The Grapevine

"*The Times*, love?" asked Mr Gwilym The Paper Shop. "Both of them sold out, this morning."

I thanked him, but sighed. I wasn't likely to find au pair job ads in either the *Echo* or The Fibs.

Trudging home, I wondered who had bought the two copies of *The Times*. Perhaps the Nelson Arm had run out of cat litter again. The pub cat, Ginger Joe, was a legend in the town, the only known survivor of a late-night tryst with Mrs Flook's broom.

Turning into our street, I noticed the Grim Sweeper wasn't out bristling, for once. But Mrs Price Opposite was on her doorstep, with her son, Mansel.

"Found a job, Holly?" called Mrs Price Opposite. "There's a pity the college couldn't get you in, teaching."

"Has my mother been chopsing?" I smiled, privately resolving to wallop Mam.

"Oh, no," replied Mrs Price Opposite. "Emlyn told us, now just."

Well, that was quicker than social media. Emlyn was our postman, a dedicated Communist, nicknamed Emlyn Kremlin. His egalitarianism extended to taking an unbiased interest in other people's businesses. We had long surmised that he read everyone's holiday postcards. He was suspiciously well informed about Carmarthenshire bingo halls.

"I would love to tour the southlands, in a travelling minstrel show," Mansel informed me.

I knew better than to question this ambition. Mansel's usual mode of communication was through obscure rock lyrics. None of us had had a sensible conversation with him since 1993.

"Will you still go, Holly?" asked Mrs Price Opposite.

"I don't know yet." I pushed our front gate open. Mam had better have found a good hiding place.

"I only told Emlyn Kremlin," argued Mam, through a mouthful of clothes pegs.

I glared at her. "Standing by the gate, clecking to everyone about my business," I growled. "What if I went round telling people about your stiff wax lumps...?"

"Go and dust your room," interjected Mam. "Some au pair girl you'd be. Remember when you tried to make toast in the oven?" She cackled and nearly swallowed a peg.

The afternoon dragged. I'd planned to spend the time improving my French vocabulary. I turned to a more pressing problem – getting ready for the slide show.

Towelling my hair, I opened my wardrobe door and sighed at the array of shapeless garments. Selecting a saggy cardigan, I caught an amused glint in the eye of my long-time bear companion, Trouble Bruin. "It's all right for you," I told him. "We can't all go around in fake fur."

"Put your cardy on," nudged Mam, setting the currant cake on to a plate.

"I'll decide if I wear a cardy," I retorted. Dad frowned at me. He'd obviously heard Mam's remastered version of my earlier speech on the individual's right to privacy.

"Don't be afraid to eat the tesen," urged Mam, indicating the cake. I cut myself a generous slice.

"All that!" squawked Mam. "No wonder you're the size you are."

"Keep it, then," I said, shoving the plate at her. "When I'm in France, you can stuff yourselves." Dad's expression grew blacker. Before he could bark, I grabbed my jacket and walked out.

"They flare up at everything I do, Lin," I grumbled.

Lin straightened the line of chairs. "Perhaps you could just go to France for a month or so, Hol."

You couldn't learn a language properly in a month. I gazed through the window, up at the sky. If I was going to get the rough edge of Dad's tongue, he'd have to use it to seal an airmail envelope first.

The door creaked open and in lurched a cardboard box, carried by a tall, grey-haired man with a long, anxious face.

"Hello, Mr Wheeler. By here?" Lin motioned to the table she'd placed behind the line of chairs. The projectionist set down his burden, wheezing.

"Them stairs," he explained. "And I had to leave the screen out by the car."

"I'll get it." Lin rushed out. We all knew what became of personal possessions left unsupervised for five minutes on the mean streets of Pontycynon.

Mr Wheeler turned to me. "Old age don't come by itself."

I hesitated between a shake of my head and a nod. It came out as an imitation of St Vitus adjusting his halo.

"Did you come on the last French trip?" Mr Wheeler was visibly struggling to place me. I explained that I'd never visited Mauvoisins, but might well be spending some time there soon. Mr Wheeler was so attentive, I'd poured out the whole story by the time Lin had returned and set up the screen.

"I've been over there a few times," said Mr Wheeler. "Last time, we stayed with the bank manager and his wife. They might know someone who needs a nanny."

I'd never had much to do with kids. The only living creature I'd ever minded successfully was Lin's hamster, when her family went on holiday. This time, I might not be able to insist that my charges stayed in their cage all day while I checked on them during ad breaks.

"'Course, there's Britishers living out there," said Mr Wheeler. "But you don't want to be speaking English with them, do you?" His eyes crinkled. I beamed. I had misjudged this Committee.

"*Holly*."

My insides curled up into a tight ball. I turned to face Mrs Hathaway.

Mrs Hathaway bared her teeth at me. "So you won't be taking up a teaching post in France?"

"I'm still going," I mumbled.

"But not teaching." Mrs Hathaway's voice rang with triumph. Other visitors, arriving, were enthralled.

"Holly might go to Mauvoisins," Lin called across the room.

Mrs Hathaway's eyebrows disappeared into her grey thatch. The silence was broken by the sound of the door creaking again. I looked up and recognised the latest arrival. My insides uncurled and broke into mad freestyle laps.

"Sorry I'm late," said the reason I'd washed my hair. "I'm parked at the bottom of the street. Do any cars ever make it up this hill?"

"Aye," said Mr Wheeler. "But you've got to put a brick behind the rear wheel, less they run back down."

My laugh came out higher than everyone else's. Kim moved towards an empty seat near where I was standing. Panicking, I stepped back and bumped into the table. Mr Wheeler's box of slides wobbled dangerously.

"Time to begin," announced Mrs Hathaway. Kim took his place, two seats away from me.

The slide show was surprisingly engaging. "This is the church," said Mr Wheeler, as one image flashed up. The building with long windows could have been the railway station. No churchyard, no garden, not even a surrounding wall.

"We went in there," remarked one spectator. "There was engravings about the history of Mavis Sins. Pity they couldn't have told us about them."

"That's right," agreed the gentleman next to Kim. "If them people in More Vosene could have spoken English, they could have told us some interesting stories."

Kim's glance met mine. We exchanged a smile.

I was still smiling when Lin switched the lights on and invited the visitors to enjoy the refreshments. I hurried to take up my duties.

"You could wait at tables, Holly," boomed Mrs Hathaway. "McDonald's recruits young people with no obvious prospects." She waved away the proffered biscuits, savouring my discomfort instead.

"Holly ain't gonna work in McDonald's." Mr Wheeler took a custard cream. "Holly can do better than that." He smiled at me.

Mrs Hathaway pounced on this. "Angeline always stays with the Mayor's family in Mauvoisins. They might need a cleaner."

I nearly dropped the biscuits. Mrs Hathaway steamed across the room in search of other hopes to sink.

"What was all that about?" I looked up and met Kim's gaze.

"It's that old battleship," I hissed. "She thinks I should spend a year picking Angeline's knickers up off the floor."

Kim and Mr Wheeler both burst out laughing. "You don't want to listen to Maggie Hathaway," confided Mr Wheeler. He winked. "She haven't even been to Mauvoisins."

"Never!" I breathed, delighted.

"Keeps saying she'll go next time," said Mr Wheeler. "I reckon she don't want to show herself up, trying to speak French."

I giggled. Kim smiled too. "Lin says you're job-seeking in Mauvoisins." He looked at me. "Have you ever done any selling?"

Before I could answer, Mrs Hathaway bellowed for silence. She thanked everyone for coming to her *soirée*: "Next spring there will be another trip to Movie Scenes for those of us adventurous enough to go."

Mr Wheeler thanked Lin for the use of the Tower. Mrs Hathaway interrupted the applause to remind everyone to give their used cutlery to Holly Gethin. She probably thought I needed all the cleaning practice I could get.

"I've got an idea," said Kim. "I know this couple - Look, come for a drink."

"I've got to tidy up here," I explained.

"I'll do that, Hol," said Lin. "You go."

I pulled on my jacket. Any idea Kim Meredith wanted to share with me, involving couples, was unmissable.

"Will we make the front page?" Mrs Hathaway asked Kim as we headed for the door.

"Can't promise," replied Kim. "But we'll try not to cut your Movie Scenes."

Mrs Hathaway looked nonplussed. I followed Kim out of the door, grinning.

I gazed fondly at Kim's left ear, the only bit of him visible through the crowd at the bar. Good-looking, charismatic man-about-valley Kim Meredith had invited out Holly Gethin, a girl so sophisticated she put Blu-Tack on the back of her earrings. I ached to comb my hair, but it was a bit late now to nip to the Ladies' for a quick blow-dry and manicure. I hung my jacket on the back of my chair. The nearest I'd get to catwalk fashion would be if Ginger Joe rubbed up against it.

Kim handed me my drink. "So you need work. There are a few businesses around here that would be glad of your help."

My face fell. Did he expect me to pull on a pinny and slice ham in the *Cwarp* all year?

Kim saw my expression and smiled. "Sponsorship," he explained. "Get local firms to sponsor you to promote their products in France. Take Welsh wine. This couple, friends of my parents, have a farm, down the valley." He paused. "Have you heard of Dewis wine, Holly?"

I nodded. Neglecting to add: yes, two seconds ago.

"If only they could sell their wine to France." Kim's eyes lit up. "They'd need someone to handle things, over there."

Selling Welsh wine to the French? The phrases "dog food" and "the Chinese" came irresistibly to mind.

"I can take you to see their vineyard," suggested Kim. "Let me take your number. Have you got a pen?"

I handed him my biro. He had such drive, such enthusiasm, such silky brown hair.

"*Château Valleys conquers France*," he grinned. "There's a story in there."

I gulped. "A story for The Fi - er, *Y Llais*?"

"I'll talk to my editor," said Kim. "Hey, it's getting dark. Drink up. I'd better get you home, or your parents will think you've left the country already."

I waved from our doorstep as Kim's rear lights winked goodnight. The door swung open. "Where have you been?" demanded Dad.

I floated past him into the living room. "Oh, hiya, Griff. Good night out? *Bonsoir*, Mam."

"I'll give you *bonsoir*," growled Dad.

"Things are looking up," I gloated. "Someone's going to find me a host family in Mauvoisins, and this - this friend of mine has got a great idea for how I can earn money in France." I perched on the arm of Griff's chair, ready to tell all.

"Mauvoisins?" said Griff. "Thought you weren't going to set dap in that place."

"I've changed my mind," I breezed. "Listen -"

"No, YOU listen," Dad barked. "Coming home reeking of drink." He glared at me. "Go, then. Go there and stay there. But don't expect any help from us."

I poked my head out from under the bedclothes. The kitchen radio was on, so Dad and Griff must have gone out. (They'd never have stomached Radio Cambria in the morning. One cuddly catchphrase in Griff's hearing and Dewi Isaac, the Housewives' Cheese, would have found himself broadcasting to the nation face down in the bin.) I heaved myself out of bed. Operation Frosties could get under way.

"What are you up so smart for?" Mam asked as I shuffled into the kitchen. "Wet the bed?" (Except she didn't say "wet", almost putting me off my breakfast.) I threw her a reproachful look and set about locating the milk in the fridge.

"Meeting your boyfriend today, are you?" Mam had adopted a strange attitude to my new acquaintance with Kim. At first amused by my eagerness to talk about him, she'd frozen when I'd mentioned the wine-selling plan.

A spoonful of cereal helped me maintain a dignified silence. Kim hadn't said when he'd ring.

"He'll be taking some other girl out drinking tonight," said Mam, comfortingly. I tucked a strand of hair behind my ear and pointedly gave my attention to Dewi, who was burbling about Sir Anthony Hopkins' latest film: *"... And if you're listening, Tony, here's one for you – Born In The USA."*

Mam tried a different, equally sharp tack. "Sit up straight. You've got a stomach like a landlord's." She banged her cup into her saucer. "Get dressed and you can go over the *Cwarp* for me."

"All right if I finish my breakfast first?" I enquired.

"No, I'll do it," said Mam, briskly and confusingly. "If you want something done tidy - Pull your stomach in."

This newly-minted proverb caught me in mid-mouthful. Mam breezed out of the kitchen, only stopping to inform me: "And I knew that boy's grandmother." She paused for effect. "His uncle married May Whiskers."

I blinked at the force of this revelation. Mam made her exit, satisfied that I had been discouraged from further acquaintance with the Meredith family.

Breakfast over, I trudged upstairs to my room. How was I going to fill the long days between now and seeing Kim again? Perhaps I could make improvements to some of my clothes. With a bonfire, for instance.

The doorbell sounded. Mam must have forgotten her keys. I sauntered downstairs, deliberately slowly. I'd make her wait.

The doorbell rang twice more before I deigned to pull the door open. My smirk faded as I recognised Mr Wheeler.

Mortified, I pulled the door open. "I thought you were my Mam," I said weakly.

Mr Wheeler was too discreet to ask questions, but Mrs Flook lacked any such inhibitions. I could see her on her doorstep, watching us, engrossed. She wouldn't have noticed if Mr Watkins the builder had got her right in the bristles with Mam's bucket of Christmas sand. I ushered Mr Wheeler into the living room.

"I e-mailed those friends in Mauvoisins," said Mr Wheeler, lowering himself on to the settee. "They wrote back this morning." He reached inside his coat and drew out a folded sheet of paper.

I opened the paper, and saw three paragraphs of jumbled type, beginning: "Ona rE+3u_".

"'Course, they've written back in French," said Mr Wheeler. "But I thought you could read it, even if I couldn't."

I read the first few lines, but had to admit defeat.

"I'd ring them up," added Mr Wheeler, "but I've got a job to understand their accent."

Accent. The French accent. French accents. "That's it," I exclaimed. "All the words with accents on - they haven't come out properly. Look, Mr Wheeler -" I shoved the letter under his moustache - "this first bit, it's 'On a reçu'. It means 'we have received'. The letter 'c' hasn't printed because it's got an accent on it - a cedilla."

Delighted, I set about deciphering the message. Mr Wheeler's former hosts signalled that some neighbours of theirs would be content to welcome a young girl au pair. Monsieur and Madame Le Floch had two children, one girl, 8 years and one boy, 6. An address in Mauvoisins was followed by a telephone number. I'd got to the closing expressions of friendship when the living room door opened.

The sight of Mr Wheeler and me code-cracking on the settee left Mam speechless. But not for long.

"Well," she said, sinking into the armchair, her shopping bags slumped on to the floor. "We don't like the idea of Holly going abroad on her own. But if they're friends of yours, Mr Wheeler - well, we'll have to see. Holly, go and make Mr Wheeler a cup of tea." She smiled at our guest. "She wants training, don't she?"

As I returned with the tea, Mr Wheeler was talking. "And there's a hotel in the town. You could come on the coach trip, with us, next spring."

Mam seemed to have taken to the idea. With Mr Wheeler under temporary settee arrest, she was grilling him. Our hostage held gamely on to his tea-cup during the interrogation. No, he had never met these Le Flochs, but if they were friends of Monsieur Benoist at the bank they ought to be all right. And Mauvoisins was pretty in the springtime. The main street had cherry blossom trees that burst into life for two weeks in May, lavishing pink confetti on the pavements. What was that? No, he couldn't say for sure if the station had proper toilets or not. But Holly could phone this family and ask them, wasn't it?

Mam smiled, visibly warming to the thought of a holiday in France.

"You said I'd be home by Christmas," I couldn't resist sniping.

"Oh, you'll be all right, as long as you've got a bit of cake in your mouth," returned Mam, grinning at Mr Wheeler. Our guest sipped his drink, then replaced his cup on its saucer, his expression more wistful than ever.

"See, with all your jawing, Mr Wheeler's tea's gone cold," scolded Mam. "Go and make him a fresh cup."

No, no, Mr Wheeler protested. He had to be on his way. He was going to the match in Aber, and kick-off was at three. I thought that if he ran, he might make the final whistle by the time Mam had finished thanking him.

"Go and send Mr Wheeler, Holly," urged Mam. "I've got to get the dinner on."

I escorted Mr Wheeler to the gate, adding my own awkward thanks to Mam's. Impulsively, I said: "You should come out and visit. We could walk through that cherry blossom confetti."

Mr Wheeler's cheeks turned bridegroom pink. He nodded, then retreated down the row.

Glancing around, I saw the audience ratings had doubled. Mrs Flook wasn't around, but Mansel and his girlfriend Shireen were on the Price Opposite doorstep.

Shireen scuffed her high heels. At just sixteen, she had pulled off the double coup of acquiring both Mansel and a full-time job in the chemist's. "You still learning French, Holly?" she inquired. "Won't be much use, when you're teaching."

Hadn't she heard? She must have been serving the customers with her iPod on. "I won't be teaching in France," I explained. "I'm going as an au pair."

"No, I mean after college," said Shireen. "Not many jobs for French teachers round here, are there?" She turned to Mansel for support. Literally. Those heels were going to give way at any moment.

"Why go to learn the words of fools?" Mansel's verdict on the National Curriculum was pithy, but I frowned. Why did everyone assume that if you studied Arts subjects at A-Level, you would automatically become a teacher? I didn't know exactly what I'd do after university, but I didn't want a lifetime of stroppy kids and staffroom coffee. Shireen clutched Mansel's arm with a kind little smile for girls who had nothing better to think about than education, travel and a fulfilling career.

A car purred down the hill, stopping in front of our house. I only turned to look at it after its horn hooted twice.

"Holly?" The driver's door opened, and so did Shireen's mouth. Kim jumped out of the car.

"Are you ready?" he asked me. "I told them we'd be there by half-past."

"There?" I stared.

"The vineyard," asked Kim. "My friends like the idea of selling their wine in France. Get in, and I'll take you to see them."

It was my turn to smile. "I'll get my coat."

I rushed indoors and called to Mam. No reply. She must have gone in the bathroom. Seizing Dad's jotter, I scribbled a note. Then I reached for my coat - no, the jacket was newer - and hurried back to join Kim. Shireen's eyes never left us as I settled in beside him.

"Haven't you got a mobile?" asked Kim, as we moved off down the road.

"I did until last term," I revealed. "But I lost it in the college laundry room. It was in my jeans pocket. By the spin cycle, it was done for."

Kim burst out laughing, but I winced, remembering how the foam had seeped from the washing machine door. Confessing my mistake had produced a similar reaction from Dad's mouth. And Griff had only just stopped humming ringtones at me.

"What did your mother say?" asked Kim.

"Not much," I replied, grinning as I remembered my note. ("Forget dinner, I've gone out with Kim. Back before midnight, unless we go pole-dancing with his Auntie Whiskers.")

My grin lasted all the way down the road, past the Workmen's Hall, down Bethel Row to the chapel, round the Hallelujah lamp-post and up Tip Road, towards the mountain.

The road was narrower now, trekking across the open mountain. On either side, rough grassland ran to meet the sky at the edge of the world.

"I love this run, don't you?" said Kim, winding his window down and resting his elbow on the ledge. "It's so wild."

I nodded. The mountain road had never inspired me before. Usually, all you noticed were mangy sheep skittering among clumps of rushes. But today I realised he was right. For a moment, I wondered if France was a good idea after all. I'd have been happy to sit beside Kim for good, driving along the mountain road into the horizon.

"These friends we're visiting," said Kim, reaching to change gear, "are called Trevor and Yvonne Davies. Trevor used to work in a factory on the estate. An analyst, in the lab. When they laid him off, he and Yvonne started growing grapes. He's his own boss now." From the forceful way Kim pushed the gearstick into its place, I wondered if his editor was a skinny, rigid man with a shiny round head.

A thought nagged me. Trevor, an analyst. Perhaps he'd been to college with Kim's Mam and Dad. They probably all had degrees. Kim must have been brought up on muesli and *The South Bank Show*. If I brought him home, Dad would grumble about the younger generation and Mam would prod my stomach. I shuddered at the prospect. Luckily, we were driving over a cattle grid, so Kim didn't notice.

"Here it is," said Kim, slowing to turn left on to a gravel track. He leapt out of the car and pushed open the gate. I followed, stepping carefully.

"Hiya, Scoops," said the hedge, from beside my shoulder. I jumped. The hedge rustled briefly, then out stepped a tall, angular lady wearing gardening gloves.

"Yvonne, hello," said Kim. "This is Holly."

"Oh, yes," said Yvonne, looking at me. "You're going to export our wine to France. Then me and Trev can retire to Provence." Her eyebrows quirked. "I can't wait to soak up the sun with my trotters in the Med."

I giggled.

"And it's coming on to rain," said Yvonne. "Who wants a cup of tea?"

In no time we were sitting at Yvonne's kitchen table with her husband Trevor, who was updating Kim on his pruning.

"You can send Holly a few dozen bottles, in France," said Kim. "She'll build up a client list for you."

Trevor and Yvonne exchanged glances. "Who would Holly sell it to?" asked Yvonne. "Restaurants and such, they'd have their own suppliers."

"Mauvoisins has a twinning committee too," said Kim. "They'd probably love Welsh wine at their events." He grinned at me. "Don't worry, Holly. Mrs Hathaway's not going to shout at you if you can't sell any."

I flushed. He thought I was a timid schoolgirl. "I'll get you your orders," I said. "No trouble."

Yvonne beamed. "Trev, we can put 'sold on the Continent' on our leaflets."

Trevor nodded. "Come round the side and see the vines. Don't mind a bit of drizzle, do you?"

Kim and I followed Trevor along the path that rounded the house, into a small field strung with neat rows of plants. Not quite the lush clusters of purple fruit I'd imagined. Kim examined the foliage while Trevor explained the subtleties of the Double Curtain method. I wondered vaguely if you had to pull a tassel to swish the vines together.

"Brolly, Holly," came Yvonne's voice from behind me. Grateful, I stepped under the umbrella she held.

"I know our vines don't look like much." Yvonne said. "But they're Trev's life, since the accident."

I looked up at her.

"Twenty years he'd been in the lab," said Yvonne. "They laid him off when he lost his leg."

Lost his leg? My mind screamed at a horrific image of white-hot metal jaws tearing human flesh, mangling white bone.

"He lost his leg - in the lab?" I whispered.

"No," said Yvonne. "He cut his hand in the lab. They sent him up the hospital. On his way out, he crossed the main road. A lorry got his leg."

31

I turned to look at Trevor, who was talking to Kim, his face vibrant.

"He was pretty down for about a year after that," Yvonne continued. "Then we decided to go for the vineyard idea." She stepped away from the mud. "Let's go back in. You can sample our farmhouse white."

"You've chosen to accept your mission, then, Holly," teased Kim as we drove away. Yvonne was waving from the gate. Trevor, his eyes touchingly bright, had presented me with two of his first-bottled, to start me on my new import-export career. I would help them, even if it meant setting up a stall in Mauvoisins town square and charging three euros the plastic beaker.

I looked at Kim, the wine warming me, inside. But he was watching the road and missed my smouldering gaze.

"You'll have a busy couple of weeks," said Kim, as we reached the mountain road again.

Not too busy to see you, I pleaded with my eyes.

"I'll be pretty busy myself," added Kim, not noticing. "Two flower shows, an art exhibition and the court case of the century - that bloke who held up the corner shop with a water pistol."

"There's a fashion show at the Tower on Tuesday," I offered, then realised this was unlikely to impress either Kim or his round-headed editor. I kept quiet for the rest of the journey.

"Good luck with the packing," said Kim, slowing as we approached my front gate.

I froze. Was this all the goodbye I was going to get?

"Oh, I forgot." Kim scrabbled in his pocket for a small card. "Here's my work e-mail. Let me know how the wine-trading goes."

"Um, did you talk to your editor about me sending news from France?" I asked. No one else in my class would have their own newspaper column.

"Not yet," said Kim. "But let us know about anything that will interest our readers." He smiled. He had great eyes. Deep, limpid pools. And that was just the sweat behind my knees.

"Enjoy the fashion show," said Kim. "I might show up. See you."

I clambered out of the car. Kim drove away, waving through his open window. Thrilled, I waved back, nearly christening the pavement with Trevor's hand-trodden vintage.

"Selling wine," sniffed Mam. "You don't want to take on anything like that."

I sighed. As usual, I was messaging talk@thewall.com.

"I know that Trevor," added Mam. "He's Huw Davies' boy. Huw Davies used to run a stall in Aber market. He had a sort of goatey thing."

"What, a beard?" asked Griff.

"No," snapped Mam. "A goat." She turned back to me. "And that Meredith boy, drinking and driving. You just forget him."

"Yes, he had almost half a glass. He'll go the same way as his Auntie Whiskers," I jeered, trying to suppress the thought that Kim shouldn't have been driving with one elbow on the window ledge.

"When you've finished," said Griff. "Anyone want to hear my news?"

"Sorry, Griff." I'd been hogging the limelight. "How was the match?" Griff had been to the rugby with his friends. They'd probably spotted someone in the crowd. An ex-international, or even a BBC Wales announcer.

"Griff have met a nice young lady," guessed Mam. Griff scowled. He was extremely sensitive about his personal life. Mam was living for the day he'd bring his first girlfriend home. Whereas she'd probably welcome Kim with open fire.

"This is for Holly," said Griff, taking a paper from his pocket. I blinked. Nice thought, but what did I want with some fly-half's autograph? I took the paper.

It wasn't an autograph.

It was a letter.

"6 rue Claude Chappe, Mauvoisins
Dear Holly,

33

Sion says you're coming to Mauvoisins. Come round and see me. (Don't believe anything Sion's said about my cooking, the no-good mule.) We'll have tea at the Café Bas de la Rue.

See you,

Chassa Brake

P.S. You couldn't squeeze a couple of orange Aeros into your luggage, could you? You can't get them here. Thanks."

4.

Generation Clecs

For once, Mam was lost for words. She stared at Griff, who sat grinning like a cat giving a press conference to *Cheshire Life*.

"Who is this girl?" asked Mam.

"She's a friend of Sion's, in work," replied Griff. "She lives in France."

"Why didn't you tell us you knew someone over there?" demanded Mam. "*And* in the twin town."

Griff raised his eyebrows. "Holly's always sworn she'd never go to that town." His grin widened. "Sion says this Chassa has been in France for a few years, working in different places. She's in Mauvoisins these days, teaching English. So when Holly said about going there, I asked Sion to let her know." He glanced at the letter. "Didn't expect her to write back so smart, though."

"And where is this girl from?" asked Mam.

Griff frowned. "Well, she went to school with Sion, and he's from Croesy." He looked at me. "You remember Sion, Holly? He came here on New Year's Eve, that time I was ill. Quite a big lad."

I remembered one winter when Griff had been laid low with 'flu. A couple of his friends had called round to cheer him up as he lay on his deathsettee. It was true that one guest had been powerfully built. In fact, he'd taken up most of the space at table as he did justice to Mam's mince pies. I remembered suppressing the less than charitable thought that we had found the man who put the hog into Hogmanay.

"Chassa Brake," repeated Mam. "Funny sort of name."

"Did you know her, Griff?" I asked. "Before she went to France."

Griff shrugged. "A lot of Sion's friends used to watch him play rugby for Croesy," he said, brusquely. Griff had always been touchy about his lack of athletic prowess. Too slight for most sports, he had had to watch his friends excel at rugby and football.

"And she have kept in touch with Sion since school," nodded Mam. "There's lucky, Holly. You'll have someone you can go to if you have any trouble with them old French."

"I don't need a nanny," I replied, my tone as curt as Griff's.

Griff snorted. "I don't think she's the Mary Poppins type." His grin reappeared. "Sion said, when they were in the sixth form, their headmaster announced that the school was going to build a swimming pool, and asked the pupils to bring in contributions. This Chassa went up to the staffroom with a bucket of water."

I giggled with delight. Mam pursed her lips, then remarked: "Well, she've probably got more sense now. What kind of school is she teaching in?"

"One with a full quota of sports facilities, I hope," said Griff. I giggled again, but had to pause to sneeze.

"There, that's traipsing around fields in the rain," scolded Mam. "Why didn't you put your Warm Coat on?"

There was no point explaining that it made me look like a hippo on a budget, so I replied with another sneeze. Mam bustled off in search of a remedy, calling to Dad that she was going to crack open his Christmas whisky: "Just a drop, with hot lemon and honey. Holly can get you another bottle, on the duty-free."

She had it all worked out, I reflected, as I headed for bed, my hot drink in one hand and Chassa Brake's letter in the other. Fair play for Griff, finding this girl was going to make life easier. Perhaps even Dad might come round, knowing another Valleys girl would be on hand. Even if she was one of them Flighty Pieces Going About The Countries.

As I pulled the bedcovers back, my mind rambled through the letter again. "Sion, the no-good mule..." If they were such big friends, why wasn't Sion supplying Chassa with her orange Aeros? Perhaps he regularly bought half a dozen to send to her, but ate them himself before he could get to the Post Office.

"Aye, you've started a cold all right." Mam hadn't sat through fifteen years of *Holby City* for nothing. "Keep in the warm today."

"Bud I god der ged by passport sordid," I said, screwing up my fifth tissue of the morning.

36

"You're not going out," said Mam. "Leave it to me. Griff, go over the Post Office and get her passport forms."

"But I need by photos taken," I wailed. I couldn't face a camera just then. My hair had all the lustre and sheen of day-old spaghetti and my nose had swollen to three times its usual size.

"You've still got a couple of weeks," Griff comforted me, putting on *his* Warm Coat, under Mam's approving gaze. "You'll need someone to counter-sign them, though. A professional person, who's known you for years. Shall I fetch Mrs Hathaway?"

Mam and I shrieked. "Don't you dare," warned Mam. "I'll take them up the surgery, one night. Dr Vaughan can sign for Holly."

"You only want to show him your wax lumps," said Griff. "Won't be long."

"You'll get your photos," Mam told me, tucking another cushion behind my head. "Dad'll run you up Morwaun in the week. There's a photo booth in the bus station."

"Dad's still sulking," I sniffed. We hadn't spoken since the row. I didn't dare approach him. He'd only cut me, raw and jagged. These days he was like a saw with a bare head.

"I'll square him," said Mam. "You cwtch up by there. Remember, you've got to ring them Le Freak people. Make sure they know when you're coming over."

I closed my eyes. I wasn't up to communicating with a strange French family just yet. Hell, I couldn't even get through to my own father.

The next day, I still couldn't ring my future employers. They'd have had trouble understanding my French on a normal day, let alone pronounced through a nose blocked thicker than the rush-hour Severn tunnel. But I couldn't put the call off much longer.

"At least the lady sounded nice, Hol," remarked Lin.

I nodded. "I understood what she was saying, but I had a job finding the words to speak back to her."

"You said who you were, though?" asked Lin, opening a cupboard door.

"I tried," I moaned. "But the tape ran out before I could finish." All that tinny voice had told me was to leave a message before the *bip sonore*. Flaming answerphones.

"Anyway..." I paused, intrigued. Lin was holding a pile of bedsheets.

"You didn't tell me this was a toga party," I cackled. "Is your boss invited? A couple of drinks and she'll end up with her laurels round her knees – "

"Hello, Mrs Whipple!" sang Lin. I turned around just in time to see that fashionable lady standing in the doorway.

I froze, but Mrs Whipple simply flashed me a magenta smile and stilted into the room on four-inch heels. I noticed the pile of folded sheets under her arm. Surely even she wouldn't have brought a change of outfit to a toga party?

"Hiya, Holly," chirped Mrs Whipple, dumping the sheets on the table. "Come to help us get ready? Owen will be pleased."

I stared. "Owen's fashion show? We haven't got to wear sheets, have we?"

Lin and Mrs Whipple yelped with laughter. "Not us. The bookshelves." Lin reassured me. "We're covering them with sheets. Owen wants a neutral background."

"Let's do it," said Mrs Whipple, straightening up to reveal a canary yellow T-shirt informing the world that *Librarians are novel lovers*. "Lin, you and Holly start by there, and I'll go down the Cwarp for the nibbles."

"Typical," I muttered as the clack of her heels had died away. "You do all the work, and she goes shopping."

"It don't matter," said Lin, hoiking the sheet up. "Why don't you write those people a letter, and then phone a couple of days later? You could use our French dictionaries." She indicated both volumes of the Tower's Foreign Language section.

"How many are coming to the show tonight?" I asked as Lin worked a hospital corner around the Reference shelf.

"A dozen, definite," said Lin. "And Owen's tutor, and another lecturer, to assess his work. Oh, and the models." She giggled. "Desree the hairdresser was supposed to help style them, but Mrs Whipple don't want her to, not since she wouldn't flick her Dido."

"And Kim said he might show up." I smiled. I loved talking about Kim. In some ways, it was better than being with him. I didn't have to worry about what I said.

"He'll have to stand at the back, then," said Lin. "The light from his halo will get in the audience's eyes."

I looked at her. It wasn't like Lin to bite back. Perhaps she was annoyed because she didn't have a man to take her squelching round muddy vineyards. A thought stabbed me. Maybe she'd try to get to know Kim herself while I was away. We worked in silence until Mrs Whipple returned.

"Good, Lin," said Mrs Whipple, nodding at the scene. "Owen's bringing the girls. They'll be here now in a minute."

"What about - the rest?" Lin asked.

"Down Below," said Mrs Whipple with a meaningful nod.

I turned away. Let them have their petty secrets.

"Holly, you can welcome the guests," said Mrs Whipple. "Sit by the door. Don't move from by there, now."

I glanced across the room at the models. All four catwalk goddesses appeared to have come straight from the shopping precinct.

"The girls are in Owen's year, at college," Lin explained as she handed me a programme. "They jumped at the chance to help him out. They say he's the nicest bloke in the class."

Fancy old Owen being such a hit with the ladies. By and large, Valleys opinion was that real men didn't stitch seams, they mined them.

"No time for chopsing, Holly," called Mrs Whipple. "The guests'll be here in a minute."

I glared at her. Wait till Kim got here. He'd put Mrs Whipple in her place. Look at her, in her fishnets. Talk about legs of mutton.

"Good evening, ladies and gentlemen," trilled MC Whipple, beaming at the assembled guests. "Thank you all for coming."

Exactly half of Lin's promised dozen had turned up. There'd be plenty of room for Kim. And I could sit beside him. The corners of my mouth turned upwards in spite of themselves.

"Mr Wheeler!" carolled Mrs Whipple, her eyes flashing as that gentleman walked in. "There's nice to see you. Oh -" as the door opened again - "it's Sonny and Cher."

"No, it's me and Mansel," said Shireen, unbuttoning her purple coat. "Holly! You haven't never come to see the fashions?"

Beneath her incredulous stare, I felt like a haystack with a scrunchie.

"Come on, Mansel," said Shireen. "Hiya, Mr Wheeler. Hiya, Mrs Stockley."

She didn't seem surprised to see the older generation taking an interest in clothes. Mansel, lolloping behind her, winked at me and confided: "Me, I'm just a lawnmower. You can tell me by the way I walk."

I nodded gravely. The music sounded and the fashion show began.

Owen's collection, *Poetry & Emotion*, wasn't bad, I had to admit. No postage-stamp tops or crocheted boots. Rachel, the star model, was teetering along in a mini red and black creation. She turned and veered back across the room, to murmurs of admiration.

"What's this got to do with poetry?" I whispered to Lin, as Rachel wobbled off. "She can't even walk in a straight line. Unless it's a tribute to Dylan Thomas?"

"Yeah, very good, Hol." Lin got to her feet. "I've got to sort some stuff out. See you."

Even my best friend couldn't stand my company these days. I stared hard at the programme in my hand. Maybe I wouldn't come back from France at all.

"And last but not least, a big thank you to the models." Mrs Whipple led the applause, her bangles jingling.

"One final thing," she continued. "One of us is about to go and make a sensation in the world capital of fashion."

I thought that was a bit premature. Wait till Owen got through his exams, at least.

"Holly!" exclaimed Mrs Whipple. "Come forward!"

All the heads turned towards me. Lin made frantic get-up gestures. I rose to my feet and walked towards Mrs Whipple, almost as steadily as Rachel.

"Holly is off to France in a couple of weeks," said Mrs Whipple. "So to round off the show, we've organized a send-off for her. There's food and drink downstairs, but first here's a little something to remember us by. Rachel?"

Rachel sashayed up to me and handed me a small box. I opened it to find an intricate Celtic ring.

"Are you all right, Holly?" Mrs Whipple flung her arm round my shoulders. "Aww, no need for that. Lin, got a tissue?"

"It's my party," I spluttered. "I'll cry if I want to." Everyone laughed except Mansel, whose eyebrows rose in silent admiration.

Downstairs, the computers had been moved into a corner and the trestle tables were laden with more crisps, peanuts and little sausages than you could shake a cocktail stick at. Shamed, I took back the harsh thoughts I'd had about everyone present.

"That's why we made you stop by the door, Holly," explained Lin. "We didn't want you going downstairs and seeing what we'd done."

"Heck, no." Mrs Whipple shook her head so violently, her earrings nearly fell off. "I was afraid you'd wander off before the special guests arrived." She glanced past me and twinkled.

I turned, and saw Mam and Griff in the doorway. This time I couldn't manage a pertinent song lyric. Everybody else made up for this with a chorus of "Aaaah" as Mam held out her arms for a cwtch.

"Tea, Mrs Gethin?" offered Lin.

"No thanks, it do keep me awake," said Mam. She indicated a jar of decaffeinated coffee. "I'll have the artificial."

"What do you keep looking at the door for, Holly?" chirped Shireen.

Fortunately, Desree saved me from replying. "Mansel!" she exclaimed. "How's that group of yours coming on?"

Mansel had spent years dreaming of managing a band, in between his DJ-ing gigs. To everyone's surprise, he gave a considered reply. "I've 'ad an idea. What Wales needs is an all-girl hard rock band."

"Needs, indeed," scoffed Shireen, plainly unhappy at the thought of Mansel devoting his working hours to young women in tight leather outfits.

41

"The Price Girls," suggested Desree. "You could have Tidy Price, Mental Price, Prop Forward Price, and all."

We laughed. Mansel, emboldened by his artificial coffee, outlined his plans for the group. They would play open-air gigs, maintaining it suitably real, so that when the backlash came against this talent show rubbish, the world 'ould be ready for 'em.

"Sounds good," said Desree, tactfully neglecting to mention that most of Pontycynon had been attending Mansel's open-air gigs for years, due to his habit of leaving his bedroom window open.

Mam sidled up to me. "Don't upset yourself, lovely," she murmured. "He didn't want to come here in front of everyone else."

I stared. Why would Kim be embarrassed to be seen with me? Then I realised. Mam thought I was hurt because Dad hadn't shown up. As if I'd even noticed he wasn't here, putting ketchup on his nibbles and telling Mrs Whipple she'd catch her death.

"He'll come round," said Mam. "But he's worried, see."

So worried, he was ignoring his daughter. And Kim hadn't even turned up. My mind threw up a few choice words that couldn't have been printed in The Fibs.

"You'll have to e-mail us the fashion news from France, Holly," called Mrs Whipple.

"Our Holly, in the fashion," scoffed Mam fondly. "Keep breathing."

"She means, 'Don't hold your breath', I translated.

"Holly won't need to e-mail," said Lin. "Holly's going to write articles for *Y Llais*. Sending news from our twin town."

Everyone exclaimed. "Never!" "Foreign correspondent, is it?" "I read the news today, oh boy…"

"Lin!" I hissed, aside.

"Well, you should do," murmured Lin. "And send it to the editor, not Kim. Show him what you can do without his help."

How much artificial had she drunk? But maybe she was right.

"Worth a try," I said. "But I doubt much sensational goes on, there. I'll have to start a riot. Get the Mayor drunk on Trevor's wine."

"What's this?" asked Mam.

"*Chien* Bites *Homme*, Mam," I told her. "*Chien* Bites *Homme*."

"To Holly," said Mr Wheeler, raising his glass. "*Bon voyage* and happy year in France."

Warmed by the chorus of good wishes, I drank my Château Cwarp. That fickle reporter. I'd get a story that would make his flower shows droop.

5.

Out Of The Fine Plan, Into The Foyer

As the footsteps died away, I gazed at the grey walls that surrounded me. Only three days on foreign tarmac, and I'd ended up in police custody.

My family didn't know yet. I'd eventually have to ring home and confess. I could already hear the triumphant chorus: *"You didn't want to have gone there in the first place."*
I shifted on my bench. I couldn't go back home after just one week. That would have beaten even Mam's prediction, as we'd stood at Bethel Road bus stop. I'd been weighed down with my shoulder bag, two suitcases and the chicken sandwiches I'd been told were my rations until the Eurostar.

"You didn't pack your Warm Coat," Mam had fretted. "Still, don' matter. You'll be home by Christmas. Here's the bus." She'd tilted her face for a quick peck. "And don't do SILLY things." This last injunction was the Mam equivalent of a comprehensive risk insurance clause.

Griff's farewells that morning had been equally ungainly. He'd allowed me an embarrassed cwtch on the doorstep, then pulled away. Dad had left for work without saying goodbye at all.

At least my university department had been more enthusiastic. Professor Havard had written back to tell me he was delighted I would be going to France, and trusted I would derive great benefit from my sojourn there. Which probably meant my adjectival endings had better have shaped up, by the time I got back. But at least he'd given me his blessing.
I'd arrived in London with my shoulder bag and a suitcase in each hand (the sandwiches hadn't made it past Newport). At the Eurostar

station, I'd checked the other passengers' labels and concluded that a) I was on the right platform and b) French handwriting had loops in places where ours didn't even have places. All that shrugging, probably.

Paris hadn't thrown me either. I'd had no trouble taking the Métro from the Gare du Nord to the Gare Montparnasse, where the trains ran from Paris to the west. There, I'd bought my ticket and found the right *quai* – platform - without any assistance.

French people didn't seem overly helpful. Two men loitering on the station had sniggered "*C'est lourd, non*?" as I'd heaved my luggage along. Parisians didn't deserve a city like this, I'd thought, gazing at the sculpted buildings and the lines of traffic proceeding down the avenues, white road signs directing them in incisive black capitals.

The journey from Paris to Mauvoisins had taken about three hours. By the time we'd arrived it had been too dark to see anything out of the window. I'd stowed away my paperback. Here it was. My new town.

Mauvoisins train station had long, arched windows. Both ticket office windows were closed, but the faded cream walls displayed an illuminated map of the town. Fair play, the French authorities had common sense. In Pontycynon, the firemen had to stop and ask you the way.

I'd found a taxi to take me to rue Jules Ferry. As we'd zipped along the wrong side of the road, shop windows had glowed behind iron grilles. I'd glimpsed names like *Miss Laura* and *Top Discs*. Not quite as exotic as I'd imagined.

At No. 12, a man had opened the door. He'd extended his hand to me. As I'd reached out to shake it, my bag had slid off my shoulder, slipped down my arm and slammed into him.

Mortified, I'd burbled apologies, but a small, dark-haired lady had appeared and taken charge of the situation. "*C'est* Ollie? Christian*, tu prends ses bagages*. Enter, Ollie. *Moi, c'est* Annick."

A few minutes later I'd been sitting at their dining room table. Madame Le Floch, Annick, was brisk, dark-haired and tanned, with little gold earrings that swung every time she turned her head. Monsieur Le Floch, Christian, had brown eyes and a hawk nose. I'd judged them to be in their early thirties.

"You are hungry, Ollie?" Annick had pronounced my name carefully.

"*C'est pas* Ollie," her husband had remarked, lounging in his chair. "*C'est Auli.*"

"Holly," I'd mumbled.

"Hholy," they'd chanted.

I'd nibbled an almond pastry as Annick had asked about my journey, my studies and life in Wales. I'd responded, pleased that I could understand her rapid French.

Pouring me a *tisane*, or herbal tea, Annick had explained that Christian was a salesman and she was a secretary: "But I am making studies of law, part-time, in the University of the Third Age."

Neither Le Floch had ever visited their Welsh twin town ("Pont-asinine", as Christian had pronounced it.) Their two children, Sébastien and Laetitia, were on holiday. "They are at my mother's house, in Bordeaux," Annick had explained. The children would be "returned" the next Friday, she'd told me.

I'd have time to explore Mauvoisins before then, I'd reflected, as I'd followed Annick and my suitcases upstairs to the spare room.

"*Voilà*, Hholy," Annick had announced, pushing open the door. I'd stepped inside and nearly bumped my nose on the opposite wall.

The small single bed took up most of the room. Annick had deposited my suitcases on the bed and turned to smile at me. I'd tried to hide my disappointment. Not room to swing a caterpillar.

Once alone, I'd sat on the bed and looked at the single framed watercolour painting facing me. If I turned round a bit sharpish I'd knock it off the wall. Looked like I'd have to go on a diet after all.

Back to this moment, in the police detention room. I shivered.

On my first morning in France, Annick, Christian and I had had breakfast together. Outside it had been raining.

"*Il fait gallois*," Annick had joked. "It is Wales weather. I have a rendezvous at the doctor's this morning, Hholy. But I take you into town centre for shopping, later."

I'd nodded and she'd departed in a juddering pale blue Citroën. I'd begun to clear the breakfast table.

"Hold!" Christian had said as I'd started washing up. He'd held out a pair of light pink rubber gloves. As I'd reached for them, he'd rubbed my fingers with his.

Startled, I'd pulled my hand back. Christian had looked hurt, placed the other glove on the table, turned and left the kitchen. I'd picked up the glove, regretting my action. Continental people were famously touchy-feely. They'd think Welsh people were plain touchy. I'd washed the breakfast things, embarrassed by my over-reaction.

That afternoon, Annick and I had climbed into the Citroën and driven to *centre-ville*. Fascinated, I'd gazed into the windows, reading the signs on display. A *librairie* wasn't a library, but a bookshop. And everywhere had been selling *soldes*.

"You lick the windows," Annick had remarked.

I'd pulled back. We weren't that primitive in Pont-asinine.

"*Non*," Annick had laughed. "When one looks, but does not buy, one licks the windows."

Ah, window-shopping. My vocabulary was growing already.

I'd bought a phone card so I could ring home and let them know I'd arrived safely. They'd been out (the nerve), so I'd tried *les Prix Opposés*. They hadn't been in either. Well, my card would have run out by the time Mansel had got to the chorus of *Si Si Je Suis Un Rock Star*. I'd left a message on their answerphone.

As we'd driven back to rue Jules Ferry, I'd remembered something. "Annick, where is the rue Claude Chappe?" I'd asked. "I know a Welsh girl who lives there."

"I know not this street," Annick had replied. "But you buy yourself a plan of the town, Hholy, and we will regard it."

And I did buy a map. But Annick never even saw it.

That evening we'd had wine with our meal. I'd giggled at Christian's stories about his visits to Britain. He had once spent three months in Southampton, selling roller-skates.

"Christian is the *angliciste* of the family," Annick had laughed, carrying our plates into the kitchen. I'd smiled. It was nice that they didn't treat me like a servant.

"I like zat smile," Christian had said, refilling my glass. As he'd handed it back to me, he'd rubbed my fingers with his.

I'd pulled away. Continental habit or not, I hadn't liked this.

I'd wondered if I should have told Annick. She'd probably have laughed at me. If only Kim had been here. That was it. I'd talk about Kim, so Christian would know there was a man in my life. Then he'd leave me alone.

As soon as Annick had returned, I'd mentioned *mon ami journaliste*.

"We will invite him," Annick had said. "Ah, Cri-Cri?" She'd patted her husband's arm.

Cri-Cri had looked distinctly unmoved. I'd smiled to myself. Looked like his battery had gone flat. That should end the digital interactive sessions.

When I'd got up the next morning, Christian had gone out. Annick had been working at the living room table, wielding a screwdriver over a lamp. The table had been spread with newspaper, an electrical flex coiled upon it. I'd bounced out of the house, my newly cut keys jangling in my pocket. My mission: to find Chassa Brake.

I'd made straight for the *Maison de la Presse*, a large newsagent's shop in the town square, and bought one of those maps that never went back the right way once you'd unfolded it. The rue Claude Chappe had been a couple of folds away. I'd set off, leaving the town square and walking down the Boulevard de l'Aquitaine, the traffic roaring past me into the west.

The day had been warm, the sunshine glinting on the pavement as I'd walked along. A sharp blast from a car horn had made me jump.

I'd turned to see a man grinning at me from his car, the window rolled down.

I'd racked my brains. How did he know me? Was he a neighbour of the Le Flochs? Or the taxi driver who'd driven me to their house?

"Bonjour, monsieur," I'd said politely.

"Tu veux que je t'emmène?" the *monsieur* had inquired. The car behind had interrupted with an impatient blast, so my pursuer had smirked and driven off.

I'd thought of my first question for Chassa. How could she stand to live in a country full of men like this?

I'd crossed a map fold into another part of town. No more little cream houses with brick-red roofs and shutters. Just worn streets and blocks of flats painted in garish purples and greens. Not far now.

I'd pushed open the heavy wooden door of No 6, rue Claude Chappe and stepped into the dark. A small button had glowed on the wall. When I'd pressed it, the light had flickered on, revealing a row of metal letterboxes in the entrance hall. I'd read the names Bonnet, Archambaud, but no C. Brake.

Maybe her name was on her door. I'd just got up the stairs to the first floor when the light went out.

"Vous cherchez quelqu'un?" Two people had emerged from a room on the landing. I'd explained that I was seeking Mademoiselle Brake, tenant of these premises.

"L'Anglaise?" the girl had said. *"Elle est partie."*

Oh, great. I'd walked all this way and Chassa didn't live there any more. I asked if they knew where she had gone, but they'd responded with an Olympic-class synchronised shrug.

I'd inched down the stairs and headed back to *centre ville*. Another thought had nagged me. If I'd complained to Annick about Christian, she might have turned me out to fend for myself. I'd have had to live in a dump like 6, rue Claude Chappe.

I wondered if the police were going to give me anything to eat or drink.

"So your friend has moved house," Annick had said, that evening. "But she has surely the telephone. You call the Information, Hholy, and they will give you her number."

Good thinking, I'd approved, as I'd washed the dishes. I'd do it as soon as Annick came off the phone. Every evening she'd called to say *bonsoir* to her children, a greeting that invariably lasted forty-five minutes.

I'd decided there was time for a bath first. Wallowing in the suds, I'd felt happier. Christian would back off when his kids were around. Maybe I'd start wearing gloves. Tell them I had highly contagious eczema.

Wrapped in my bath towel, I'd left the bathroom and headed upstairs to my room. Drat, the towel had got caught in the bathroom door. I'd turned to free it.

But the towel hadn't got caught in the bathroom door. It had got caught in Christian's right hand.

I'd stood rooted to the spot. Then, with his other hand, he'd tried to make sure my assets got some fresh air and exercise.

"Huh?" My yelp had been one of amazement rather than fright. I'd tried to cover myself with the towel, but he'd held on to it. Panicking, I'd pulled off the towel and shoved it over his face, leaving him reeling while I'd hurtled away in my natural state. I'd shot into my room, slammed the door behind me and pushed the bed against it as a barricade, shaking uncontrollably.

I'd pulled on my clothes without drying myself. That was it. I was leaving this house. What was the French for *ménage à trois*? I wasn't going to hang around and find out.

What was I going to tell Annick? She'd been so nice to me. And where was I going to go?

There was only one thing I could do.

I'd sneaked down the stairs to the bathroom, panicking in case Christian was there. He'd probably told his wife I'd tried to pull him into the bath with me. I'd shuddered. The French went in for *crimes passionnels*. I'd pictured Annick striding up to my room, her electrical flex stretched between her hands.

I'd written a note to Annick, explaining what had happened. By the time she read it, I'd be out of reach. I'd known exactly where to leave the note - somewhere she would find it, but Christian would never look. I'd left my keys in my room, tiptoed downstairs with my luggage, wrenched the front door open, rushed outside and fled. They could keep my towel.

"So, *mademoiselle*," said the police officer, reappearing in the detention room, "you have left your lodgings and you have no job."

"Yes," I repeated. "I can stay here tonight? In a cell?"

"*Non, mademoiselle*," said the officer firmly. "We have not the right to put you in a cell. But I have the number of a refuge for women. You may telephone from here." He ushered me out of the detention room and into the reception area of the police station.

My spirits rose. I'd done the right thing, coming to the police station. I picked up the telephone receiver and dialled the number of the refuge.

Ten minutes later a lady in jeans and a sweatshirt had arrived at the police station, asking for me. This Françoise listened to my story, her eyes thoughtful behind her glasses.

"I can take you to the shelter," she said. "But you cannot stay there indefinitely without a job."

"I will find work," I promised, warmed by the thought of a safe bed for the night.

Françoise took my suitcases and soon we were driving away. Even in a strange car, with a stranger, in the dark, I felt secure for the first time in days.

The shelter looked like every other house in the street, with its double front doors and long windows.

"We do not give the address of the *foyer* to others," said Madeleine, the lady in charge, as I stood in the hall with my baggage. "In cases where the husband pursues the wife, you understand."

I nodded. Françoise wished me *bonne chance*, then drove away. I wondered what her link with the shelter was. Perhaps she was a volunteer there. Or could she have been a former resident?

Madeleine led me down the hall. I saw a room with a large expanse of lino, a single bookshelf and a television. This must be the day room. Through another open door I spotted a camp bed and a folded blanket.

"The dormitory," explained Madeleine. "The *salle d'eau* is next to it. Tomorrow we will speak of your situation. *Bonne nuit.*"

I sank on to the camp bed. Tomorrow I'd have to look for another job, another place to live, and – there was no escaping it – ring home to explain why I'd left the Le Flochs.

I lay back and closed my eyes. Lacking the energy to undress, I pulled the blanket over myself and breathed deeply. Whatever hands I'd fallen into, they didn't seem the kind to stray where they had no business.

6.

Ex-Pat Timing

"*Jeune fille au pair*," said Madeleine, looking up from her desk. "There is the agency of employment in *centre ville*. You have a *résumé?*"

I'd make one, I decided, as the doorbell rang. Madeleine rose to heed its summons and then reappeared, escorting a tall lady with two small children into the hall. I fetched my coat. Madeleine had enough to do. The sooner I could get myself a job and lodgings, the sooner I'd be off her hands.

The *Agence National de l'Emploi* was my first stop. My hopes sank as I studied their noticeboard. I wasn't a trained mechanic, nor had I had five years' experience as a nursing aide. But the *agence* had a computer. With much gesturing, I asked the man in charge if I could type out a CV. He agreed, probably relieved that I'd have something to keep my hands occupied for the rest of my visit.

Straight away I hit a problem. Where did I live? I couldn't give the address of the shelter, I'd promised to keep it quiet. A Post Office box would cost money. But I wasn't going to run back home with my tail between my leggings. I'd think of something.

Then I remembered. I hadn't rung *L'information* to find the number for Chassa Brake. I attacked my CV with renewed vigour.

That evening I trudged back to the refuge, my spirits low. *L'Information* had told me they had no listing for anyone named Brake. At the library I'd found a municipal notice board that displayed cards offering apartments to let. I'd felt ill just looking at the rent required.

I'd even gone into a couple of schools and explained I was a native English speaker who could give English lessons. In each case I had been politely informed that the staff team was complete.

Back at the refuge, I went into the day room. The two kids I'd seen that morning were wrangling over a comic book. I picked up a newspaper and sat in an armchair with it.

"You are here since a long time?" The tall lady, the children's mother, addressed me from behind the ironing board she had set up in the corner of the room.

Reluctant to tell the whole story, I said I was a British student searching for work. The lady, Valérie, considered this while her kids squabbled.

"There is an employment agency, rue Jean Jaurès," she finally said. "Companies will perhaps need English speakers to answer the telephone."

I sat up. Not a bad idea.

"You are from which corner of England?" asked Valérie.

"I am not from England. I am from Wales," I replied.

"Portugal?" Valérie looked surprised.

"*Non, non. Pas Portugal - Pays de Galles*," I enunciated. *Mon Duw*, my accent would need some working on before I answered any company calls.

As Valérie's kids shouted, I turned the pages of the newspaper. Ah, here was a word I recognized - "*cinéma*". I'd go to the pictures.

Outside the cinema. I looked at the two posters. One of the films, *Midi à quatorze heures*, appeared to be a complex, intriguing story of modern relationships. I glared at the stills. I'd had enough of forbidden liaisons for a while.

The other film, *Les Diaboliques*, looked more promising. "*Un grand classique du cinéma français*", read the press cutting. From what I could make out, it was about two women who plotted to murder a nasty man. That was more like it. I strode into the cinema.

Les Diaboliques turned out to be an old black and white thriller. I couldn't understand everything they said, but I could follow the story. A couple of times I almost jumped out of my seat.

It was getting downright scary, now we were approaching the *dénouement*. This flickering effect was most dramatic. Hold on, why had the screen gone black?

When the grumbling sounded around the room, I realised that this wasn't part of the story. The film had broken down.

"*Messieurs – dames*," buzzed a disembodied voice. I couldn't make out the explanation that followed, partly because it was too rapid, and partly because the woman next to me was complaining loudly to her escort.

The lights came on. The discontented rumble grew louder. Now we'd never find out how the film ended.

But then came the twist.

A cry of "*ATTENDEZ!*" rang out. I looked up. Heads were turning to face the far aisle. A red flash flickered through the crowd, moving down the aisle to the front of the hall, where it stood revealed as a girl in a bright red sweatshirt.

"*ATTENDEZ!*" shouted the girl again. The room quietened. The girl held both palms up to the audience, then turned and beckoned. A tall young man ambled up to her, apparently fascinated by his trainers.

The girl – she was blonde, about my age – stepped forward and pulled a couple of surprised front-row spectators to their feet. Surely she wasn't the manager, she looked too young. And what did these poor people have to do with the film breakdown?

The girl waved her hands, then addressed her friend. She clutched her chest and swayed, as if she was ill. Laughter rippled through the room. Then I realised what was happening. The girl, her friend and the front-row spectators were acting out the end of the film.

I watched, entranced. As they ran through the action to the *dénouement*, the spectators broke into applause. "*Chapeau!*"shouted the woman next to me.

The blonde girl took her friend's hand and bowed to the crowd, her face aglow. Her friend gave a quick nod to the audience, then tugged his hand free and hurried back to his seat.

I wanted to thank the girl, but she was surrounded by admiring cinemagoers. I trudged up the aisle towards the exit.

Outside, the evening was cool, but clear. I watched people strolling down the street, laughing and talking together. I drew back into the shadows and watched them walk off into the twilight.

I didn't want to go back to the shelter and listen to Valérie's kids screaming. There was a café on the corner. I'd have an ice cream.

I pushed open the café door and saw that one table was free. I hurried over, sat down and buried my face in the menu.

"*You ain't gonna learn much French like that.*" Dad's voice sounded in my head, grimly amused. "*You want to talk to some of 'em.*"

I glanced around. The place was full of student types. I couldn't just go up and talk to them. I stared at the menu. Was it was *'un'* or *'une' limonade*? I'd have to buy two, then I could order *'deux limonades'* in correct French.

A shout rang out from the corner table. "*Dégage!*" laughed a girl's voice.

And then, the most startling sound I'd heard all week.

A Valleys accent, declaring: "Give over, you daft rabbit."

I swung round in my seat, promptly knocking the menu to the floor. Diving to retrieve it, I nearly tripped up a passing waiter and his tray. Squeaking an embarrassed *pardon*, I got up and came face to face with the two people sitting at the next table. It was the blonde girl from the cinema and her reluctant co-star.

"*Ca va?*" asked the girl, looking at me.

"Umm, hello," I blurted. "I saw you in the cinema. You were great."

The girl's eyes widened. She replied with a single word: "Whereyoufromthen?"

"South Wales," I said. "Pontycynon." *Go on, ask her.* "Is your name Chassa Brake?"

The girl looked surprised, then burst out laughing. Her companion looked from me to her, bemused.

"Yes," said the girl. "And you're Holly."

"I've got some Aeros for you," was all I could think of to say.

Chassa jumped out of her seat, put her hand on my shoulder and pressed her cheek against mine.

"I'm Chassa," she confirmed. "This is Didier. *Lapin* -" she turned to her friend and rattled off a burst of French. Didier, her friend, reached over and shook my hand as Chassa seized another chair and pushed it against their table.

"Come and sit by'yere," she said, looking closely at me. "Yep, you're Holly all right. How long you been here?"

However long *she'd* been there, she hadn't lost her accent. I took a deep breath. "I arrived on Saturday," I began. Looking at Didier, I paused and translated: "*Je suis arrivée ici*, um, *samedi dernier…*"

"*C'est bon, j'ai compris*," said Didier with a grin. I went pink.

"Don' worry, Holly," Chassa reassured me. "He understands what I say in English. Usually when he's not supposed to. Bad rabbit." She shook her head at him. I wondered where the rabbit reference came into it. Didier didn't have buck teeth or unusually long ears.

"You were great now just," I ventured. "Acting out the film."

"Well, we'd seen it before," explained Chassa. "Didier's seen it – how many times, Laps? He's doing Film Studies at college. He wants to direct a film one day."

"*Science-fiction*," nodded Didier dreamily.

"Where are you living, Holly?" asked Chassa.

I poured out the story of how I'd moved in with the Le Flochs, then moved out twice as fast. They listened wide-eyed, the only interruptions from Chassa, translating an occasional phrase for Didier. She seemed to know when he needed help.

"So I went to the pictures to cheer myself up, and then…I saw you," I finished.

Chassa and Didier exchanged glances. Now they were going to tell me they'd endured much worse treatment from French landlords. They'd probably had their doors burned down, their pillowcases hidden and their biros confiscated, yet carried on undaunted.

"Well," said Chassa, sitting back in her chair. "The creepy git. Right, you can't stay in that shelter all year. Laps, *on va chercher ses bagages?*"

Didier replied in calm, measured French. Chassa flashed back her answer. Her French came out a lot faster than his, for all she was the foreigner. While they talked, I studied their faces. Chassa had a pointed chin and bright eyes, while Didier had a steady, placid look.

Chassa leaned forward to make a point, tilting her face up to his. Soppy couple. The thought of Kim stabbed me.

I put on my screensaver face to hide my discomfort. But they didn't kiss. Chassa looked like an eager kitten reaching up to paw the nose of a patient Labrador.

"Holly," announced Chassa, "we're taking you out of that hostel. Rabbit's got the car outside. We'll drive you there, you pack your stuff, then you can come and stay with me. I'm working at a cafe in town."

"She's a waitress at the Bad Café," snickered Didier.

"The studio's above the café. The owner won't mind you staying. We'll go now, is it?" Chassa jumped up from her chair.

A waitress, not a teacher. And what was this Bad Café? But she was from home. And she knew Sion. Sion knew Griff. Griff knew Mam and Dad. Surely they'd agree I was doing the right thing. I picked up my handbag and followed Chassa and Didier through the café and out into the street.

"*Monte*, Holly," invited Chassa, as we stopped beside a silver whale of a car. I tugged open the door and clambered into the back seat. Chassa dived in beside Didier, the doors clicked, and we were off. Didier reached for the dashboard controls. The sound of crackling filled the car speakers.

"Not Static FM again, Laps," sighed Chassa.

"*C'est pour que vous appreniez le français*," grinned Didier.

"We won't learn much like that," said Chassa. "Now, Holly, which way to your hostel?"

"Umm, I think you turn left here," I volunteered.

"Ah! *Sens interdit*," noted Didier, braking sharply. I cringed. I'd nearly sent us down a No Entry road.

"Nearly got you, Laps," said Chassa. "We'll have you driving on the left in no time. Won't we, Holly?"

At the shelter, Valérie and the kids were nowhere to be heard. I wanted to ask where they'd gone, but the angle of Madeleine's eyebrows made it clear that, like our recent left turn, this was an avenue better not pursued. I collected my things, which didn't take long.

As we drove away from the shelter, I realised I hadn't asked where exactly this café was. Maybe it was miles out of town. How many map folds would I have to cross? What if it was near the rue Jules Ferry? I shuddered at the thought of bumping into Christian and his fingers.

"Chassa," I began. "Where exactly...?"

"Here we are," interrupted Chassa. "It's just by'yere."

I stepped out of the car and looked around. The street was deserted, but the lights of the café were subtly inviting. I stepped closer to the window and peered inside at a sandwich bar, with high chrome stools and a drinks shelf, amply stocked. I smiled. This looked nice.

"No, by'yere, Holly," called Chassa.

I turned to look across the street. My smile faded.

"I know it don' look grêt," said Chassa.

Estée Lauder would have had a job to soft-soap this. I took in the dun-coloured frontage with "CAFE au BAS de la RUE" above the window in thin letters.

"We call it the *Café Bas d'* for short," explained Chassa. "The Bad Café." She pushed open the door and we walked inside.

I looked at the empty walls beyond the tables. One corner boasted a dingy sofa of dubious upholstery. I wondered if any local buses were missing their back seat.

"*Alors? C'est à c't'heure-ci qu'on rentre?*" grated a voice from the other side of the room.

I looked up and saw a young, fair-haired man wearing a spattered pinafore apron.

"Patrice," Chassa ran over to him and poured out another torrent of French. I'd never be able to speak it that well. She even waved her arms grammatically.

Patrice didn't look at all pleased at the prospect of a new lodger. I folded my hands, trying to look quiet and reliable with the rent.

Chassa wound up her narrative on a pleading note. It clearly didn't work. Patrice grunted, flicked his pinny at us and stomped back into the room he'd just emerged from. I felt sorry to have caused such trouble. It had been a valiant effort.

"I'll go back to the shelter," I offered. "Thanks for trying."

"Oh, you can move in," said Chassa. "But he says if we want dessert, we'll have to get it ourselves, 'cos he's going home. Anyone want some ice cream?"

Soon the three of us were squashed on to the bus seat, making inroads into Patrice's mint chocolate chip supplies. Chassa had found some clean white bowls and we'd all dug in. We'd even sampled a bottle of red wine she'd produced from the kitchen.

"All right, Holly?" teased Chassa, as I refilled my glass.

"Yes." The wine had kicked in. I raised my glass, embarrassed, but determined to thank them properly. "Thanks to you, Chassa, and you, Monsieur Lapin, er, Rabbit -" I floundered. "How do you call, er, why -"

"Why do I call him Rabbit?" asked Chassa. She looked at Didier. "Only one reason."

Didier looked resigned. Oh, no. I was going to hear some intimate detail that only their Relate counsellor should be privy to.

"To annoy him," said Chassa. "I said it once, last summer, and the name stuck. Didn't it, Bunny?"

"Yes, Lolotte," replied Didier solemnly.

"He calls me that to get his own back," explained Chassa. "Ever since he found out my real name's Charlotte. Makes me sound like a poodle."

"*Miss Lolotte*," snickered Didier.

"Oh, give over, Mr Garden," replied Chassa, waving a threatening spoon.

They weren't very romantic, I thought. But other questions were more pressing.

"And the studio, where you live...?" I began.

"Upstairs," said Chassa, spooning up her choc chips. "It's a nice little room. I've even got a roof garden – or I will have, when Rabbit brings round those cyclamens he's been promising this long time." She paused to take another mouthful.

"Doesn't Patrice live above the café, then?" I asked.

"No, he lives with his Mam and Dad," explained Chassa. "They've got a big house in Mauvoisins. His Mam's a grêt cook. I've been round there for tea..." she smiled, apparently remembering a meal. "And his dad's a maintenance man. He comes round here to unblock the sink and stuff."

"Do you get many customers?" I asked.

Chassa and Didier laughed. "Not many," admitted Chassa. "These days everyone's going to that new sandwich bar down the street."

The one I'd admired, I thought, with a guilty blush.

"This place needs brightening up," admitted Chassa. "But whatever I suggest, old *Pas Triste* grunts that it's too dear. You'll have to back me up. Tell him how nice his café would look with new tablecloths. Even the moths won't eat here."

"Have you been in Mauvoisins long?" I asked.

"About a year," said Chassa. "I was in Brittany before, then I found a job in a school here. English language assistant."

"Asylum seeker," teased Didier. "Immigrant, from behind the Coal Curtain."

"I've been looking for a teaching job," I said eagerly. "Which school were you in? Would they want someone else for this school year?"

"Well, I was at the agricultural college," said Chassa. "But I dunno if they'll want another assistant."

Didier cackled and swished his hand through the air. Chassa shot him a warning frown. I looked from one to the other. Chassa must have smacked a pupil and lost her job.

"But you could try," said Chassa. "The English teacher there is Virginie Tessier. They call her Vicky. I've got her number somewhere. I'll find it for you."

"Agricultural college," I said, intrigued. "You didn't have to teach them about corn, and ploughing, did you?"

"Oh, no," said Chassa. "I'd get them to act sketches, or watch a video and answer questions. I'll dig out my lesson plans for you, if you like."

This was getting better by the sip. Two new friends, one of whom had teaching experience and could point me towards a job. I gave them both a big smile. Won over by my charm, Didier got up to leave, saying something about his bedtime.

"See you, Laps," said Chassa, getting up to accompany him to the door.

"And the next time, I will bring the plants for your garden," promised Didier.

"Same old song the cuckoo got," said Chassa. "'Bye." She pecked him on both cheeks, stroked his arm, then stood aside. Didier leaned towards me. I restricted my farewells to a skirmish with his face.

"This way," said Chassa, pulling open a door to reveal a staircase. We heaved my bags up to the top. Chassa unlocked the door at the top of the stairs, pushed it open and we lumped the bags inside the room.

"You are now setting foot on Welsh territory," joked Chassa, switching on the light. I was surprised by how spacious her room was. One small bed, a table, a compact shower unit, shelves and a cooker. I marvelled. I'd never managed to keep my room so neat.

"Let's put your stuff by'yere for now," suggested Chassa. She rounded the table and disappeared from view. I followed and stopped short in front of a large wardrobe which was almost obscured by a mountain of carrier bags.

"Haven't finished unpacking yet," explained Chassa. "I only moved in three weeks ago. You can have the bed and I'll move my mattress onto the floor. I've got clean sheets somewhere."

In a daze I looked on as she moved around, dragging one mattress into the corner and powering her way through the bags to get to the wardrobe. I sat on the bed, drained by the late hour and the swift pace of events.

"And I've thought of a way we can make some money," added Chassa. "Tell you about it tomorrow."

I looked around the room, now my home. My life was rearranging itself around my ears.

7.

Waitressing For Godot

On waking, I turned over in bed and came eye to bead with Trouble Bruin.

I sat up and looked across the room. Chassa was nowhere to be seen. A sheet of graph paper fluttered from the mirror: "Gone to the bakery. Chassa." Well, either she'd dressed on tiptoe, or she'd gone shopping in her pyjamas.

My eyes were drawn to Chassa's mountain of carrier bags. She must trust me, she'd left me alone with all her possessions. Not that I dared touch them, the heap looked too precarious. One false move and the whole tip might come down.

I unhooked the wooden window shutters and drew them back. Outside was a wide ledge.

I clambered over the sill and stood for a moment, looking at *les toits de Mauvoisins*. I leaned forward, holding on to the railings that surrounded the ledge. People walked up the street, directly beneath me.

Chassa had set up a chair on her ledge, with another folded beside it. It would be nice to sit out here on a warm night.

There was so much I wanted to ask Chassa, I thought, closing the window and turning my attention to the shower. How long she'd known Didier, where she'd met him... And I hadn't even found out exactly where she was from. Griff had said she'd gone to school with Sion in Croesy, but Mam and Dad would want to know the lot when I wrote home. They'd probably asked Mr Wheeler to e-mail the Le Flochs to make sure I was wearing my Warm Coat of an evening.

I shivered. Mr Wheeler was bound to contact the Le Flochs eventually. What would they tell him? Annick might not believe what she read in the note I'd left. And Christian wasn't going to confess. I'd just have to get another job and convince Mam and Dad that it had all been for the best.

Once washed and dressed, I ventured downstairs. I found Chassa in the kitchen with a pinniless Patrice and an older man.

"Holly!" whooped Chassa. "Breakfast?"

"*Alors, c'est vous, la nouvelle pensionnaire?*" said the older monsieur, smiling at me.

Who was he calling a pensioner? He was more than twice my age. No, hold on, *pension* meant a guest house, so maybe *pensionnaire* meant boarder. I greeted him in French, shaking his hand firmly to make up for my off-key accent.

"Serge Chazalet," he introduced himself. "*Ch'suis le papa de Patrice.*"

"I met Patrice's dad in the *Oulangerie*," explained Chassa.

Ah, the sink-unblocking dad. Now I could see the resemblance. Monsieur Chazalet seemed friendlier than his son, though. He had a twinkle. Patrice looked me up and down, clearly disappointed with the view.

"*Vous travaillez à Mauvoisins?*" inquired his *papa*. I explained that I was going to go and look for a job. "*A l'agricole école. Er, à l'école agricole.*"

"*Le Lycée Agricole,*" nodded Monsieur Chazalet. "*Eh, bien, bonne chance.*"

"I'll walk you to the bus stop if you like," offered Chassa. "But have some breakfast first."

As Chassa cut me a generous slice of baguette, Patrice grumbled something about a back gate that wouldn't lock. The Chazalets, *père et fils*, pulled open the kitchen door and walked into the back yard.

The coffee Chassa poured me was considerably stronger than Lin's artificial. But the bread tasted grêt, as my countrywoman would have put it. I was on the point of saying so, but she got in first. "French bread's good, i'n it? The bakery's just round the corner."

"Where's the museum?" I asked. "The one where you met Patrice's dad now just. The Orangerie, wasn't it?"

"Oh, that wasn't a museum!" cackled Chassa. "That was the bakery – the *boulangerie*. We call it the *Oulangerie* because the letter B's dropped off the sign." She grinned. "Could catch on. We'd get our hair done at the *Waffeur*'s, and save money in the *'Anque*."

I chewed slowly to give myself time to translate this. I got the impression that Chassa's thoughts travelled at twice the speed of most people's, even first thing in the morning.

"The poor greengrocer," I said, after thinking for a while.

Chassa's face lit up. "The *Pissier*," she said. "Good one, Holly."

I smiled and chewed, hoping this game never caught on in Pontycynon. Poor Derek Pugh would be a laughing stock.

It was an effort to keep up with Chassa's feet as well as her mind, I thought, hurrying along the street behind her.

"You can catch the 42 bus from the main square, Holly," explained Chassa. "But it doesn't go all the way to the *Lycée*. You'll have to – ooh, hold on." She skidded to a halt in front of a shop window displaying bangles and beads.

"Just thought of something," Chassa called back over her shoulder. I followed her into the shop, which looked like the sort of place Shireen spent most of her wages.

"*Et avec ça?*" enquired the assistant, as Chassa handed her something shiny and golden.

"*Ce sera tout*," replied Chassa, turning to hand the wrapped package to me. "Here, Holly. Pin your hair back with this."

Opening the paper bag, I beamed. The hair slide was slim, golden, pretty.

"Um, Holly," added Chassa, scrabbling in her pockets. "I've got nearly enough change, but I'm a bit short. Could you - ?"

I was delighted to lend her enough money to buy me such a nice present. Hairslide in place, I glided out of the shop after Chassa.

"I've got to go to the *'Upermarché*," explained Chassa. "Get some food in for the café. See you later. Good luck with the school."

Using a combination of stealth, skill and sheer animal courage, I asked a passing French person where the 42 bus stopped. In the shelter, I sat on the slidey bench and waited. Posters for a local election covered a nearby board, but I didn't recognise any of the acronyms the candidates were representing.

I wondered if Chassa had been here long enough to vote. And why was she waiting tables in a rundown café? It wasn't much of a job.

For an agricultural college, they didn't have a lot of livestock, I thought, walking up the tarmac drive to a large cream-coloured building. But then look at Trevor and Yvonne, their vineyard was their back yard. Maybe this school grew grapes too, I thought, checking the brass plate by the door. *Lycée Agricole de Mauvoisins*. I pressed the bell and tried to look employable.

"*Non, mademoiselle,*" said the secretary, for the third time. "We have no English *assistante* here. Never."

"*Mais –*" I hesitated. I'd better not say that *mon amie* Chassa had held the position the year before. They might not employ friends of people they'd fired. "*Je peux parler à votre professeur d'anglais? Madame Virginie Tessier?*"

"*Y'a pas de Madame Tessier ici,*" replied the secretary, giving me a strange look. "*Notre professeur d'anglais, c'est Monsieur Garcia.*"

Taken aback, I had to ad lib my *au revoir*. Stumbling out, I prepared to trek back down the drive and take the next bus back to *centre ville*.

Why were they saying they'd never had an assistant? Had Madame Tessier left too? Why had that secretary lied to me? Didn't they want to hire any Brits? I stomped towards the bus stop, hoping a freak drought would wither all their grapes.

Getting off the bus just before the main square, I meandered around the streets. There were some great cake shops in this town. I stopped to admire some biscuits shaped like penguins.

Turning my head from the temptation, I noticed another brass plaque, similar to the one outside the *Lycée Agricole*.

"*Ecole Vallentin*", read the plaque. "*Ecole Privée de Secrétariat.*"

I felt in my bag for my CV. A mixture of pique, perseverance and penguin-avoidance pushed me through the door and up a flight of stairs to the school.

"It is Madame Vallentin you must see," said the small lady in grey who let me in. She looked like a secretary, except for the dustpan in her left hand.

Sitting in the entrance hall, I peered through the windows into the adjoining classrooms, all whiteboards and desks. I noticed a row of typewriters in one.

I wondered how Chassa handled job interviews. She seemed to face most situations in life head-on. If only some of her charisma could rub off on me.

Madame Vallentin, the *directrice*, beckoned me to enter her office. She was a tall, imposing woman, with strands of grey in her dark hair. I thought I'd seen her somewhere before. Maybe because her height and her dark colouring reminded me of Valérie, the mother from the refuge. Madame Vallentin looked like a woman of means, though. Her office was smartly furnished, from the black leather swivel chairs to the aquarium in the corner.

I found myself sitting upright in my chair. Madame Vallentin made me feel distinctly downstairs maid. Any minute now I'd be bobbing a curtsey and agreeing to black-lead her range.

Madame Vallentin didn't seem unfriendly, though. She even let out a giggle when I said I lodged in a café in Mauvoisins.

"*Un café*," she said, amused. "Well, you will be able to take your lunch there. *Tenez, mademoiselle.* I am going to ask you to do a written translation."

The French text she handed me was about declining educational standards since 1980. Not easy to convert into elegant English prose. By the time I submitted my ink-stained page, I was drained.

"*C'est bien*," nodded Madame Vallentin. "*On vous prend.*"

A job? I shrieked and jumped out of my chair. Madame Vallentin looked on, smiling.

"But, *mademoiselle*," her tone was firm. "In this school, we use the Méthode Vallentin of teaching. In each of your lessons, you will follow the Méthode Vallentin. You will not bring in your own materials."

67

Fair enough, it was her school. I wondered what the Méthode Vallentin involved.

"You will return tomorrow and Madame Lesourd will explain the method to you," said Madame Vallentin. "When you will have acquired the method, you will teach one class, three mornings a week."

Oh. Only a part-time job, then.

"We do not have thousands of students," explained Madame Vallentin, seeing my disappointment. "Unless you prefer not to return?" she teased.

Oh, I'd return all right. I was going to come to this lovely school every day. Thrilled, I beamed around the room and noticed a lone goldfish in the aquarium.

Madame Vallentin followed my gaze. "*Il s'appelle Cousteau.*"

That did it. I burst out laughing.

"It is my husband who has chosen the name," explained Madame Vallentin, smiling at my reaction. "He has found it amusing."

Smart people, with a sense of humour too. This was going to be great. Mam and Dad would be amazed that I'd found another job all by myself. Lin, too – I'd e-mail her the second I could, with my news. And Kim…My thoughts melted into pure chocolate.

"When you return, you will bring your *carte de séjour* and your bank account number," instructed Madame Vallentin.

I skipped down the stairs. I was a teacher in France. Now Mam could hold her head up, whoever she next met across the dustbins.

"Hiya, Holly," Chassa greeted me from the corner table, where she was finishing her lunch.

I sat down next to her. Patrice appeared from the kitchen, gave me a dismissive glance and then retreated.

"You've missed the midday rush," joked Chassa, nodding at the empty tables. "Did you make it to the *Lycée*?"

I related my adventures, gratified to see how impressed Chassa looked.

"Fair play, Holly," she nodded. "You've done grêt."

"But why did the agricultural school say they'd never had an assistant before?" I pointed out.

Chassa looked away. Then she turned back to me, her face thoughtful. "Show me on the map where you went," she said. Obligingly, I unfolded the Flap of the Town and traced the bus route with my finger.

"Well, no wonder," said Chassa. "You went to the other *Lycée Agricole*. I forgot to tell you there were two. The one I was at is by'yere – hold on –" she unfolded another couple of flaps. I gave a little gasp. The area she was pointing to was out in the country. Never mind cows, they probably raised coyotes out there.

"I wondered how you'd taken the bus there," said Chassa. "As far as I know, there's no bus goes all the way out to Juillac."

"How did you used to get there, then?" I asked. "Did you have a car?"

"I don't drive," said Chassa, with a shudder.

"I can't either," I confessed. "Although my – someone – er, this friend, said I ought to take the test here, buy a car and drive it home." Thinking of Kim made me smile.

"Oh! Who's your Someone?" asked Chassa at once.

Blushing, I explained who Kim was, and the plans we'd made for my year in France.

"We thought I could advertise their wine in Mauvoisins," I concluded.

"We could sell some here," said Chassa. "*Hé*, Patrice!" she bellowed. "Shall we sell Welsh wine, in the café?"

"I do not wish to poison the clients," returned Patrice, from the kitchen doorway.

"It could be a speciality," argued Chassa.

"Already we cannot sell what we buy from the hypermarket," pointed out Patrice. "You would do better to talk to individuals," he said, suddenly addressing me. "Friends, who want to offer a present at Christmas. To their little rabbit," he turned back to Chassa with a sneer.

"Oh, give over," said Chassa. "But that's an idea. I'll have some for Patrice's Mam and Dad, for Christmas. Put me down for a couple of bottles, Holly."

"Right," I said, happily. "I'll have to check the prices, though."

"You have the money to buy imported wine?" Patrice teased Chassa.

"Well, not with my salary from here," replied Chassa smartly. "But I've got this great idea for earning some more money. I just need to sort summat out with Rabbit," she added, looking at me. "Then I'll tell you. Oh, and Holly, you busy on Monday evenings?"

"Ah," Patrice turned to me. "The Miss –" he gestured towards Chassa – "has decided she wants her Monday evening free. She says you can serve at table."

I was about to say I hadn't served at table since Lin and I had teamed up for the school ping-pong tournament, but a green flash of Chassa's eyes stopped me. Just then the phone rang in the kitchen, and Patrice went to answer it.

"It's only one night a week," Chassa encouraged me. "Go on, Holly – I really want to go to this first aid class, and it's on Monday evenings."

"If I'm anywhere near that kitchen, most of your casualties will be in here," I sighed.

"Let's start now," suggested Chassa, gathering the plates. "I'll show you how to work the dishwasher. Cranky old thing it is, too. It'll wash the floor as soon as look at you."

In the kitchen, Chassa introduced me to each piece of equipment, speaking softly and miming so as not to disturb Patrice while he talked on the phone. Her demonstration of how to mix the perfect *apéritif* while swigging a bit on the quiet had me stifling giggles.

"Here's the menu," said Chassa, leading me back into the cafe. "There are three set meals, see – *Menu Un*, *Menu Deux*, and *Menu Trois*. And at least once a day, someone's bound to ask for *Le Menu Quatre*. They think it's the highest form of wit."

I obediently looked at the bill-of-fare, but I was more interested in Chassa's past. "Was your school in Croesy?" I asked.

"Croes-yny-Pant Comp," said Chassa, banging clouds off the stacked menus. "Our rugby team was called the Panthers, until they lost to Aber Juniors, then they became the Pants. Sion was captain," she added, as I giggled. "We've been in the same class since the Infants."

"Did you come to France straight after school, then?" I asked. "What did your family say?"

In the silence that followed, I glanced at Chassa and went cold all over. Chassa's face had gone white, her features set in a chilling mask.

"I don't do families," said a strange, harsh voice where Chassa's lilt used to be.

Stunned, I took a step backwards. Chassa turned abruptly and made for the bar.

"Chassa, I'm sorry," I pleaded. "I just wondered how you ended up as a waitress. In a place like this –"

Chassa picked up a cloth and began polishing glasses. She didn't look at me.

I couldn't think what to say. Luckily, Patrice reappeared: "*Les Miss*," he announced. "You are both invited to eat chez Chazalet one of these Sundays, at midday. *C'est chez mes parents*," he confirmed. "*On va manger en famille*."

"Grêt," said Chassa, almost brightly. "Tell Sophie we'll be delighted to attend. Sophie is Patrice's Mam," she explained, without looking at me. "She's Polish."

"Oh," was my well thought-out, incisive comment.

Patrice, oblivious to the tension in the air, waved a notepad at his second-in-command. "Show Holly the system of the tables," he ordered her.

Chassa took the pad and squeezed past him. "Holly," she began. "Each table has a number. When you take the customer's order, write down the meal by'yere, and the drinks by'yere –"

She went through the whole waitressing process, but I hardly listened. I was tearing myself to shreds. Her family affairs were none of my business.

"Got that, Holly?" The colour had almost returned to Chassa's face.

"Oh, yes," I said hastily.

"Grêt." Chassa was brisk again. "You wouldn't mind doing an hour tonight, would you? I'd like to pop out for a bit –" She smiled at me. I found myself nodding like a windscreen puppy.

"Grêt," said Chassa. "I'll show you how to work the till."

Perhaps she was meeting Didier, I thought. I wanted to ask how they'd met, but I didn't want to see Chassa's face tighten like that again.

71

Happily, she brought up the subject herself. "Rabbit might pop in after work," she remarked, flicking a duster over the bar. "If I'm not back, just pull his ears from me."

"You're not very romantic," I said.

Chassa cackled. "You thought we were a couple? Neeer. A lot of people think we are," she added, rearranging the glasses behind the bar. "But we're just friends. So don' worry, we won't be mooning on the balcony every night, quoting Verlaine."

My relief must have shown on my face. Chassa smiled. "Tell you what. After closing time tonight, let's have something to eat upstairs. I've got some Thai food. And don' worry about serving, we probably won't get many in."

"Holl-eeee!!" Patrice bellowed for the third time as I shoved menus at a group of diners, almost knocking over their *apéritifs*.

"*Je prends le Menu Quatre,*" sniggered one man, perusing the menu. I smiled like a drain swallowing cabbagewater, then rushed back to the kitchen.

"Table Three," barked Patrice, handing me two steaming plates. "Then the washing up. *Vite.*"

I'd have sworn if I'd had any breath left. I'd been led to believe this place was dead in the evenings.

Hurry up, Chassa, I pleaded silently. The café had been empty for the first two hours, except for a young bloke who'd sat in the corner nursing a coffee and a book. I'd hung around, scuffing my heels on the kitchen tiles, watching Patrice going through his accounts.

But now Waitressing for Godot had become From Rush Hour With Love. I retreated to the kitchen, bumping into a table that had got in my way.

"In at the deep end, was it?"asked Chassa, whipping her jacket off.

"Glug, glug, glug," I replied succinctly. Patrice had been highly uncomplimentary about my performance. I thought he'd exaggerated. The customers hadn't seemed to mind opening the wine bottles themselves.

"Five whole customers?" said Chassa. "That's our national and Olympic record."

"I reckon they waited for you to go out," I grumbled.

Chassa laughed. "Patrice told me about you spilling the gravy."

"He went mad," I grumbled. "Anyone would have thought that lady didn't own another skirt."

"It'll get better," encouraged Chassa. "You'll still do Monday nights, won't you? I'm gonna sign up for my first aid course tomorrow." Her face was flushed with the night. I managed to stop myself from asking where she'd been.

"I've just thought," said Chassa. "Want to phone your Mam and Dad? They won't be in bed yet, will they? Britain's an hour behind France. Patrice! Holly wants to telephone."

The phone was ringing. I pictured it, on its little table in our hallway. Mam would be so pleased to hear from me. I danced a few steps in spite of my aching feet. Soon I'd bathe them in cool, refreshing water. Well, we all would, if the dishwasher was true to form.

"Hello?" said Mam cautiously.

"Mam," I burbled. "I'm all right. I've met that girl from Croesy, Chassa Brake, Sion's friend. And I'm living in a café with her, AND I've got a teaching job. Not bad, is it?"

"But why have you left them Le Flushes?" asked Mam.

I briefly explained the situation with Christian. There was an ominous silence.

"Well," said Mam. "What did you want to move out for? After all the trouble Mr Wheeler took for you! And I have to see him in the fish market on Fridays! Here, talk to your father." After a pause, I heard Dad's voice, asking: "Holly? What's the matter?"

"Plenty," I said bitterly. "That man I was staying with was groping me, behind his wife's back."

"People don't do things like that," was my father's authoritative reply.

"*And* Mam says it's all my fault," I snarled.

There was a short silence. Then a sour voice said: "I know whose fault it was."

I recoiled, then slammed down the receiver and marched back into the cafe. I was beginning to understand Chassa's stance on families.

"You go upstairs and have a rest," said Chassa, looking at me. "I'll help His Nibs clear up, then we'll have some Thai food."

The bed creaked as I sat down on it and prised my swollen feet from my shoes. Tomorrow I had to train as a teacher. Whatever the Méthode Vallentin was, I fervently hoped you could do it sitting down.

"*Hé*, waitress," carolled Chassa, entering the room. "A bottle of red, please, with your finest corkscrew. Patrice told me," she sniggered. "We'll have to practise opening wine bottles every night, up here. Right, kettle on."

"What Thai food have you got?" I asked, suddenly hungry. I quite fancied some of those white puffy crisps with the savoury tang.

"No, I said *Ty-Phoo*," explained Chassa, producing a red box. "Proper tea. There's a bloke who sells it at Talensac market. He's got a cat named Voyou," she added, filling the kettle. "And one day he wants to drive in the Paris-Dakar rally."

I sighed. I'd never settle into French life like Chassa had. French people didn't talk to me, except to ask why their dessert was taking so long to arrive.

And on top of that, Mam had blamed me for letting Mr Wheeler down. Well, she'd just have to brave the Friday fish market until things settled down. I wasn't putting up with abuse, not even to facilitate Pontycynon seafood commerce. Mr Wheeler would have to accept this, however great his piscine angst.

"Here," said Chassa, handing me a mug of tea. "It's nice to have peace and quiet, in' it?"

Just then a tremendous crash rocked the balcony. The force of the blow flung the shutters open. Chassa reeled back against the wall. From outside the window, a man's hand appeared, and grasped the shutter. A scream ripped from my throat.

8.

Dial 'Em For Merde

I froze, but Chassa hurtled to the window.

"*Qu'est-ce vous faites là?*" she shouted.

"*Pardon, Madame,*" came a voice. A male one.

Chassa pulled open the shutters. On the balcony were two teenage boys.

"*Madame,*" began one of them.

"*Hé!*" exclaimed his friend. "*C'est Mademoiselle Chassa! Du lycée!*"

"Yes," said Chassa, sounding more surprised than frightened. "What are you doing?"

"*On fait Le Parkours, Mademoiselle,*" explained the taller boy.

To my astonishment, Chassa burst out laughing.

"*Entrez,*" she invited them. The lads clambered over the sill and into the room.

"Holly," said Chassa, turning to me. "These are two of my old pupils, from the *Lycée Agricole* in Juillac."

"*Moi, c'est Benoît,*" said the taller boy.

"*Matthieu,*" added his friend, shaking my hand.

"The boys were practising free-running," explained Chassa. "They jump from building to building."

"Not quite," admitted Benoît. "But I have once landed on a dustbin."

"We jump on public benches too," added Matthieu.

"*Allez, les sportifs,*" said Chassa. "Come and drink a cola, and tell us all."

The boys greeted this idea with enthusiasm. I wondered if I'd fallen asleep and was dreaming this whole encounter.

"We will run a race three weeks from now," explained Benoît, squatting on the floor. "We run against a team from the other *Lycée Agricole.*"

"We make the tour of the town," added Matthieu. "But, Mademoiselle Chassa, we will avoid your balcony."

I studied the athletes. Benoît had the standard French dark hair and big brown eyes. Matthieu looked more Celtic, stocky, with reddish-brown hair.

"Mademoiselle Chassa," said Matthieu, "we do not see you any more at the *Lycée*."

"I am no longer a teacher. I'm a waitress," Chassa told him, sticking the neck of the bottle of cola in the hinge of the door. She held the door with one hand and twisted the bottle with the other. I watched in admiration as the top, now loosened, came off easily in her hand.

"*Et vous*, Mademoiselle." Benoît turned to me. "You are a waitress too?"

"No, I am not a waitress. I am a teacher," I said. And enjoyed the confused expression on his face.

The time flew by as we chatted. Both boys seemed eager to make amends for having startled us. Matthieu told us we should come and visit him on his farm, outside Mauvoisins. Not to be outdone, Benoît invited us to his sister's wedding reception that month, at the *Salle des Fêtes* in the town centre.

"It is the day after *Le Parkours*," he added. "I will be witness at the marriage."

"If you do not break your leg the night before," joked Matthieu.

"*Bof*," replied Benoît with a shrug.

"*Bon*, we will break ourselves," said Matthieu, getting up. I thought they probably would, if they swallow-dived on to many more balconies. Ah, it was another French expression: "*On va se casser*" meant "We'll be leaving now."

"Take the stairs this time," Chassa suggested. Both boys shook my hand before Chassa escorted them down the stairs. To think I'd taken them for armed terrorists, at the very least.

"Sion likes running," remarked Chassa, on her return. "I heard from him the other day." She reached for her handbag, drew out a postcard and gave it to me.

The postcard showed a lady in Welsh costume smiling gappily outside a dilapidated wooden hut.

76

"We've got a competition," explained Chassa. "Who can send the worst postcard. Read it if you like, Hol."

I flipped the Welsh lady over. "*Bore da, Mademoiselle,*" read the card. "Went to Penarth for the day with the Wesleyans. Nice tearooms, our driver had a puncture. New fixture: Inverness, April 25th. Love, Gran and Sion xxx."

"Sion writes to me for my Granny Chappell, now and again," explained Chassa, settling on her mattress. "Her eyesight's bad, so she tells Sion her news and he writes a card from both of them. Mind, sometimes it's a job to work out who's got the hypertension and who's got the hangover."

So Chassa had a granny. But she'd said she didn't "do" families.

"Does your Granny live in Croesy?" I ventured.

"Nearby," Chassa didn't seem annoyed. "She's lived in the same house for nigh on 80 years. Won't hear of going in a home. Says if they knock her house down, she'll crumble with it." She gulped her cola. "Croesy's first fifteen are touring Scotland, next spring, so Sion's training with them. And he helps coach the old school team. Can't leave his Pants alone."

"He wants to keep his hand in," I said, without thinking.

Chassa exploded, spraying the floor with her drink. I smiled, relieved she hadn't turned on me for asking about her family.

"Look at the time." Chassa scrambled to her feet. "And you've got to educate the youth of today, tomorrow." She closed the shutters. "No more Wuthering Heights tonight."

"Excuse me, *mademoiselle*," murmured Madame Lesourd. "I am not sure of when to say 'much'."

I went blank. I'd spoken English all my life, but didn't have a clue about the rules. "Er," I began. "One cannot say 'I have much money'. But one can say 'I haven't much money' and one can say 'Have you much money?' So 'much' is used with the negative and with the interrogative."

Madame Lesourd beamed. I sat a little taller, facing her across the classroom table.

"You are *intrépide, mademoiselle*," whispered Madame Lesourd. "Madame Vallentin has told me how you came here to seek work, and live in a café."

I glowed. You hadn't lived until you'd left your country and moved into a catering establishment, without a proper job. We women of the world knew that.

Madame Lesourd clutched the school's manual, the 300-page *Méthode Vallentin de l'Enseignement d'Anglais*. "Could you –" she began. Then the door opened and Madame Vallentin walked in.

"Mademoiselle Holly makes progress, Madame Lesourd?" enquired Madame Vallentin.

"Great progress," gasped Madame Lesourd. "Soon she will be able to teach the *baccalauréat* class." The manual shook in her hands.

"Have you told Mademoiselle Holly about our business?" asked Madame Vallentin. Madame Lesourd flushed.

"I have the catalogue in my office." Madame Vallentin motioned to me. "Come, *mademoiselle*."

I followed her into her office.

"Our clients may obtain the Méthode Vallentin by correspondence," explained Madame Vallentin, producing a glossy brochure. "We have recorded the English dialogues of the Méthode, on cassette audio and compact-disc. We have sold them to clients, even overseas."

I was impressed. Madame Vallentin's smile widened. "We are not just a school, we are an *entreprise*," she told me. "And your papers, Mademoiselle Holly? Have you brought me your *carte de séjour*?"

Wasn't that a brand of ice cream? No, it was a residence permit. I gulped. I hadn't even applied for one.

Madame Vallentin looked pained. "Mademoiselle Holly, you will go to the police station this afternoon, and get a temporary card. I will also need the details of your bank account."

What bank account? I thought, nodding fervently.

"Otherwise, I cannot pay you," teased Madame Vallentin. Wishing me *bonne continuation*, she waved me back to Madame Lesourd and the Méthode.

"She didn't say how many of those tapes they've sold, Hol," said Chassa, over lunch in the Bad Café. "Probably only three."

"What about this *carte de séjour*?" I was worried. "What do I have to do to get one?"

"Just ask at the police station," said Chassa. "You must be on first-name terms with them by now."

"But they'll need proof of my address," I wailed. "I haven't even got a gas bill."

"We'll get Patrice to sign a document," said Chassa. "*Hé*, Patrice!"

But that *monsieur* proved singularly unhelpful. When asked to write a letter confirming that I was living in the Bad Café, he refused, insisting that the police would be round in seconds flat, arresting him for housing Welsh asylum seekers.

"They'll think Patrice is charging you rent, Hol," Chassa explained. "Without telling the taxman. But hold on." She pulled open the cellar door and hurried down the steps.

Surely a crate of wine wouldn't be enough to bribe the police? But Chassa reappeared with Patrice's *papa* in tow.

"Serge will write a letter for you," explained Chassa. "He'll say that you live in his home. You can be their au pair girl."

It was a daring scheme. Monsieur Chazalet *père* twinkled at me as he scribbled the letter. "*Voilà*, Mees Holly," he presented it to me. "But this document is only valid on condition that you come to my house and iron my shirts."

"You're *génial*, Serge," Chassa told him.

I sighed with relief. "As long as the police don't come round and check that I really live at –" I checked the letter again – "17 rue Jacques Cartier."

"They won't." Chassa was confident. "And, if they do, Serge can tell them your washing up's so bad, he's sent you to the café on a refresher course."

"What if I'm illegal," I worried aloud, as we walked through *centre ville*. "What if they send me home?"

"They gave *me* a permit," pointed out Chassa. "Oh, I've got something to tell you. Let's sit down by'yere a minute."

We settled on to a bench in the town square. Around us, orange and white buses negotiated the traffic.

"Here's my idea for making money." said Chassa. She handed me a small white card.

"Allô! English," read the card. "English by telephone. Learn without leaving your home."

There followed two mobile numbers I didn't recognise. I looked at Chassa.

"Aye," said Professor Charlotte Higgins. "You and me's gonna teach English. Rabbit's bought me a new mobile. You can have my old one, it still works fine."

"How will we teach people English, over the phone?" I asked.

"Simple," said Chassa. "I've got some English textbooks. We'll photocopy a couple of lessons and take them round to our students. Then they'll phone us, and we'll go through the lessons over the phone, correct their pronunciation, whatever. I bet lots of people would do this in their lunch hour. S'worth a shot. Here, take some cards. We can put one in the *Oulangerie* window, and I'll put another in the *tabac* on the way home."

So she thought of the Bad Café as home. I didn't think I'd ever feel at home in France. I still looked in the wrong direction when I crossed the road.

"*Merci, madame,*" said Chassa, sticking the card in the bakery window.

"*Et vous, madame?*" inquired the assistant.

"*Non, merci,*" I indicated that I was with Chassa.

"*Non, Mer See,*" repeated the other, younger assistant, snickering.

"Whatever happened to being polite to the customer?" I bristled, as we left the shop.

"They don't do that, here," said Chassa. "The other day, at the '*Upermarché*, the checkout girl didn't even look at me, just talked with her colleague all the time she was serving me. And her badge said '*Je vous écoute*'. Hey, *salut!*" She stopped and smiled at a passer-by.

"*Salut,*" replied the girl Chassa had greeted. She looked younger than me, but more sophisticated.

"You start your first year of BTS, Milou?" asked Chassa.

"Maybe not," said the girl. "But I take singing lessons at the moment." She smiled, suddenly looking younger. "*Et vous?*"

While Chassa was explaining her circumstances, I studied the girl. That skirt was far too short. I wondered where she'd bought it.

"This is my friend Holly," said Chassa. "Holly, Milou was one of my pupils at the *Lycée Agricole* last year. *Eh, bien*, Milou, *bonne chance.*"

"*Vous aussi, merde!*" laughed Milou.

"Chassa!" I hissed, as Milou walked away. "She swore at you!"

"*Merde* can mean 'good luck'," explained Chassa. "Pity she's leaving school, she's bright enough to do a BTS. That's a diploma, a *Brevet de Technicien Supérieur*, – a two-year course after A-Levels."

"Oh, not Bit Too Sexy?" I sniffed, resolving to buy a skirt like Milou's as soon as I got my first month's pay.

Then I remembered. "Chassa, I've got to open a bank account," I fretted.

"Aye," said Chassa. "Let's get you legalised first."

Next stop was Monoprix department store, where I discovered that French photo booths were no more forgiving than the British ones.

"I look like a camel with mumps," I grumbled.

"At least people will recognise you," said Chassa. "Only joking, Hol. You should see the photo on my driver's licence. You'd think my dinner wouldn't go down."

Driver's licence? But she'd said she didn't drive.

"Did you take your test in Croesy?" I began, but Chassa was already heading for the police station.

Sitting in an interview room, I ran through my cover story of how I'd come to my twin town to help the Chazalet family. The *agent* filed Serge's document next to my mug shot. He didn't even ask for my fingerprints. Mind, the way I'd gripped my chair as I'd talked, he could easily get them off the armrests.

In no time I was the proud owner of a temporary *carte de séjour*. I clutched the yellow card, relieved. Perhaps they gave you a red one when they deported you.

"Nice one, Holly," said Chassa. "I'm meeting Rabbit in a bit, but I can come to the bank with you first, if you like."

"Oh, I can manage." I wasn't going to cling to her. "*A bientôt.* Stay *merdeux.*"

"*Vous êtes d'Angleterre?*" said the bank clerk.

At least his guess was closer than Portugal. I explained where I was from, adding for good measure: "It is the twin town of Mauvoisins."

The clerk sat up: "I have a friend in the twin town. Geoffroi Huillière."

I was about to say I didn't know him when the cent dropped. The name-plate on the desk confirmed that this bank clerk was none other than Monsieur Benoist, friend of Mr Wheeler and arranger of lodgings with Christian and Annick. My mouth went dry.

"*Oui*, Monsieur Wheeler," I admitted. "It was he who asked you to find me a room here. You suggested Monsieur and Madame Le Floch."

"Ah!" said Monsieur Benoist, scrutinising me. "But I did nothing, me – it is my wife who knows Madame Le Floch." He glanced at my completed forms. "But how is it that you live at a café?"

"Oh," I mumbled. "I have met another Welsh girl, and she has asked me to share her *studio.*" I tried to look pathetically homesick.

Fortunately for me, Monsieur Benoist didn't ask any other awkward questions. The deal done, I thanked him, grasped my papers and hurried back to the café.

"*Chassa n'est pas là,*" said Patrice as I walked in. "But one of the clients from Monday evening was here at midday. He asked where I had found such a bad waitress. I said: 'I advertised, and there was only she who answered.'" He grinned, delighted with his wit.

I shrugged (perhaps I was getting acclimatised after all) and went upstairs. I'd have a quiet evening in, and study the Méthode Vallentin.

After five minutes I'd switched to lying on my bed studying the ceiling. Was I going to stay in, alone, every evening? I could have done that at home.

The shops here stayed open until quite late. I'd go and buy Chassa a thank-you gift for all her help. I grabbed my jacket and ran down the stairs.

I walked along, studying each shop window display. I didn't want Monsieur Benoist inviting me round for a chat about my overdraft so soon after we'd met.

A small jeweller's shop was squeezed between *Tarte Marie* and *Coupe Coupe* the hairdresser's. Did Chassa have pierced ears? I'd go inside and ask if they had any clip-on earrings.

The door closed behind me, the bell echoing round the shop. I shifted from one dap to another. Someone was bound to appear in a minute and be rude to me.

A strange noise came from the back room. At first I thought it was French telly. Then I realised it wasn't.

It was the sound of a woman crying.

I edged past the counter. Peering around the door, I saw the woman slumped at the table, her head in her hands, her shoulders shaking.

"*Madame*," I said.

Madame sat up. Her face turned from pink to white.

"*Qui êtes-vous?*" Her eyes were terrified.

"I came to buy some earrings, Madame," I faltered. "But..."

I noticed her hands. Her pale skin, the blue veins. The small bottle she was clutching.

Automatically, I held out my hand, adopting the firm look I wore whenever Griff borrowed my CDs without asking.

Madame looked at me, then meekly handed me the bottle.

I didn't recognise the name printed on the label, but I was pretty sure that a few of these capsules would knock you out. Too many, and you wouldn't get up again.

Two minutes later, I was boiling a small saucepan of water while Madame blew her nose. Patting Madame's shoulder, I hurried back into the shop, closed the front door and flipped the sign over to *Fermé*.

I sat down beside her and set two cups of coffee before us. Madame managed a smile.

"*Qui êtes-vous?*" she asked again.

As brightly as I could when talking to a knife-edge suicide, I told her my name and what I was doing in France. The mention of ordinary things like the café, the teaching job and the customers seemed to relax her.

I grew bold. "What is the matter, Madame?"

Madame's lip trembled. "If I tell you, it must go no further," she said.

"I will say nothing to nobody." I promised. Should that have been "nothing to anybody"? Why hadn't I listened in grammar lectures? Too late now.

"It is my daughter," began Madame. "She has gone to study in Paris. We have family in Paris. I have asked if Eliane can lodge with them. But –" her face crumpled again, "they have said no."

And for that Madame had been about to take her own life.

There had to be more to it than that.

I didn't know what to say. The shop bell sounded and a tall, greying man walked into the room. Here was Monsieur, I surmised.

"The *dentiste* says -" he began, then noticed I was there. Madame sat up, shooting a nervous look at me.

Whatever Monsieur thought of finding a stranger in his back room, he didn't say. Ten minutes later we were all sitting down to a bowl of steaming *potage*. (Monsieur had just come from the dentist's and refused to prepare anything chewable.)

Monsieur - his name was Monsieur Silvain - asked a host of questions about me, but none about his wife's stained face. I wasn't going to let on about what had happened earlier, so I responded politely.

"Before, I was an English teacher," Monsieur Silvain informed me. Well, he knew how to make Madame shut up when he entered the room.

"You please yourself, in France?" asked Monsieur Silvain.

"*Beaucoup*," I said. And realised I meant it.

"You speak very well French," said Monsieur Silvain. "Your parents are French? You have a French accent."

I nearly choked. If he thought I had a French accent, it was his ears that needed seeing to, not his teeth.

The meal was unexpectedly jolly. The Silvains chuckled at my description of Emlyn Kremlin filling his kettle, ready to steam open my correspondence and recount my misadventures up and down the valley.

"Come back and see us," invited Monsieur Silvain. "We have her telephone number, Elisabeth?"

I took one of Chassa's English lessons cards out of my bag and handed it to Madame Silvain. "Would you affix this in your window?"

"Allô! English," read Madame, smiling properly. Monsieur Silvain promised to display the card, then escorted me out of the shop.

Madame Silvain's confidences echoed in my head as I walked along. Surely the daughter could find other lodgings. Still, at least Madame cared where her daughter lived, unlike some parents.

I walked into Chassa's room to be welcomed by a clod of earth whizzing past my head.

"Sorry, Hol," called Chassa from the balcony. "Rabbit's brought my plants, so we're chucking dirt at each other."

"That's a relief," I quipped. "For a minute, I thought you were gardening."

"You work late at the school, Holly?" asked Didier.

I joined them on the balcony and related my adventure.

"Oh, Hol," breathed Chassa, looking quite pale.

"You should have let her swallow her tablets, Holly," teased Didier. "Then you could have seized the jewellery."

"Shut up, Rabbit," snapped Chassa. She turned away and leaned over the balcony for a moment, facing the traffic. When she turned back to us, she was herself again.

"You should go back and see that lady, Hol," she said. "But don' buy me anything. I'm bad at jewellery," she explained. "Brooches tumble off me, and necklaces unclasp. If I put on earrings, you can venter one of them'll land in someone's dinner."

"You have a story for your newspaper," remarked Didier, bumping his head against the balcony railings.

"That sort of thing is no joke," said Chassa. "Not when you've - hé, Mr Garden! You'll get your head stuck in the railings."

"You can flatten it, with the *machin-chouette*..." replied Didier. I wasn't sure what he meant, but Chassa stifled a giggle.

"That flat thing in your suitcase, Hol," she said. "We wondered what it was." She nodded towards my belongings.

"Oh, that's my *luchwen*," I explained. "For making Welsh cakes."

"We'll get Patrice to put Welsh cakes on the menu," suggested Chassa. "Introduce the French to them."

Now that would make a story for The Fibs. As Chassa and Didier turned back to the plants, I went to find a page of Chassa's squared paper. Putting pencil to graph paper, I began to plot my ascent.

9.

My Tailor Is Rich

"Mademoiselle Holly," Madame Vallentin, greeted me, as I hung my jacket on a corridor peg. "Today you will take the *classe baccalauréat*."

She walked up to the classroom door and pushed it open. The hubbub faded.

"*Je vous présente Mademoiselle* Gay-tan," announced Madame Vallentin to the twenty or so young women seated at four rows of tables. Every pair of eyes in the class was staring at me. Perhaps these girls hadn't seen a foreigner in the flesh before. I stood up straight and tried to look less fleshy.

"*...l'Entente Cordiale*." Madame Vallentin finished her speech. "*Bon, à vous*, Mademoiselle Gay-tan."

She closed the door behind her. This was it.

"Hello," I said. The girls looked at each other and giggled.

Bad start. I clutched the Méthode, my lifebelt. "Today, we will study Lesson Four," I announced. "Page 20. At the railway station. Who wants to begin?"

Silence. You could have heard their grades drop.

The Méthode didn't include a chapter on how to make reluctant pupils work. It was up to me. With no training, no qualification, no experience.

I turned to the blackboard and chalked the opening sentence across it. A murmur at the back of the room caught my ear. I turned. A girl with long brown hair was lounging in her seat, chatting to her neighbour in a studied show of indifference. I noted her scrap-metal earrings and glossy sneer of a mouth. This one had "troublemaker" graffiti-sprayed all over her.

"*Nous allons lire le premier paragraphe,*" I began. "*Si vous avez des questions, vous...er, vous levez la patte.*"

The girls screamed with laughter. The brown-haired girl's face was bright with amused contempt.

"*Bon.*" I pointed at a girl in the front row. "Read the first paragraph, please."

To my surprise, she obeyed. When she'd finished, I motioned to her neighbour to continue. The giggling at the back of the class eventually subsided when I wrote another sentence on the board. Heads bent, the girls copied it into their notebooks. My knees relaxed slightly. As long as I wrote something down, they'd keep quiet and copy it.

The lesson dragged on until midday. As the girls jostled out of the room, the next class arrived for Madame Vallentin's lesson.

"Anne-Laure, *c'était bien, avec la nouvelle prof?*" I heard one newcomer ask.

"*Non, c'était chiant,*" replied the brown-haired girl, knowing full well that I could hear her.

"Hmm," Chassa put down her mug of tea. "Thing is, Hol, they ain't gonna learn much English if they just write things down."

I bristled. "Tomorrow I'll give them a written test."

"But Hol," pointed out Chassa, "they're not speaking English, that way. That's what you're there for – to teach 'em to speak. That headmistress took you on 'cos you're a native speaker. She'll expect you to speak English to them, and make them speak back."

"But they don't understand me, unless I speak French," I argued. "And they just giggle at that." I told her how the girls had gone into hysterics over my spoken French.

Chassa chortled. "Oh, Hol. You told them to *lever la patte?* That's what a dog does against a lamp-post."

Well, that was my authority down the drain for the rest of the year.

Chassa drained her mug of tea. "I used to get the kids to act sketches," she said. "They like to show off."

"But I've got to use this Méthode," I grumbled. "I'm not allowed to bring in my own material."

"Thing is, Hol, it's a private school," said Chassa. "And that usually means the kids were too thick for a normal *lycée.*"

"Brilliant," I groaned.

"They might not all be hopeless," Chassa tried to reassure me. "Maybe their parents just reckon secretarial skills are more useful on the job market. Sad but true. You could spend years studying 17th century poetry, then end up serving in MacDo's. From Du Bellay to *double lait*."

"MacDo's," This sounded very French. "That's where my old schoolteacher thinks I belong." I described Mrs Hathaway's attitude to my year in France. Chassa's grin widened as I acted out the scene at the slide show when Kim had put Mrs Hathaway in her place.

"She can't stand anyone competing with that niece of hers," I growled, while Chassa chuckled. "To hear her, you'd think Angeline owned France."

"We had an Angeline at our school," said Chassa. "Angeline Taylor. Right bossy madam."

"Taylor?" I squeaked. "But that's *my* Angeline. I mean, Mrs Hathaway's Angeline. She went to school with you?"

"She was a couple of years below us," said Chassa. "But she used to hang around. Around Sion, mainly, him being captain of the rugby team." She grinned. "Their classroom overlooked the rugby pitch. She used to press herself up against the pane, to watch the boys playing. We used to call her Windowlene."

I giggled.

"Oh, forgot to tell you." Chassa added. "I got a phone call yesterday from this bloke who wants English lessons over the phone! Our first customer! I said I'd do the first one. That all right?"

"Yes, you do it," I urged her, mindful of my performance in the Vallentin classroom that morning. "Who is he?"

"He says he's an actor," said Chassa. "His name's Patrick Degermann. I've never heard of him, though." She jumped up. "Oh, I promised you my old mobile, Hol. I'll fetch it." She pushed aside her chair and rushed upstairs.

A mobile phone of my own again. I brightened. I could surprise Lin, and Griff. Not Mam and Dad though – they'd moan. I could hear Mam's voice already: *"Teaching by mobile? Think of the bills you'll have! And you'll fry your brain."*

They still hadn't written, either. Unless…

I squeaked out loud, turning the heads of my fellow readers. The library computer had displayed my e-mail home page, and from there I'd reached my in-box in double-click time.

The middle-aged librarian frowned at me. I clicked as quietly as I could on the e-mail I'd received from Lin.

It was great to read news of home. Owen's fashion show had won him good marks. He was now working on a collection with a rural theme – "pastures and meadows." I dreaded to think what Lin might have to cover the Tower's shelves with, next time. Mansel, under Shireen's guiding fist, had abandoned his dream of managing a girl group. Instead, he was planning to form a new electronic pop outfit he had already christened Blorenge Juice.

"Lucky you've met Chassa," wrote Lin. "Have you met any nice Frenchmen? Not still brooding over Kim, I hope? I haven't seen him since the slide show."

I wondered how to word my reply. Lin thought I was flourishing on the Continent. How could I admit I couldn't say three words in French without getting two wrong, and I was making a mess of my teaching?

I decided to gloss over the awkward bits. "Life is full of surprises and I'm kept busy by my job," I typed back. As for romance, I added truthfully that I had met two nice Frenchmen on a balcony by moonlight, and one of them had asked me to a wedding.

Re-reading my message, I thought it was a wonder my pants hadn't spontaneously combusted. I must have stretched the truth to twice its original length. I cheered up as I opened my second e-mail, read it, and sent a quick reply.

Waitress duty tonight, I remembered, walking back to the cafe. I wondered how Chassa was getting on with her first aid lessons. The other night, she'd demonstrated how to tie a bandage round one's rabbit's mouth when he annoyed one, but I had a feeling this wasn't a mandatory module.

"*Hé!*" I looked up and saw the group of teenagers crowded around the nearby bus stop.

"*Lever la patte!*" shouted a voice. Yelps of laughter followed.

I walked on, cursing inwardly. My pupils must have told their friends about my mistake. Now I'd have to put up with this everywhere I went.

"*My tailor is rich*," shouted another voice, as I passed by.

Was that a comment on my clothes? I flushed. I couldn't afford the outfits I'd seen in the boutiques here.

On impulse I turned and headed down another street. I knew someone who would welcome me, however I was dressed.

Madame Silvain was standing behind the counter, sorting watch straps.

"*Vous allez bien, Madame?*" I asked.

"*Je vais mieux*," replied Madame Silvain, smiling shyly. "*Et vos parents? Ils vont bien?*"

I thought she was probably still too fragile to cope with hearing about Mam's impending interview with Mr Wheeler in the Friday fish market, so I just nodded. But, raw from the street heckling, I asked her if she thought my clothes looked odd.

Madame Silvain seemed intrigued. When I explained, she giggled. It was nice to hear her laugh.

"But they were not mocking your clothes," Madame Silvain assured me. "It was because you teach English. In France, we have a classic textbook for learning English. And the first sentence we learn is a simple one: 'My tailor is rich'."

"Oh!" I got it. "It's like *la plume de ma tante* – one of those sayings everybody knows."

I thought about it. A strange choice of phrase, when you considered the British reputation for style. "My tailor is blind" would have been more apt. But I had to get the pupils to learn a bit more than that.

Madame Silvain looked at me intently. "Mees Holly," she began. "Can one be too old to begin to learn English? I have a friend...she has almost the age of retirement..." She looked at me expectantly. I assured her that this lady's age was not a problem.

Madame Silvain leaned closer to me. "It is me who wishes to learn," she confided. "Would you give me private lessons?"

"Of course," I beamed. "Lucky I didn't say your friend was too old."

Madame Silvain giggled. I glowed. Chassa would be pleased. Now we'd have one pupil each.

Madame Silvain thought telephone lessons would be awkward. She did not wish her husband to know she was learning until she had acquired the basics. But, she suggested, I could come to the shop at certain lunchtimes, when Monsieur was out, and we could study in peace.

I practically skipped out of the shop. This teaching idea was really taking off. I could meet some new French friends, that way. Not that I'd dump Chassa. She'd done so much for me. I smiled as I remembered the other e-mail I'd received.

"Hello, Holly,

Good to hear from you. And you've got us an order already!

We'll send the bottles of Dewis red for your friend. Hope you're having a good time over there. I met Kim in Aber the other day, told him we were in business in France, thanks to you. Take care. Thanks again, Yvonne."

So Kim had heard my name. And Chassa would have her present for Patrice's parents sooner than she'd thought. At least I wouldn't be tempted to drink it first – I wouldn't able to open the bottles.

"Patrice! *Tes coudes*!" screeched the fair-haired lady. *"Devant les invitées!"*

I wanted to snigger at Patrice, but thought better of it. After all, we were guests in his parents' home, and would shortly be enjoying his mother's cooking.

"Mees Holly," invited Serge, pouring me a glass of *sirop*. I smiled at him. It was great to be in a French home, with a family.

"Qui c'est, ça?" came a querulous voice. I looked up to see an elderly lady standing in the doorway. She had a wooden stick and a steely expression.

"C'est Holl-ee, Maman," explained Sophie, Patrice's mother, pulling out a chair for the grey-haired arrival. *"C'est la petite amie de Chassa."*

Patrice sniggered suggestively at this. I braced myself for some unsavoury remarks about the sleeping arrangements in Chassa's room. Fortunately, his grandmother screeched first. "Sophie," she bellowed. "I do not want to sit at the head of this table. I cannot hear what these girls are saying."

I wondered what juicy secrets she was expecting to hear. All we'd talked about so far was the maintenance work Serge was doing at Mauvoisins fire station.

But Chassa was unruffled. "*Bonjour, Madame Chazalet,*" she called. "*Comment allez-vous?*"

This kept Gran Chazalet busy for the next ten minutes, regaling us with the details of why her doctor was getting her medication all wrong. Serge, at the other end of the table, winked at me.

"I suffer still," concluded Gran. "My poor legs, and my poor feet."

Next would be her poor neck, the way she kept craning it to stare at me. Happily, Sophie produced the ratatouille, which swiftly became the centre of attention.

"That was grêt, Sophie," declared Chassa, cleaning her plate. "Patrice, why don't you cook ratatouille in the café?"

"I am the chef," said Patrice, coldly. "It is me who decides the menu."

"*Voyons*, Patrice," urged Serge. "A change from time to time would be good. *N'est-ce pas*, Mees Holly?"

Patrice sniggered. "Holly knows her food, *non*?" He mimed a huge stomach. I flushed deep red.

"Patrice!" barked Serge. "One does not speak of guests like that! Even when one thinks it," he added, with a grin.

"*Qu'est-ce que vous dites?*" Gran was querulous again.

"I say that she is - *forte, Mémé*." Patrice was enjoying my discomfort.

His granny sniffed. "*Et alors*? I would like to be a plump chicken. But with this medicine, I am nothing but a sparrow." She looked at us, inviting sympathy.

"Better keep out of Patrice's kitchen, then," replied Chassa. "He'll cover you with sauce and pass you off as duck *à l'orange*."

I couldn't help giggling. Serge cackled. Gran pursed her lips.

"But why will he say a sparrow is a duck?" Sophie looked blank.

Patrice snorted. He turned to me. "What do you eat, in your country, Holly?"

Everyone's eyes were on me. "Er," I began, trying to remember a special meal. Birthdays. Mam heaping a plate with warm golden creations.

"*Les* pancakes," I replied. "Um, *les crêpes*."

"*Comme les Bretons*," nodded Serge.

"*Crêperies* – pancake houses – are big in Brittany, Hol," put in Chassa. "They do savoury fillings as well as sweet. And cider to drink."

"So you prefer *la cuisine bretonne*, Mees Chassa," sniped Patrice. "After I employ you in my café, give you a home, welcome your friends. I collect your letters…"

"What letters?" snorted Chassa. "You only ever give me the electricity bill. With my share calculated in red."

"And the letters of Mees Holly," added St Patrice Of The Indeterminate Poultry.

What was he on about? I hadn't received a letter since I'd been in France. Not that I thought about that, first thing every morning.

Patrice looked at me. Something flickered in his eyes. He got up, went into the hallway, returned with a brown envelope and handed it to me.

"*Mes excuses*, Mees Holly." Patrice smiled, suddenly looking like his father. "I thought I had given this to you. I have found it in the letterbox of the café a few days ago."

I took the envelope. It was marked "Miss Holly, the Wales".

Inside was a small white card. The handwritten message read: "Miss Holly,

The Lycée Agricole de Juillac requires an English language assistant, to teach some hours a week. Come to the school and ask for Madame Virginie Tessier."

"Wow!" said Chassa, handing it back. "Another job, Hol."

"But who could have sent me this?" I exclaimed. "Who knows where I live?"

"Benoît and Matthieu?" suggested Chassa. "Maybe they told Vicky Tessier about you. Ask her when you go there."

Well. It wouldn't hurt to go and see this Virginie – Vicky, as Chassa called her. And *they* were asking *me*. No risk of getting turned away at the front door again.

"A salary increase," joked Serge. "I will demand rent from my au pair girl."

I giggled. I'd forgotten that, for the purposes of my residence permit, I lived and worked at Serge's house.

"But why would she pay us rent?" Sophie again. I got the impression she was a couple of hours behind the rest of us.

"Don' matter, Sophie." Chassa was quick on her feet. "Let me help you clear the table."

"And you just found this note in the letterbox, Patrice?" I asked him again.

"I have said it." Patrice sounded impatient.

"Patrice!" Gran complained. "I do not want to watch the television."

"I want to see it," insisted Patrice. He switched the set on and began flicking through the channels.

"You should get a television, Holly," said Serge. "You might see your actor, Patrick." This meant another ten minutes explaining to Sophie how a thespian had contacted Chassa for English lessons.

"Perhaps he wants to play Shakespeare," remarked Serge. "At least, on the telephone, Holly, you will not know if he lifts his *patte*!"

"That *lever la patte* joke will follow me around all year," I grumbled, as Chassa and I walked back to the café. Patrice must have mentioned it to his father.

"Serge is so much nicer than his son," I mused. "I reckon Patrice takes after his Gran."

"He's not like either of his parents," agreed Chassa. "I mean, Sophie's as slow as the school clock, but she don' pass remarks like he does."

I sighed. "I hope they won't all mock me in this Lycée."

"They won't," Chassa reassured me. "Most of the teachers are nice. Vicky's a laugh."

"How come she didn't ask you to come back?" I regretted the question as soon as I'd asked it, but Chassa sauntered on.

"Oh, they won't want me," she replied, apparently unconcerned. "They'll be much better off with you."

"If I get the job," I pointed out. "And what am I going to wear?"

"Just go as you are," said Chassa. "And tell them your tailor's gone on a Caribbean cruise."

10.

It's One Small Crêpe For A Man

Vicky Tessier raised her eyebrows. "And you do not know who sent you this? *Bizarre!*"

Not knowing what to say, I nodded.

"And you are a friend of Chassa," said Vicky Tessier. She looked at me. "We will need you three afternoons a week."

I gasped with delight.

"You can begin next week?" asked Vicky. "The time to prepare the contract... I have told Jean-Paul that we need an *assistant*," she added, turning to the school secretary. "And now we have someone on hand. Come, Holly, I will show you the *Lycée*."

"This school's quite a way from Mauvoisins," said Vicky, as we walked down a corridor. "You could arrange a lift with a teacher. Or a pupil – they all have cars."

"Not with a pupil." I was horrified at the idea. Imagine depending on some little madam with a lip-ring to drive you to work. She'd tell the whole class how you overslept and had to rake on your mascara in the car. Better to keep a professional distance.

"Come and meet the TS2," said Vicky. "They're the main class I want you to teach."

She pushed open a door. I followed her into the classroom.

"*Un peu de silence, s'il vous plaît,*" shouted Vicky.

The boys in the room stopped their lively talking and turned to us.

Except these weren't schoolboys. These were hod carriers.

I looked at them, aghast. Even sitting down, they were all bigger than me. Some of them had *beards,* for heaven's sake.

"*Voici la nouvelle assistante de langue anglaise,*" announced Vicky. She turned to me. "*Mademoiselle –*"

"Holly," I supplied automatically.

"*Au lit,*" shouted one of the boys. The others exploded with laughter.

"*Ca suffit*," said Vicky. She explained that I would be taking the class for two afternoons a week. The lads' eyes gleamed.

I was relieved when my new mobile phone rang. I stepped out into the corridor to answer it.

"Hol?" It was Chassa. "Have you found the school? What did they say?"

"I've got the job," I told her. "But Vicky says she didn't write that note."

"Weird," said Chassa. "Anyway, can you stick one of our telephone cards up in the staffroom? I bet some of the teachers wouldn't mind practising their English. A couple of them have been to Britain. They used to ask me about pubs and stuff."

Heartened by the thought of chatty conversations about licensing laws with my new colleagues, I agreed. Chassa wished me good luck and rang off.

Chassa always knew what to do, I thought. She'd have breezed into the school, charmed the staff, and had the pupils eating out of her handbag.

"*She was here, once,*" said a voice in my head. "*Teaching. You can do it too. And not get the push, like she did.*"

"At lunchtime, I drive home," said Vicky. "I'll give you a lift back to town."

I thanked her. It would take me forever to find my way round this school, I thought, pushing through swing doors into yet another corridor. A group of pupils, loitering there, turned to stare at me.

"*Holly!*" said a voice. I turned. There was Benoît. And close behind, Matthieu.

I greeted them, and asked: "Was it you who wrote to me about the job here?"

Their surprise was genuine. I explained about the note and my new job.

"*Mais c'est génial,*" enthused Matthieu. "You will teach our class, the TS1? We will take our BTS next year. We need to learn much English with you."

"My sister marries, this month," Benoît reminded me. "I will bring an invitation to you and Mademoiselle Chassa. *Elle va bien?*"

"*TS1, en classe*," barked a voice. Another teacher had arrived. From the leather elbow patches on his jacket, I deduced that the geography lesson was about to begin.

"*On va en histoire-géo*," Benoît confirmed.

I watched as he and Matthieu jostled into the classroom with the others. It was a long time since I'd been part of a class. I turned away as the door closed behind them.

The staffroom was empty except for a couple of middle-aged men smoking and rumbling at each other in deep French. They didn't look at me.

I went over to the staffroom noticeboard. One spare drawing pin, and *voilà*. Now the entire teaching staff could ring us for a chat about closing times.

"You are the new *assistante anglaise*?" The soft voice came from behind me. I turned to look at a girl even smaller than me.

"*Vous faites Anglaise*," smiled the girl, reading my mind.

"*Sauf que je suis Galloise*," I smiled back.

"*Ah!*" The girl looked at me closely. "We have had an *assistante* here last year, she was *Galloise* –"

"Mademoiselle Chassa," I supplied.

"You know her?" The girl's eyes were round. "What is she becoming?"

"She works at the Bad Café," I replied. Taking the opportunity to practise my French, I explained about the café and its nickname. The girl smiled, showing dimples I'd have ached to charm Kim with.

"You speak very well French," commented the girl. "*Moi, c'est* Arielle. *Je suis laborantine.*"

I was about to ask what that was when she turned, opened one of the lockers near the wall and took out an off-white garment. As she slipped it on, I realised she must be the lab assistant.

A bell rang. "You eat with us at the canteen?" asked Arielle.

"Um, *pas aujourd'hui, merci*." It was a kind offer, but I was thinking of my lift home. There was a lot I needed to ask Vicky.

"How do I cope with them?" repeated Vicky, nudging her Peugeot between the school gates. "Well, experience, really."

I sighed. All I'd learned at the chalkface so far was to roll my sleeves up in case they got covered in the white stuff.

"You'll be fine," Vicky reassured me. "I'll give you some texts you can use, until you find your feet. And if anyone misbehaves, send him out of the room."

"The corridor will be full," I said darkly.

Vicky laughed. "It's good to have an assistant again," she said. "Chassa was great, even when she – Did you come to France to visit her?"

"No," I admitted. "I came here as an *au pair*. But there was a problem." I briefly explained about Christian's advances to me.

Vicky burst out laughing. "Weren't you flattered?"

I stared at her, not knowing what to day.

"Shall I drop you here, Holly?" inquired Vicky.

"Um, yes, please." I was still staggered by her reaction. "Thank you for the lift."

"See you on Monday." Vicky was giggling again. "I'll tell the pupils to keep their hands off you."

I went into the supermarket, still irritated by Vicky's attitude. I'd show her I didn't need any help in coping with those boys.

"Don' worry about her," came my inner voice again. *"She wouldn't laugh if some man was groping her daughter. And if them boys get out of hand, just chuck 'em out."*

"She'll think I can't cope," I grumbled to a shelf of free range eggs.

"It was her that said to do it," pointed out the voice.

This made sense. I glanced at the other baking products. It was funny seeing ordinary things like flour billed under exotic names like *Moulin d'Or*. Although *Béghin Say* didn't sound particularly French, more like an exotic delicacy.

I reached for the sugar, packaged in a cardboard box with a spout in the side. A woman on a mission, I loaded up my *chariot* with eggs, butter, milk and – yes, there they were. I picked up the packet and admired the contents. Little black gems.

Silence reigned in the cafe. I glanced at Patrice. For once, his face had lost its bored expression as he concentrated on what was at hand.

It was Chassa who finally spoke. "Holly, they're grêt," she said.

I beamed. I hadn't thought my Welsh cakes would go down so well. Or so quickly. That was Didier's third, by my reckoning. He hadn't ventured an opinion yet. Perhaps he was like Dad, planning to wait thirty years before he gave his assessment.

"You've got to put these on the menu," Chassa urged Patrice.

Patrice nodded. He picked up another cake and bit into it. I marvelled at his change in attitude. One taste of home cooking, and Mr Scoff had turned into Mr Scoff.

"What is in these cakes?" asked Didier, between bites.

"Butter, flour, milk and sugar," I recited. "But no eggs."

"*Pas d'oeuf?*" Patrice stared at me. "*Des gateaux sans oeuf?*" For the first time since I'd met him, he was looking at me with something approaching respect.

Chassa's eyes were suddenly round. "Eggs," she blurted. Pushing her chair back, she jumped up and rushed into the kitchen. Perplexed, I followed.

"Eggs," muttered Chassa, wrenching random cupboards open. "Oh, here they are. Right, Hol, stand back."

"Chassa!" I begged. "Don't do it. You've only just cleaned the floor."

"I'm not gonna throw them at him," Chassa chortled. "I'm not gonna do anything with them. You are."

"Me?" I squawked.

"You," said Chassa. "Where's your luck thing?"

"*Bravo*, Holly," said Patrice, taking the plate from me. "This one, he can test it for us."

I watched in trepidation as Patrice marched across the café. He stopped before the corner table, where the young man was engrossed in his hardback.

"*Monsieur*! *La maison veut vous offrir ceci*," said Patrice smoothly, setting the plate on the table before his customer.

The customer looked up. "*Oh! Mais c'est tres aimable de vot' part...*" he eventually replied. He looked from Patrice to the plate.

"My own creation," said Patrice unblushingly. "*Une crêpe maison.*"

Beside me, Chassa bristled. "The fibber," she hissed. "*You* made that pancake, Hol, not him."

"Ssh!" I was watching the customer. "He's eating it, Chassa! He likes it!"

We gazed, enthralled.

"It's one small *crêpe* for a man..." I breathed.

"...One lying creep for mankind," finished Chassa, glaring at Patrice as he sauntered back into the kitchen.

"*Ecoute*, Chassa," said Patrice firmly. "I must say it is my own creation. What will my clients think, if I say it is the part-time waitress who has cooked the meal?"

"It was Holly's idea," Chassa argued.

"*Your* idea," I pointed out. "What made you think of serving pancakes?"

"You said about your family treat," explained Chassa. "Let's ask him what he thought."

The four of us walked over to the corner table. Our taster looked up, disconcerted at the sight of this procession.

"*Alors*, Monsieur, *cette crêpe?*" inquired Patrice.

"*C'etait très bon*," replied the customer, who had remarkably large brown eyes.

"*Et avec ça, un bol de cidre?*" asked Chassa. "*C'est la maison qui vous l'offre.*" She moved off, shepherding Didier and Patrice with her.

Left to explain matters, I turned back to the brown-eyed customer.

"We want to put *crêpes* on the menu," I explained in my hesitant French. "But this is the first time I have made them to..er, the, er, *spécifications françaises.*"

Our customer started laughing. All very well for him. He hadn't had to stand at the stove for twenty minutes while Patrice moaned that the mixture was still too thick, try again, lemon juice didn't go with pancake mix, and *que diable* was I doing with those currants.

"We will not add the *crêpe* to your bill, Monsieur," I reassured him, holding up my waitressing pad with its perforated pages. "I will tear off *le*...er, *le slip.*"

My listener's eyes grew even bigger. When he finally spoke, it was to explain: "*Pardon*, Mademoiselle, but... *le slip* – it means, one's knickers."

Well, that sledgehammered the ice. Soon Bruno – that was his name – and I were chatting away. It turned out he was a fan of *les Monty Python*.

"The guy who is interviewed on television," Bruno reminisced dreamily. "He has composed a symphony, but they only wish to speak about his *abri de jardin*."

"That's Arthur 'Two Sheds' Jackson," I supplied, happily. Normally you couldn't tell a French person anything they didn't already know.

But meeting Bruno was different, somehow. Usually, when speaking French to a French person, I stumbled over my grammar and whether nouns were masculine or feminine. Now the words flowed out of me.

When Bruno finally left, he promised to come back and sample some more of my pancakes. He even presented me with a tip. I smiled at the coin as I turned it over in my hand.

"*Bon*, Holly." Patrice approached the table. "Chassa will clear the kitchen and then we will discuss the new menu."

"Here is my idea," said Patrice, placing a sheet of paper on the table before Chassa, Didier and me.

Chassa seized the paper. "*La Bretonne*," she read. "*Le Forestier?*"

"I have decided," announced Patrice. "Given the success of Miss Holly's *crêpe* tonight, *Café Bas De La Rue* will become a *crêperie*." He winked at me, suddenly full of charm. "Some of these *crêpes* are known, others will be our speciality."

"*Le Diable*," read Chassa. "*Le Saint-Jacques. Le Grand Chazalet!*" she yelped in disbelief. "You've got a nerve. Naming a *crêpe* after yourself."

"Chassa, if you do not like it, the door is wide open." Patrice looked smug.

"It is a good idea," said Didier, the voice of calm. "There is not another *crêperie* in Mauvoisins."

"*Exact*," said Patrice. "We will offer *crêpes salées* and *crêpes sucrées*."

"If the bill is not too *salée*," joked Didier, catching my eye. I looked back, blank.

"It is a joke," he explained. "When the prices are too high, we say the bill is *salée*."

Fair play, the French had some weird expressions. How could you have a salty bill? Maybe it came from the customers' comments when they saw the total amount, plus VAT.

Back in our room, Chassa's language was so high in sodium content, I feared for her blood pressure. When she voiced her opinion of Patrice, I nearly covered Trouble Bruin's ears.

"That man," grumbled Chassa through a mouthful of toothpaste. "Taking all the credit. He is getting *beyond*."

"You're not quitting, are you?" I asked.

"No," said Chassa, "But he better make a decent job of this *crêperie*." She switched off the light. I heard her cross the room and settle on to her mattress.

"Bruno enjoyed the trial pancake," I remarked.

Chassa's voice brightened. "You were getting on well with him," she said. "Did you get his phone number?"

"It's not like that," I said primly.

Chassa cackled. "Write and tell Kim you've met a good-looking Frenchman who's been giving you tips."

I laughed obligingly.

Then I turned away. Kim wouldn't care how many Frenchmen I met. Even if I did write to him, I'd have no real relationships to tell him about, just superficial encounters, exaggerated to sound as if they meant something. The only time I'd see two become one was when the clocks went back.

Was it always going to be like this? I was glad Chassa couldn't see my expression, in the dark.

"It is good that you have another *mi-temps*," nodded Madame Vallentin. "At the Lycée Agricole, too. The headmaster is an acquaintance of my husband. We have dined with him and his wife – that is, his companion."

So she didn't mind about my second job. I sighed with relief.

My contentment was short-lived. "*La classe baccalauréat* will have an oral examination at the end of term," Madame Vallentin informed me. "I will inform you of the date."

I shuddered. That class, sitting an oral. The only English phrase they'd have learned by heart would be "shut up".

I walked into the classroom, where the girls were busy lounging at their desks and chattering amongst themselves.

"Hello," I greeted them. "Today, we will revise Lesson Four – at the station."

"*On l'a déjà fait,*" shouted someone in the back row.

"This time," I announced, "we will revise it without looking at our books." I took the copy of the Méthode Vallentin that lay open on Corinne's front row desk, and turned it face down. From the shocked silence, you'd have thought I'd asked them to read the lesson naked.

"Corinne." I motioned to her to stand up. "You are selling travel tickets. Isabelle –" she was tractable enough – "you're in London. You want to go to Brecon. Ask Corinne the times of the coaches and the buses."

Isabelle managed to say: "What time is ze bus to Bre-*con...*" before collapsing with laughter. The other girls joined in, drunk with the hilarity of hearing a naughty word. I put on the patient face my French teacher, Mrs Tina Jones, had worn when dealing with our class as giggly eleven-year-olds. We'd regularly wet our school regulation bottle green knickers the second someone said "*Oui, oui.*"

Sylvie and Viviane had managed a longer exchange than Christine and Brigitte, who had followed Corinne and Isabelle. Now they'd all be able to travel to Brecon, changing at Bristol where necessary. I smiled at them. Naked reading was the way forward.

But, looking around the class, I realised that not everyone had been listening to the dialogues. At the back, old Full Metal Earrings was absorbed in a private conversation with her friend.

"Anne-Laure," I snapped. "Come to the blackboard."

Anne-Laure remained in her place. Only a flicker of mascara showed that she had understood me. Silence fell as the other girls turned to look at her.

"Anne-Laure," I repeated. "To the blackboard."

Anne-Laure stared back at me. Her friends began to giggle.

"Anne-Laure," I resorted to French. "Come here and work, or go outside."

Anne-Laure lolled in her chair, staring back at me. Her friends gasped with admiration at her daring stand, or rather, slump.

"If I am run over by a car, it is you who are responsible," Anne-Laure informed me, her malicious grin widening.

I hesitated. At that moment the bell sounded. Anne-Laure, face alight with triumph, got up and sauntered out of the classroom, passing me without a word. Her classmates followed, giggling.

Still brooding as I walked into the café, I almost collided with two people who were leaving. I stomped upstairs and flung myself on to my bed.

"You all right, Hol?" Chassa had flown up the stairs behind me. "You look terrible."

"Thanks." I spat out the story of how Anne-Laure had humiliated me in class.

I expected Chassa to flare up in my defence, but she seemed lost in thought.

"Don't you think she's a nasty little thing?" I prompted.

"Oh, yeah," said Chassa absently. "But, thing is, Hol, it's no good losing it with people like that. You're the one that comes off worst in the long run."

"What would you have done?" I grumbled.

"Well," replied Chassa. "I wish I'd – you could talk to Madame Vallentin. Get her on your side."

"I can't ask her to sit in class with me and make them all shut up and listen," I grumbled.

"No, no," said Chassa. "But you can tell her one pupil won't work. Next time this little show-off plays up, pack her off to the headmistress. Throw in a slab of extra homework, and she won't bother you again."

"Madame Vallentin might think I'm not up to the job if I can't control the pupils," I pointed out.

"*She's* not up to the job of headmistress if she don't support her staff," argued Chassa. "Mind, some head teachers..." She paused.

"Some of them only care about their favourites, and everyone else can go to - Hol, did you see your letter? Came this morning." She handed me an envelope.

Putting my worries aside, I sat up and tore open the envelope.

"From Kim, is it?" teased Chassa.

"No, from Mam," I laughed. "She's finally – hey, Chassa, have you done something to your face?"

"Foundation, that's all," said Chassa. "Otherwise I look like death microwaved."

"And have you got mascara on?" I was intrigued. "I don't think I've ever seen you wearing any before."

"Oh, I went a bit mad in the '*Upermarché*," said Chassa. "Found this other stuff as well – you dab it on your T-zone to stop it shining. It works, too. Now my nose is so matte, a cat could sit on it. Well, got to go and wash up, Hol. We had two whole customers this lunchtime. Wait till we're serving your pancakes, then we'll have three. An' don' worry about that little squirt." She hurried out.

But now I was more intrigued by Chassa's little squirts – of lotions and potions on strategic places. A few days ago, she wouldn't have known her T-zone from her U-bend.

Had Chassa met a man? This sudden beauty treatment couldn't be for Didier's benefit. That burst of chatter was covering up something more than Celtic pallor.

Mam's letter didn't disappoint. Not quite a classic like the postcard she'd once written from Llandudno ("*Dear Holly, Arrived safely. Our hotel is very nice, our head waiter looks like Dustin Hoffman. Love, Mam and Dad*"), but still a clip of home life.

Things were fine with them, wrote Mam, except that the house was strangely quiet these days. She was glad to hear I had picked up with another Valleys girl, although she had never heard of anyone from Croesy called Brake, so couldn't think who Chassa was belonging to.

Dad had complained of headaches, but was refusing to see Dr Vaughan about them. Mam blamed the small print in The Fibs, and advised me to write my column in capital letters, how was it coming on? Mr Wheeler hadn't been in the fish market last week, and so remained blissfully unaware of interpersonal tensions across the Channel.

"Your café sounds nice," wrote Mam. "Me and Dad will eat there when we come out to visit, so keep practising opening the bottles, eh."

Mam had to close before the Cwarp did, but hoped I would send a proper letter soon. Dad sent his love, hoped my French was coming on and warned me not to talk to anyone I didn't know.

Still trying to work that last one out, I unfolded the page Griff had scribbled.

Griff's letter consisted of questions. Had Chassa introduced me to other friends? What were they like?

I smiled. Dear Griff, always so protective. He ended on a Dad-like note, "Any trouble and I'll post you the fare home."

I re-read my letters, savouring the taste of home. I'd write back tonight. Mam would enjoy hearing how a class of French kids could now buy coach tickets to Brecon. Come to think of it, it was funny that a Welsh town should be named in a French-made teaching method. Maybe the author had once been to the Brecon Jazz Festival.

I decided not to tell Chassa that Mam had asked about her family. But one thing reassured me. Chassa's family couldn't have any really dark secrets. If they had, the whole valley would know the details and Mam would have spilled the lot. I folded my letters, smiling.

11.

Shop Window Modelling For Dummies

"*Encore du café*, Mees Holly?" Madame Silvain refilled my cup. I smiled. Individual tuition was much nicer than dealing with a class of sniggering teenagers.

"Your husband, he is well?" I asked.

"He thinks to retire soon," sighed Madame Silvain. "We would like to spend time with the family. But when the family is not there…"

I risked the question. "Have you news of your daughter?"

"She studies, in Paris," said Madame Silvain. "She makes her *Maîtrise*."

Her Masters. I nodded, pleased that I recognised this term.

"And our son, he is in Australia," added Madame. "I would visit him, but it is far."

I made sympathetic noises. The gilded clock on the wall struck, signalling that our time was up.

Saying goodbye on the doorstep, I remembered. "Madame, this is for you." I handed her a slip of paper. "Our café becomes a *crêperie*. The first evening, the drinks will be less expensive."

As Madame Silvain took the invitation, a light "*Bonjour*" caught my ear. I turned and saw a young girl approaching us.

"*Vous êtes l'amie de Mademoiselle Chassa*," remarked the girl.

I recognised her. It was Chassa's friend, the one with the short skirt, what was her name?

"Milou," supplied the girl.

"*Ah, oui*," I smiled. It seemed polite to introduce her to Madame Silvain too.

"You offer yourself a gift?" Milou asked me, as we walked away from the shop.

"*Non, non,*" I said. I hesitated to reveal my arrangement with Madame Silvain. After all, she didn't even want her husband to know.

"*Non*, we discuss…things…" I glanced behind me. Madame Silvain was cooing at the sight of a lady wheeling twin babies in a pram.

"I have left the *Lycée*," remarked Milou.

"And I have started there," I grinned. Milou's eyes widened as I explained about my new job.

My handbag was still open. "Milou," I said. "Would you like to come to the opening of Mauvoisins' new *crêperie*?"

"*Avec plaisir*." Milou accepted gracefully. If only my pupils were as polite.

"These are smarter than ours," I sighed, handing the gilt-edged card back to Chassa.

"Well, we wouldn't be the Bad Café without cheap invitations," pointed out Chassa. "Got to maintain our reputation." She looked at the card again. "Nice of them."

I agreed. Monsieur and Madame Auguin of Talensac had decided that the marriage of their daughter Agnès would not be complete if *Mesdemoiselles* Holly *et* Chassa were not present. They'd never met us, which explained their reasoning. But, on their son Benoît's recommendation, here was our invitation.

"We should get them a present," I fretted. "And what should we wear? Have you ever been to a French wedding?"

"No," said Chassa. "But they're probably much like British ones. The Best Outfit competition, then muttering about how Our Amy had *her* reception at a much better hotel. Then, a twelvemonth later, the lovebirds split up. They ought to make two separate wedding lists in the first place."

"Not all marriages break up," I argued.

"Aye, well, if you see Benoît at the *Lycée*, ask him about their wedding list," suggested Chassa.

I nodded. Inwardly, I'd drawn up my own wish list for my new job, starting with cool authority and shakeproof knees.

I stepped up on to the platform next to the blackboard. The class – mostly boys, two or three girls – were in their seats, staring at me.

"Hello, Mrs," said one of the front row, who looked as if he occupied the same position in the school's first XV. Another held out his hand to me. Taken by surprise, I shook it. The boys sniggered.

"Today we will read these texts." I brandished the photocopies of a newspaper article Vicky had given me. "Then there will be questions." I handed the papers to Prop Forward, indicating that he should pass them round.

"*Madame, vous vous appelez comment?*" asked Handshake. I ignored him.

"Ask her what she is doing tonight," snickered the girl next to him.

"*Je rentre chez moi*," I informed her.

The girl squealed. "*Elle a compris!*"

"*Moi, c'est* Nicolas, Madame," announced Handshake.

"*Moi aussi, c'est* Nicolas," added his neighbour.

"*On s'appelle tous* Nicolas," sniggered Prop Forward.

I picked up the register Vicky had given me, listing each pupil, alongside their mugshot. A quick glance showed that there were indeed about five Nicolases in the class.

"*Bon*," I nodded at them. "Nicolas *Un et* Nicolas *Deux – on va faire comme* Rocky I, Rocky II..."

The pupils' laughter was genuine. I relaxed a little.

But, looking up, I saw that while I had been talking, some of the boys had pushed their desks together. Four of them had started a game of cards.

I nearly fell off the platform. At my school, even daydreaming in lessons had earned you a swift reprimand.

I marched over to the little group and seized the pack of cards. "Out," I barked, pointing at the ringleader. "*Dehors*. Now."

The cool, individualistic rebels turned to look at their leader. He was twice my width. I wouldn't be able to sling him out bodily.

Fortunately for me, he got up and walked towards the door, tossing a "*Salut*" to his mates. I breathed again.

But the trouble wasn't over yet. His friends were getting up and leaving their desks.

"*C'est la solidarité*," one of them explained to me, kindly.

A few other pupils, grinning broadly, had risen too. Alarmed, I realised half the class was leaving.

"Hé, les gars." Prop Forward was on his feet, but to admonish his friends. "We have laughed enough. Come back."

But the rebels were having none of it. If this foreigner was going to insist that they work, they weren't going to stay. Who did she think she was, their teacher?

Left with the few remaining pupils, I attempted to recover my authority. *"Bon,"* I began. "We will read the text and then I will ask you questions." My voice sounded thin in the half-empty room.

I had never been so glad to see the end of an hour. The pupils who had stayed had worked amiably enough, but I was burning inside.

"You come back next week, Madame?" inquired a tall thin boy, depositing his photocopy on the teacher's desk on his way out.

I bristled. "Evidently, since I am employed here," I snapped.

The tall boy didn't seem offended. *"Bon, à la semaine prochaîne,"* he replied, sauntering out of the classroom. His voice was deeper than Bruno's.

I wanted to lash out at the lot of them. Unfair, I knew, but I couldn't decide who I felt more annoyed with, the insolent pupils for walking out, or the ones who had stayed, for humouring me.

I supposed I should go and tell Vicky what had happened, but I wanted to calm down first.

Striding down the corridor, I noticed an open door. The room was dark, the blinds drawn. "CDI" read the gilt letters on the door.

I slipped inside the room, closing the door behind me. I just wanted a minute in the dark to cool down.

I moved over to the window. I was never going to make a go of teaching. Frustrated, I lowered my head and banged it on the window sill.

Suddenly, the lights came on. I swung round and saw a lady in a dark suit standing in the doorway, carrying a pile of books. I looked around me. The rows of bookshelves revealed that the CDI was in fact the library.

"Pardon, Madame," I began. "I have come in here, to...um, er, I have come in here to bang my head on the window sill."

The lady's finely curved eyebrows didn't twitch, but her lips did.

"You have had an English lesson with the TS2," she remarked, depositing her books on the table.

I stared. Head-banging was clearly standard therapy after teaching that particular class.

"Most of those pupils have passed in front of the CDI this afternoon," observed Madame. "When they should have been *en classe.*"

Madame looked somewhat severe, but just then I'd have talked to a stone pond statue if it had stopped piddling long enough to listen.

"That class, they do not work, Madame," I began. Yes, it was embarrassing to admit I couldn't control the pupils, but, dammit, the woman had just seen me head-butting her library.

Madame listened until I'd finished my tale.

"The best, it is that you speak of this with Monsieur Chevalier," she remarked. "You will need to make an appointment."

Oh, *non.* The headmaster wouldn't be at all impressed with an assistant teacher who wouldn't say boo to a goose, or as the French probably put it, wouldn't say *Oi!* to a *oie.* But Madame had picked up the telephone receiver and was dialling.

"*Merci,*" concluded Madame, replacing the receiver. "Monsieur Chevalier will see you at four o'clock, *mademoiselle.*"

Setting aside her books, Madame beckoned to me. Soon we were walking downstairs to the school secretary's office.

Madame Stern – that was the librarian's name – was taking a close interest in my case. She informed the secretary that *Mademoiselle l'assistante* had experienced the most disgraceful behaviour from a class both insolent and lazy. I sat in the office swivel chair, and rather enjoyed seeing the secretary so obsequious.

Madame Stern's example was inspiring. When I was admitted to the headmaster's presence, I explained what had happened without mumbling or looking at my daps.

Fair play for Monsieur Chevalier, the headmaster. He nodded gravely: "Mademoiselle, I apologise for the behaviour of this class."

I eyed him warily. He wasn't being sarcastic. Nice-looking too. No wonder I'd had to make an appointment. The female teachers must have been queuing up to go through their timetables with him.

"I will address myself to this class tomorrow morning," concluded Monsieur Chevalier, opening the door in a kind, but firm gesture of dismissal.

My smile lasted all the way up the corridor. Things were going to be all right.

"I've always said librarians are great," I gabbled to Lin, from a phone box in the town centre.

"Good move, Hol," came Lin's voice, clear as rain. Light-headed, I talked on about the future *crêperie*.

"Is that Bruno coming to your launch night?" asked Lin.

"Lin," I groaned. "Don't keep going on about Frenchmen."

"I just think you should meet someone," Lin replied. "Help you get over your Kim obsession."

Obsession, I seethed, as I eventually hung up. I had feelings, not a mental problem. One day Kim would realise I'd be good for him. And Lin would be on the Own Words Diet before she knew it.

"Some pupils are *insupportables*," whispered Madame Lesourd.

So I wasn't the only teacher who had problems with discipline.

"I have heard the girls talking, *mademoiselle*," continued Madame Lesourd. "They say how much they are bored by your English lessons."

I bridled. But little Madame Lesourd's face was so cherubic, I couldn't believe she was getting at me.

"It is not me who has written the *Méthode* Vallentin," I pointed out. "Oh, Madame –" a thought struck me – "have you seen Madame Vallentin today? I need to talk to her."

I wanted a few details about the school to add to my article for The Fibs.

"I have not seen her this morning," said Madame Lesourd. "She has said she receives a friend from England."

Perhaps she'd bring her English friend to the school. If he was a good-looking man, my little academics might realise that English could be useful.

The jaded intellectuals had trudged into the room. Anne-Laure had seated herself in the back row, sneer already in place.

"A competition for all the class," I announced. "With a prize. Today, everyone will practise a business conversation in English. The pair that improvises the best dialogue will win a meal, with free drinks, at Mauvoisins' new *crêperie*."

The class rippled with excitement. All except Anne-Laure, who was scowling, annoyed that her friends were actually interested in something I'd said.

I smiled to myself. Patrice wouldn't be thrilled at the prospect of giving away free pancakes, though. I could imagine the business conversation he'd be improvising with me.

"You will practise in pairs, then I want to hear your dialogues." I reached for Corinne's copy of the *Méthode* and flipped it over. "Without the book!"

The girls were putting real effort into their work. Maybe I should step up the bribery. A pile of cakes every week and they'd be fluent by Christmas.

Anne-Laure was leaning back in her chair, her arms folded. Her neighbour nudged her as I moved around, listening to the dialogues.

"She will not reprimand me," sniffed Anne-Laure. I wondered if she left her lip curlers in overnight.

The prospect of free *crêpes* had spurred everyone on. Christine and Nadia were incisive in their portrayal of office manager and goods supplier, finalising the time when the photocopier would be delivered. Brigitte and Isabelle thrashed out the problem of reserving a first-class seat on the next day's 10.30 plane to New York. But the honours went to Corinne and Viviane, who held us all spellbound with their attempt to book a conference room for lingerie salespeople.

"That was worth a *Crêpe Bretonne*," I told the duo, who sat pink-faced and smiling at the spontaneous applause. "But I cannot give you the prize."

"Euh?" inquired the class.

I shook my head. "It was a competition for all the class. Nobody will have the prize, because Anne-Laure and her friend Maryline did not participate."

Corinne, Viviane and the others stared in disbelief. As heads turned towards the back of the class, I knew I'd won.

"Pourquoi t'as pas joué?" *"Egoiste!"* spat the girls. All the curl went out of Anne-Laure's lip. As the bell sounded, I allowed myself a quiet smile. The queen bee had been reduced to a heap of royal jelly.

Corinne and Viviane wouldn't lose out, though. I'd slip them their invitations, later. I left the classroom, light-hearted.

"That deserves a drink, Hol," said Chassa, delving into one of Patrice's new crates.

"We mustn't drink all the cider before the Grand Opening," I protested.

"Relax, mun," said Chassa, pouring *cidre doux* into one of the café's new brown mugs. "Plenty to go around. When's that Welsh wine of yours getting here? I'll need it for Christmas dinner at Serge's. You'll come too, won't you, Hol? Less you're going home?"

"I haven't decided yet," I admitted. Christmas seemed a long way off.

"If you're here at Christmas, they'll invite you," Chassa reassured me. "They won't leave anybody out."

It was Chassa who wouldn't leave anybody out, I thought, as I sampled the *cidre doux*. For the hundredth time, I wondered what her relatives could have done to drive her away.

Except the granny, I remembered. Chassa seemed fond of her.

Perhaps Chassa had had some minor disagreement with her clan, and, with every week and month that had passed, hurt pride had grown harder to swallow. Unlike this cider. I took another gulp.

"Messieurs-dames, bonsoir et bienvenue." Patrice greeted the guests. "I hope you will enjoy the *crêpes*, my creations."

I winced. Saying that in front of Chassa was nothing but a polite, carefully worded request for trouble. I wouldn't put it past her to christen the venture by smashing a bottle of *cidre doux* over Patrice's head. Fortunately she was busy welcoming a late arrival, a small balding man I didn't recognise.

"And *bon appétit* to all," finished Patrice. The guests applauded.

Chassa turned to me. "Hol. Can you hand the drinks round? I'll give out the menus."

I hurried into the kitchen, where Patrice was demonstrating his cocktail making skills to his parents. There was an art to it. When I'd tried, a few days before, I'd forgotten you needed to turn the glass upside down to sugar the rim *before* you filled it with the drink.

"The establishment looks fine, Holly," said Sophie. "Patrice has worked hard, *n'est-ce pas?*"

I nodded. Patrice had even hung pictures on the café walls. He'd wanted sepia prints. Chassa, ever resourceful, had offered to spill tea over Didier's holiday snaps, but in the end her employer had shelled out for some paintings of the Breton coast. The Café wasn't looking too Bad tonight.

Madame Silvain was seated at the corner table. I'd be too busy to look after her. Fortunately Milou was sitting with her, chatting. I smiled. Provided Chassa was on hand to open all the bottles, things should go fine.

"*Ça va*, Mademoiselle Gethin?" Corinne and Viviane approached me.

"*Ça va*," I told them. "This way, girls."

The two girls went pink as I ushered them to Benoît and Matthieu's table. Perhaps they'd hit it off. With the café's quaint charm, exciting cuisine and two bottles of *cidre doux*, who knew what might happen?

"Holly." Patrice was beckoning, from the kitchen. "Tell people to sit by the windows."

"*Quoi?*" I managed.

"We want the passers-by to see we have people," hissed Patrice. "Make them move."

I looked at the diners, then at the empty tables nearest the windows. I couldn't drag people out of their seats and shove them across the room. Chassa was handing out menus. The guests would be ordering soon.

I supposed I'd have to ask Corinne and Viv to move. A shame to separate them from the boys though.

"Hol?" Chassa was at my elbow. "You all right?"

"No one's sitting in the window," I fretted. "Patrice wants the customers to be on show."

"S'all right." Chassa took my notepad from me. "You sit there. Be the customer."

"I can't sit down and watch you doing all the work," I protested.

"Serge'll give me a hand," said Chassa. "Hey, here's someone to keep you company. *Bonsoir, Monsieur*."

I turned and saw Bruno closing the café door behind him.

"*Par ici, Monsieur*." Chassa swept us both towards a window table. Next thing I knew I was seated opposite Bruno. From *bonsoir* to *bon appétit* in 60 seconds.

Bruno placed his ever-present hardback on the table. I squinted discreetly, but couldn't make out its title. Probably something heavy, like *Teach Yourself Autodidacticism*.

"*Monsieur, madame*." Serge handed us a menu each. He glanced at Bruno and winked at me.

"*Un Mixte, s'il vous plaît*," I said faintly.

Serge left with our order. I couldn't think what to say to Bruno. He wasn't very forthcoming either.

"Are you studying?" I eventually asked.

"*Non*," replied Bruno. "I teach yoga, in evening classes. You have done yoga?"

I shook my head. A light shone in Bruno's eyes.

"Yoga is so important," he began. "I would like to set up a practice, teaching people to breathe." His eyes, large and brown, hinted at a profoundly sensitive nature. I treated myself to a long gaze into them.

"*Voilà* Holly, *une Salade Mixte*," announced Serge, setting a plate of salad on the table before me. "*Et pour Monsieur, une Complète*."

I gasped. I hadn't wanted a *Salade Mixte*, but a *Crêpe Mixte*. Why had Serge assumed I'd wanted a salad? My face burned. He'd assumed I was trying to lose weight. Which meant he thought I needed to.

"*Hé! Madame!*" I looked up and got a shock. A face was pressed up against the window. White, with staring eyes.

As I recoiled, another voice from outside shouted: *"C'est l'assistante!"*

Peering through the window, I made out two or three figures in the dark. Oh, no. My pupils. And, judging by their voices, the ones from the agricultural school.

"Elle a un petit copain!" shrieked another voice. *"Hou les amoureux!"*

Great, now they'd seen Bruno. I cringed.

"I love youuu..." giggled a high-pitched voice.

And one of them was a girl. How would she have liked a gang of blokes to hassle her while she was dining out?

"I am sorry, Bruno," I explained. "It is my pupils."

Bruno set down his *kir-cassis*. He would sort these rodneys out. He'd get up, go outside and send them back to prune their geese, or whatever farmers did at this time of year.

Outside, the shouts and giggles continued. Bruno looked thoughtful.

"Don't they bother you?" I ventured.

Bruno turned his gaze on me. "Each should be free to do as he wishes," he pronounced.

I nearly rubbed my ears. The window-tapping continued.

Someone make those idiots go away. I looked round for Chassa. She'd been here a minute ago, now she'd vanished.

No good turning to Patrice. I'd have to rely on myself.

I got up, pushed my chair back, and walked to the *crêperie* door.

But as I pulled the door open, I saw that the rowdy gang had moved back from the window. Their leader, whom I vaguely recognised as a possible Nicolas, was having words with another, taller, boy.

"M'enfin, Gilles, we only laugh," argued Possible Nicolas.

"You annoy *la Miss*," returned the tall boy.

Hearing a shout from above, I looked up. But not fast enough. I gasped as a sudden blast of icy water drenched me.

"Cassez-vous!" rang out Chassa's voice.

Wiping the water from my eyes, I saw Chassa on her balcony, a bucket in her hand. The pupils burst into hysterical laughter.

"Oh, hell fire." Chassa had realised what she'd just done. "Sorry, Hol."

I didn't trust myself to reply. Chassa's window slammed. Through my dripping fingers, I saw that the tall boy was wiping his face too.

Before I could speak, Chassa came running out of the café, with Serge behind her.

"Holly," yelped Chassa. "I didn't mean to soak you, I was after those kids. Are you all right? *Et vous, monsieur?*"

"Dry yourselves," invited Serge, offering us towels. He'd moved fast. He'd only just been waiting at table.

The tall boy – the others had called him Gilles – strolled into the café. Chassa whisked us through the café and kitchen, then up the stairs.

"We will offer you a free meal, *monsieur*," Chassa called over her shoulder as she rushed around our room, smoothing down my bedcover. I'd never seen her so flustered.

But Gilles didn't seem bothered at all. Towelling his hair, he looked around him and remarked, "*Vous êtes bien installées.*"

Now I remembered where I'd seen him before. He was one of the agricultural pupils who hadn't walked out of my lesson. The one who had asked if I was coming back to teach the class the next week. Suddenly I didn't feel so awkward.

Before I knew it, we were sitting on chairs in Patrice's warm kitchen while that gentleman, amused, served us up a pancake each. (This time I'd insisted on a **Crêpe Mixte,** to avoid another plate of bunny food). Serge, filling the dishwasher, chatted with Gilles about his studies. I sat and munched, strangely content, despite the unexpected shower.

"Oh, Hol," said Chassa, charging back into the kitchen. "Someone I want you to meet."

Behind her I saw the small, balding man she'd welcomed earlier.

"This is Patrick Degermann," said Chassa. "Our telephone pupil."

So this was him. I shook his hand.

"Patrick's been an actor for thirty years," announced Chassa. "But he's still unknown."

"*Totalement,*" nodded the visitor, proudly. He poured out a torrent of French about theatrical productions he had been in. Gilles and Chassa nodded, but all I could think about was how Patrick's moustache moved with a life of its own. Perhaps it could audition for a remake of *Cat People*, playing the whiskers.

Looking at Gilles, I wondered if agriculture was his true calling. I couldn't picture him jumping up and down, purple-faced, shouting "Get off my land."

Sitting on my bed that night, I reviewed the evening. It hadn't gone quite as planned, but everyone had had a good time, even old Patrice. I wasn't even cross about the bucket of water incident. It had felt so much friendlier, chatting in the kitchen with Serge and Gilles.

And meeting our telephone pupil too. I automatically turned to my mobile phone.

A text message was waiting. Vicky or Madame Silvain, perhaps.

But the message that appeared surprised me.

"RENTRE CHEZ TOI" read the text.

I pressed buttons, but the sender's number was unavailable.

Must be a wrong number. I switched off the mobile and returned it to my handbag, then flopped back on to the bed.

My gaze fell on my letter from Mam. I smiled, thinking of home. I'd tasted life in a completely different culture. One with nosey neighbours, sudden downpours and misunderstanding dads.

12.

Saint-Cloud For Having Us

"*La demoiselle d'honneur!*" Serge exclaimed as I walked downstairs in my least worst outfit.

"*D'horreur, plutôt.*" Patrice sniggered.

"*Merci*, Serge. Are you still working at the fire station?" I asked Serge, deliberately ignoring his son's remark.

"At the fire station, yes," said Serge. "Between serving *crêpes*." He winked at me.

"And when will my back gate be repaired?" grumbled Patrice.

"When your workman has finished your front door and your tables," replied Serge.

Patrice really was an ungrateful git, I thought. With Chassa and me going to Benoît's sister's wedding, he would have been stuck if Serge and Sophie hadn't agreed to help him for the day. And he was going to need the help. Since we'd become a *crêperie*, we'd been getting a steady stream of customers, at lunchtime and in the evenings. Bruno had been back, although I hadn't been around to serve him. Chassa reported that he was keeping his nose to the hardback.

"Won't talk to me," she'd teased. "He wants his Holly."

"Well, he should have sorted out his Holly's pupils," I'd grumbled. I hadn't appreciated Bruno's attitude. Talk about *laissez-faire*. (Not that I would, in case I mispronounced it).

I hadn't seen Gilles since opening night, either. Monsieur Chevalier, the headmaster, had given the TS2 a lecture on classroom behaviour. I hadn't been present, but Vicky had assured me he'd had a few things to say about respect for teachers and the importance of learning English. The week after, they'd been away on a field trip, but I'd have to face them soon.

The *Salle des Mariages* at Mauvoisins Town Hall looked like Ponty jobcentre, with fewer chairs.

"So that's Benoît's sister," I mused, gazing at the bride. That was the shortest wedding dress I'd ever seen.

"There's Benoît." Chassa whispered back. "And his Mam and Dad. Oh, they're starting."

The Mayor tall and dark, looked impossibly French. His ribbons gleamed cherry red in a daring attempt to upstage the bride. On my big day, I'd make sure I outshone the vicar. Although no one in the congregation would be looking at me. They'd be admiring Kim in his suit. Actually, no, they'd all be staring at where Mrs Whipple had put her carnation.

A couple of questions from the Mayor and that was it. Two were now officially one. Not like chapel. Once Bethel choir got started, you were lucky to get out before evening had broken, let alone morning.

The guests stood up, applauding, as the newlyweds left the *Salle*.

"They'll be off to the park to take photos," said Chassa. "We'll go and wait for them at the *Salle des Fêtes*. But let's say hello to Benoît and his Mam and Dad first."

"*Alors, c'est vous, les petites Anglaises,*" remarked Benoît's dad, shaking hands with us. Chassa explained that we were *Galloises*, and managed to look as if she'd never heard the *Galloise blonde* pun before. My admiration for her acting ability grew.

"You look nice, Benoît," I said. "Hey, did you run your race last night? You didn't hurt yourself, jumping on the roofs?"

"*Ah, oui*, I broke my leg," teased Benoît. "*Non,* I did not run, my sister was worried that I would break my neck and she would be without a witness. It was a friend who ran in my place. We won the race."

"*Bravo!*" I said.

"My replacement joins us later, to celebrate with us," said Benoit. "Now I have to rejoin *les jeunes mariés* for the photos. *A t'à l'heure!*"

"Mees Holly!" Matthieu wasn't going to waste time in the park when there was a buffet to be sampled. He led Chassa and me to the food tables.

"This is for you," joked Matthieu, indicating the salad. *"L'assiette anglaise."*

"You French people," I griped. "You think Britain is only England."

"But in Wales, you speak English, *non?*" asked Matthieu. "At the end of the year we have the *examen oral* in English. I am very bad. In class, I score three or four."

I hoped that wasn't his percentage. He continued: "If you will read aloud some texts in English, I will record them. Like that, I will improve my pronunciation."

I hesitated. Should a teacher help one pupil, and not the others?

"I have a *magnétophone* at home," said Matthieu. "I will invite you *chez moi*, to my parents' farm, one Saturday."

I accepted, glowing quietly. He'd asked me for help, not Chassa.

"This year, *en anglais, je vais faire un carton*," Matthieu announced, turning to the small pieces of toast topped with salmon.

"What does he mean, he'll make a cardboard box?" I asked Chassa, who had filled her plate.

"He means he'll do really well," said Chassa. "I can't see two free seats, together. We'll have to sit separate. There's a seat for you, at that table b'there. See you later."

As I moved towards the table, a shiver ran down my spine. Seated there were a big blond man and a little dark-haired lady. For one horrible moment I thought they were Christian and Annick Le Floch. As they turned to me, they must have wondered what they'd done to provoke such an inane smile of relief.

I introduced myself as the teacher of Agnès' brother, at the *Lycée Agricole*.

"Jacques was a pupil at this *Lycée*," explained the wife.

"A very long time ago," joked Jacques. "Monsieur Archambaud, he is still there?"

I explained that I didn't know all the teachers, I was only there part-time. "But I have another *mi-temps*," I added. *"A l'Ecole Vallentin. L'école de secrétariat."*

"Tiens, c'est pas là...?" From their rapid exchange, I gathered that Jacques and Madame Jacques were also acquainted with the Vallentin establishment.

"Before, Jacques worked with the husband of Madame Vallentin," explained Madame Jacques.

Heck, Jacques knew everyone. Good thing he hadn't been up against me at the job interview.

"*Homme d'affaires*," said Jacques dryly.

His tone discouraged me from inquiring further into Monsieur Vallentin's business.

"And you will have seen her brother today, also," remarked Jacques. "*Le Maire de Mauvoisins* - Monsieur Grebot."

I thought I'd misheard. Jacques explained that the Mayor who had married Agnès and Philippe was Monsieur Grebot, the brother of Madame Vallentin. Now I realised why Madame V had looked so familiar. I'd seen her brother's face on the election posters.

"You have not yet been invited to the *Mairie*?" teased Jacques.

"They have more important guests than me," I told him, thinking of the English visitor Madame V had gone to collect at the airport. Probably another businessman embroiled in dodgy dealings with Monsieur V.

"That filled a gap." Chassa rubbed her tum as we sat on the steps of the *Salle des Fêtes*, digesting our meal.

"Don't you miss the food from home? Or anything else?" I asked on impulse.

Luckily, Chassa was too contented to get annoyed.

"Orange Aeros," she grinned. "And my Granny Chappell. And old Sion."

"Nothing else?" Sometimes, even walking uphill brought a lump to my throat.

Chassa was about to answer when the door of the *Salle des Fêtes* swung open and Benoît and Matthieu appeared.

"We wait for the *pièce montée*," Benoît explained. "Then we will hear the speeches, and then dance." I wondered what in the world a Mounted Piece was.

"*Les mariages, chez vous,* what are they like?" Matthieu asked me.

"We stand outside the chapel and hold brooms," answered Chassa, before I could speak. "The bride carries a bucket to catch the good wishes. Then the newly-weds run round the chapel backwards while we all stamp our feet."

Benoit pretended he hadn't been taken in for a second. Matthieu cackled, and invited Chassa to join us for the day on the farm.

"I will fetch you in the car," he promised. *"Et Monsieur Lapin aussi."*

So Chassa and Didier would be there too. I scuffed my shoes.

"What's wrong?" asked my inner voice. *"Want him all to yourself, do you?"*

I thought it over while the others chatted. It wasn't that I wanted Matthieu to myself. It was just that when Chassa was there, people talked to her, instead of me.

"Holly," Chassa nudged me. "Your friend's here."

I looked up. Gilles was shaking hands with Benoît and Matthieu.

"You have met each other in the shower," grinned Matthieu.

So he'd heard about that. Seemed like none of my mishaps had gone unnoticed in this town. Shop assistants probably mimed the *lever-la-patte* incident to each other every time I left their premises.

I rose to greet Gilles, but sneezed before I could speak.

"Told you to dry yourself after your shower," teased Chassa.

The boys laughed. I smiled sourly. She was at it again, charming everyone while I lumped through life. I decided I must never introduce Chassa to Kim.

A small van was pulling up near the building. Benoît hurried down the steps to greet the driver.

Three men emerged from the van. They were all carrying large flat containers.

"What is it that they bring?" I asked Gilles, as Benoît ushered the new arrivals into the hall.

"It is the *pièce montée*," explained Gilles. "It comes in three or four layers. They will construct it –" he made expressive gestures – "so that the bride and groom can cut it."

So the mysterious *pièce montée* was the wedding cake. I laughed at the thought of it travelling in style, in its own vehicle.

"Is Gilles in your class at the *Lycée*?" I asked Benoît, aside.

"Non," replied Benoit. "He is a year older than me."

Now I remembered, Gilles was in the TS2, the naughty walk-out class. Benoît and Matthieu were in the year below.

"Our team needed a runner," continued Benoît. "For *Le Parkours* last night."

"So Gilles stood in for you." I glanced across at Gilles. Long legs must be an advantage in free-running.

"*Vive la mariée*," warbled Chassa, managing to stumble down the pavement in spite of its perfectly flat, level stones.

One evening out and I had a shameless lush teetering home beside me. I caught her arm before she could start shoving late-night buses out of the way.

"*Pint-glass figure*," sang Chassa, pinching the roll of fat above my waist.

I pulled away.

"Only joking, Hol," hiccupped Chassa. She clasped my shoulder. "Bit of exercise, that'll shift the weight. I've got a book on aerobics, somewhere." She hiccupped again. "*Flatten Your Stomach*, it's called."

"Shall we go in the back way?" I steered Chassa away from the front door of the Bad Café. This would spare any diners the sight of their regular waitress three sheets, a candlewick bedspread and several pillow cases to the wind.

Although the back gate opened easily, Chassa still climbed over it to undo the catch.

"Open the back door, will'ew, Hol," she yelled, swinging back and forth on the gate. "The key's under the mat."

"That's right, tell all the neighbours." I looked around the yard. "Where's the mat? It's not here, Chassa."

Chassa chortled and slid off the gate. As she lay giggling on her side, the café door opened. Serge stood in the doorway.

"Hiya," carolled Chassa, trying to stand up, but missing the ground by several centimetres. I braced myself for a telling-off. But Serge just beckoned us inside. I hurried Chassa through the kitchen and up the stairs.

"You'll get us both the sack," I hissed, propelling her into our room and closing the door.

"Oh, don' create," cackled Chassa, swaying across the room and crash-landing into her stack of carrier bags.

"You'll ruin your shoes," I scolded. I'd spent most of the reception making conversation with the older guests, while Chassa had danced with everyone else.

"Don't go all chapel on me, Hol," yawned Chassa, curling up at the foot of Mount Binbag. "You used to fall asleep after the party. Oh, no, that wasn't you, was it?" She giggled, turned on to her side and shut down for the night.

My mouth tightened. We'd had this at home every Christmas, when Griff would return from the office party around teatime, flop on the settee and snore for the rest of the evening. Mam would tiptoe round him. I had to be the helpful one, who gathered gloves from the floor and stashed away discarded shoes.

I turned away from Chassa. One of us had had a wild time. I wondered when it was going to be me.

"La campagne française, ça te plaît, Holly?" asked Matthieu, creaking into fourth gear beside me.

"Beaucoup." I smiled.

"You see how beautiful the *Pays de Galles* could be," teased Didier from the back seat. "If you flattened your mountains."

Chassa snorted at this. The ensuing backseat scuffle sounded more like *Flatten Your Rabbit.*

Saint-Cloud-les-Roseaux, read the road sign. We'd reached Matthieu's village, then. Field after field, dotted with grazing cows. Matthieu turned the car and guided it up a path that gradually widened to a track. At the far end, I saw the farmhouse, with its stone walls.

As we parked, the front door of the farmhouse opened and a little old lady appeared, wearing a coat and rubber boots.

"Ma grand-mère - Mémé," explained Matthieu.

After shaking hands with the three of us, Matthieu's *Mémé* got into a little car parked near the house and promptly drove away down the track. I nearly fell over.

"Matthieu.... she has what age, your grandmother?" I asked.

"Eighty-six," said Matthieu, without batting an eyelid. "Come inside. Today roast chicken is the *plat du jour.*"

"Here, we are the Good Café," joked Matthieu, serving us coffee as we sat around the living room table digesting his roast chicken. All clucked and plucked on the premises, he'd assured us.

"It's a beautiful house," I said out loud, gazing around the room. There was even an old-fashioned dresser with plates on.

"Holly is homesick," teased Chassa. "A Welsh dresser and a real coal fire."

The boys laughed.

"Shall we make the recording of your texts, Matthieu?" I asked, pointedly reminding the company that it was my help he had asked for.

"I will fetch the *magnéto*," promised Matthieu. "And after, I will show you the farm."

Matthew's texts all seemed to concern social and economic issues.

"Most urban societies are faced with the problem of homelessness," I enunciated into Matthieu's tape recorder's external mic. He listened as I read, even asking me how I would phrase some of the sentences as questions. I was gratified at the close attention he paid.

"Matthieu, you are planning to travel to Britain?" I asked. "Ah, I know. You've got a girlfriend *anglophone*, haven't you?"

"*Non, non*," replied Matthieu, looking so innocent that I didn't believe a word. "*Merci infiniment*, Holly." He switched off the tape recorder. "We will go to join the others?"

We found Chassa and Didier in the kitchen garden, talking with Benoît. A near neighbour, it turned out.

"He only lives five *kilomètres* from here," explained Matthieu, as Benoît and I did the French cheek-kissing greeting I'd learned was called the *bise*.

Matthieu, Benoît and Didier promptly organised an obstacle race over walls, gates and sheds. Chassa commentated, and I awarded marks for speed, style, and artistic interpretation.

Didier, bursting to keep up with the two free-runners, leapt from shed to wall, injuring his toe in the process. First Aider Chassa was on the case, offering to saw off his foot and suspend it from her handbag as a lucky charm.

"Go on, Laps," she coaxed. "Don't you want to bring me luck?"

"With men?" asked Didier. "You will need more than a rabbit's foot."

My turn to smirk. Annoyingly, Chassa didn't seem to mind.

"*La galanterie française*," she observed with a Patrícean shrug.

Matthieu got up from the patch of nettles where he'd landed. "We shall take tea? Somewhere in the world, it is five o'clock!"

We retreated to the farmhouse. Matthieu searched for his slippers, getting quite cross when he couldn't find them.

"You have hidden them, Holly," he accused me.

"I have never seen your slippers," I protested.

"They are violet," said Benoît helpfully.

Matthieu stomped around, looking for his missing footwear, then gave up and stoked the fire. "You're getting warmer," teased Chassa. Didier claimed that the slippers had burned beautifully, throwing up magnificent purple flames. I couldn't stop giggling.

Benoît entertained us with tales of midnight rides around Mauvoisins in Matthieu's car, stopping occasionally at advertising billboards to take down a poster they fancied for their bedroom walls. The salad cream adverts were the best, he reported.

"Salad cream?" I was surprised. "I would have thought you'd want the underwear ads."

"On the salad cream posters, the girls wear fewer clothes," explained Benoît, cheerfully.

After tea, the boys wanted to play a card game, *belote* – "We four will play and you can watch, Holly," said Matthieu. Thankfully, Chassa saved me from being left out by declaring that she had never got to grips with *belote*.

"It's not a patch on Whot," she said. "And we ought to get home before dark."

Saying *à plus* to Benoît, we bundled back into Matthieu's car and headed down the track. As we reached the main road, a solitary figure passed us.

"*Tiens!*" said Chassa, waving at the pedestrian. "There's Milou. My old pupil, remember? She came to our opening night."

I was surprised. I wouldn't have thought Milou would take country walks, in her high heels.

"Maryline Guilbaud," nodded Matthieu. "She lives in Saint-Cloud too."

"Bright girl," commented Chassa. "Pity she left school."

Matthieu gave a short laugh.

"She has left school, all right," he said. "It is because she expects a baby. And there is no boyfriend to recognise the child. And her mother goes to *la messe* – the church service – every day. It is a shameful thing for her, to have a grandchild that has no father."

13.

Feuds Reignited

"Madame, a piss of cack?" asked a hopeful voice.

"When you have finished the exercise, Isabelle," I said gravely. "Then you may take a piss, er, a piece of cake."

"*Moi aussi*, Madame," Brigitte, Corinne and the others weren't going to be left out.

They'd worked for the last hour with only half the usual giggling. Nothing like the carrot cake and stick to make my little donkeys trot along.

I was handing out the last slices – even Anne-Laure wasn't above a nibble – when the bell rang for the end of the lesson. The girls snatched up their books and headed for the door.

They were so young, under their mascara and airs of boredom. Milou wasn't much older. What sort of a life would she have now?

"Mademoiselle Holly!" Madame Lesourd crept into the classroom as if she was being stalked by her own shadow. "Madame Vallentin wishes to see you."

Brushing telltale crumbs from my jumper, I shoved the cake box into my carrier bag and went into my employer's office.

Madame Vallentin greeted me with a smile. "We have a visitor," she said. "An old acquaintance of yours."

"Holly doesn't recognise me," observed the young woman sitting near her. "Well, it has been a long time since schooldays."

My mouth fell open in a promising imitation of Cousteau, who was swimming serenely in his tank.

"Angeline?" I breathed.

Mrs Hathaway's voice echoed in my head: "*When Angeline goes to Movie Scenes, she stays with the Mayor's family.*" So that was how she knew Madame Vallentin, and had heard I was working at the school.

Angeline's features were smooth with an evenly applied glow. Her plaits had given way to a glossy black bob.

"We'll have lunch, and catch up, Holly," said Angeline. She took her leave of Madame V with a theatrical *bise*. Dazed, I followed her to the door.

"We'll go to the *brasserie* in rue Alleinde," remarked Angeline.

I followed, still stunned. Lunch with Angeline Taylor. We hadn't eaten together since she'd snatched my tube of Smarties in the playground, then graciously thrown one back at me.

"So, Holly." Angeline looked up from the menu. "What brought you to Mauvoisins?"

I suspected she'd heard Mrs Hathaway gloating over my Plan B, but played along.

"I needed to spend time in France for my university course," I explained. "It seemed reasonable to visit the twin town."

"You can't beat spending time in the country," agreed Angeline. "My work placement in Freiburg really paid off."

"*Using her French AND HER GERMAN.*" I braced myself. She'd start showing off about places she'd been.

"It can be hard to make French friends," remarked Angeline. "But join something like Amnesty International and you meet native speakers."

I was astonished at her friendliness. Time must have softened her.

"And how did you start teaching?" asked Angeline.

I ran through the story of Christian, the shelter, finding the school and landing the job. Now she'd be impressed by my initiative.

"I'd have been on the first train up to Paris," remarked Angeline. "There's always bar work. Cigarette?"

"Er, no thanks." I was eight years old again, discovering that one's roller skates were only socially acceptable if they had been bought in Cardiff, and not ordered from the back of the cornflakes packet.

"You don't need to do a TEFL course either," said Angeline. "I never did."

133

Her voice was carefully accentless. You'd never know she'd come out of the same valley as me. The waiter arrived and Angeline began ordering for both of us.

"This wine's pretty cruddy," remarked Angeline, setting down her glass. "Francis has a decent cellar. Francis Grebot, that is. The Mayor."

"How do you know the Mayor's family?" I asked.

"I met his daughter, Marine, on a school exchange, when I was thirteen," said Angeline. "Where are you living, by the way?"

"I'm lodging with a girl from Croesy," I replied. "Chassa Brake."

Angeline sat up. "Charlotte Brake!" Her eyes narrowed. Suddenly I recognised the girl who used to pull the smaller children's hair in the dinner queue.

"She's a waitress in a *crêperie*," I explained.

Angeline's smile widened. "Well, well. Ms Spotlight, cleaning tables."

I bit my tongue.

"She fancied herself as a star, at school," said Angeline. "She only got to be head girl because the teachers liked her. Heaven knows why."

"I didn't know she'd been head girl." I was surprised.

"I shouldn't think she's told you everything," sniffed Angeline.

"Do you know why she left Croesy?" I asked.

Sensing my interest, Angeline pointedly sipped her wine.

"Which café does she work in?" she asked. "It will be nice to see Charlotte again. Especially after she left school so suddenly."

Walking back to the Bad Café, I shuddered. Angeline would be coming round to gloat at Chassa's menial job. And Chassa was impulsive. One too many taunts, and Angeline might end up discovering how decent the Bad Café's cellar was. Head first.

"Angeline Taylor?" said Chassa. "Never!"

"She wants to come and eat here," I sighed. "Says she wants to catch up with you."

"Probably just wants Sion's phone number," said Chassa. "She's never forgiven me for the end-of-term concert in my last year. She was due to sing in it." She grinned at the memory.

"What happened?" I asked.

"I was in a sketch," said Chassa. "I played this sprinter, training for the Cardiff Olympics. I was talking about drug testing, holding up my bottled sample. I dropped the bottle and it smashed."

"So?" I said.

"Angeline was on next," said Chassa. "She stepped into the puddle. 'Cept it wasn't water. Sion's friend Gareth had filled the bottle, but not from a tap. Believed in realism, he did. Angeline slipped, landed on her bum, and the audience burst out laughing."

"Did she storm off stage?" I asked.

"No, she started her song," said Chassa. "But the damage had been done. Gareth lost it, bounded on to the stage and ran around mooning the audience, shouting out that he was Peter Purves. The whole place collapsed."

I giggled.

"Angeline fancied Sion," said Chassa. "So she put the fault on me. Claimed I'd put Gareth up to it."

"She said you were head girl," I ventured. "And you left school suddenly."

Chassa manufactured a smile. "Yeah," she breezed. "Once the A-levels were in the bag, I shoved off to France. Oh, got something to show you." She darted behind the bar and emerged with a large scroll of paper.

"Patrice reckons we need a logo, now we're a *crêperie*. I've drawn one." She unrolled the paper.

"Nice," I nodded. "I like the cucumbers."

"They're croissants," groaned Chassa. "I'm no good at drawing. You have a go." She thrust a black marker pen into my hand. "Time for Patrick's telephone lesson." She raced away.

Could Patrick, the actor, be the reason Chassa was wearing make-up now? He wasn't going to notice it, over the phone.

I studied Chassa's drawing. We'd learned lettering at school. I tilted the marker pen to the correct angle and began forming the letters. B…A….D, then a rounded C…A…F…E….

My handbag beeped from the chair. I set down the pen and scrabbled for my mobile. Probably Madame Silvain, texting about our next lesson.

What I read made me gasp. I hadn't encountered that sort of language since I'd arrived here.

I re-read the message, then erased it. It had to be an error. Like that last text, the one that had told me to go home. I pushed my mobile back into my bag.

"*Hello!*" The voice was deep, masculine. I turned to glare at the speaker. I was at the bus stop, waiting for one of those accordion buses to squeeze round the corner. I didn't need Frenchmen bothering me. Some of them took a foreign passport for a written invitation.

Seated at the driving wheel of a little cream car was Gilles. My glare vanished.

"You are going to the *Lycée*?" he enquired.

I nodded. Seconds later, I was sitting beside him and the streets of Mauvoisins were rushing past us.

A lot of the pupils had cars. I remembered Matthieu telling us he'd passed his driving test after only thirteen lessons. He'd learned to drive in the countryside, though. They probably only had to reverse around a cow.

"Normally, I run to school," remarked Gilles, reaching to change gear.

I raised my eyebrows. "You jump from gate to gate?"

Gilles laughed. "I am training for a race that will take place next summer, in the region. I try to encourage Benoît and Matthieu to join me. "

"You like sport?" I asked, as the fields sped by.

"*Bof*," replied Gilles. "It is especially to make some money."

"There is a prize?" I was surprised. He hadn't struck me as being mercenary.

"*Non, non,*" explained Gilles. "The race has a charitable aim. There is a clinic, near my home that needs money. My nephew receives care there. So, I run in the race."

He drove into the *Lycée* grounds, picked out a space and parked the car neatly. I was certain he'd excelled at cow reversing.

136

"*Merci*, Gilles, *et bonne journée*," I said, stepping out of the vehicle with a smile. It would have looked quite regal had I not got my coat stuck in the car door.

"Madame, *vous venez au bal?*" asked one of the prop forwards, indicating the poster on the classroom wall.

I walked over to read the poster, which was advertising the *Lycée*'s Christmas dance.

"November, it is early for a *bal de Noël*," I remarked.

"*Elle sait lire!*" squeaked a long-haired girl. I looked at her. She was the scarf who always sat draped round her boyfriend.

"The school will be closed for the *vacances de Noël*, Madame," explained Prop Forward. "So we organise the *bal* in advance. Monsieur Giraud sells the tickets. You will bring your fiancé!"

The pupils laughed, but nicely. I smiled back. They were much better behaved since Dressing Down Friday, when the headmaster had rebuked them.

Except one, or rather, two. Returning to my desk, I glanced at my class register. It listed the entwined couple as Moulin, Thierry, and Lanthier, Nadine.

"*Bon*," I began. "Today, we will form two teams. This side, you will be Team A. And over here, Team B. Thierry, move to the other side."

Nadine gave a horrified yelp as her boyfriend moved a whole metre away from her.

"A quiz," I announced. "One point for the right answer, another point for the correct English. First question: which is the biggest planet in the solar system? Mars, Venus or Jupiter?"

Cue much cheerful arguing before a Nicolas bellowed out the answer. I relaxed. All those hours in Séverine's library with the Internet and the *Livre Guinness des Records* were paying off.

The time passed quickly. The second the bell rang, Nadine flew out of her chair and flung herself on Thierry. I watched them leave the classroom. They'd soon be in the *Livre des Records* themselves. The world's first voluntary Siamese twins.

"My daughter, Eliane, liked to go to the *bal*, with her friends," Madame Silvain told me. Caught up in her reminiscences, she eventually noticed my expression.

"*Ah!* You have no dress to wear to the *bal*," she said. She patted my arm. "*En haut*, I have some clothes of Eliane's."

I beamed, and followed her through the back room and up the stairs to the family apartment.

Madame Silvain rifled through the wardrobe in her room as I waited nearby. "*Tenez!*" She pulled a black creation from the rail.

I took the dress and held it against me. It trailed along the carpet. Madame Silvain had neglected to mention that Eliane stood six feet ten inches tall.

"*Trop long*," noted Madame Silvain. "*Et celle-ci?*" She held up a long-sleeved creation in a hideous burgundy. I shook my head, taking care to look regretful.

"*C'est dommage*," said Madame Silvain. "But if you buy an evening dress, it will serve for other occasions."

I ambled round the upper floor of Fauret, Mauvoisins' largest department store. Even the simplest dress on the rack would cost me most of my monthly salary. Maybe Chassa had an outfit I could borrow, somewhere in her binbags. I'd ask her when I saw her.

Which was ten seconds later, when I passed the jewellery counter. Two girls were examining the goods on display.

"Holly!" said Chassa. "What d'yew think?" She pointed at a bracelet in one of the display cases.

"That'll look nice on you," I nodded.

"Not for me," said Chassa. "For Milou."

Her companion smiled at me. Chassa turned to the cashier. Two minutes later the bracelet was in a box and the box was in Milou's clutches.

"To cheer her up, see," murmured Chassa, while Milou examined handbags. "She's taking me to the record shop next."

To the cleaners, more like. But I smiled and returned their *à tout à l'heure*.

"Holly!" Patrice rasped. "A customer. Fetch the menu."

"But I am not in service this evening," I protested. "It's Chassa who works tonight."

"She is not back yet," said Patrice. "*Vite!*"

I took a menu from the pile and turned to welcome the customer. My smile froze.

"Holly!" said Angeline. "So this is your *crêperie*." She looked around, amused. "Where's Charlotte?"

"She's not back yet," I explained, handing her the menu. "She's – er, she's gone to –"

Looking round for inspiration, I spotted the transistor radio Patrice had left on the bar. "She's gone to record her radio programme."

"Charlotte is on a radio programme?" Angeline's jaw dropped.

"Yes, it's on, er, Radio Eliane," I improvised wildly. "It's for students." My pies were becoming porkier by the minute. Fortunately Patrice appeared, eyes gleaming. I introduced Angeline as an old classmate of mine from home.

"Holly," smiled Patrice. "Fetch your friend an *apéritif. Un kir-cassis, Mademoiselle?*"

Angeline accepted gracefully and sat at a window table. Hurrying to the kitchen to prepare the drink, I noticed a vase of white carnations on the dishwasher. I grabbed the vase, carried it to Angeline's table and set it down with a flourish.

"How pretty," said Angeline, examining the arrangement. "Francis always has flowers on his coffee table. Although his are fresh."

It was only then that I noticed the dust on the carnations.

"What are you playing at?" hissed Patrice to me, aside. "I found those old plastic flowers in the cellar this morning. I was going to throw them out."

I went pink, but managed not to spill Angeline's drink as I placed it on the table.

"Bring her an ashtray," ordered Patrice.

I rushed back to the kitchen. As I rummaged in the cupboard, Chassa burst in through the back door.

"Hol!" she carolled. "Look." She rolled her sleeve up and revealed a large black panther loping down her arm. A striking image, except that the majestic beast appeared to be wearing a nappy.

"They're boxer shorts," explained Chassa. "It's for the Pants, see? Sion's rugby team. I'm gonna suggest it to him for the club badge."

"You got a tattoo?" I was startled. "Didn't it hurt?"

"Neeer. It washes off," explained Chassa. "Here, you sit down. I'll do that." Chassa twitched the ashtray out of my hand and bounded into the café. I followed, but too late to warn her.

"So you're a waitress, Charlotte?" Angeline put down her drink to smirk at her former schoolmate.

"Yep," replied Chassa, apparently undisturbed.

"Well," Angeline gleamed. "I always knew you'd go far. Not quite this far, though." She looked at me, delighted to have a witness.

"You haven't lost your socialist ideals, then," remarked Chassa. "Or were they just borrowed for that one debate? When Sion was speaking?"

Angeline looked discomfited, then returned to the attack. "Mrs Seed will be thrilled to know how well her prize pupil has done."

"Oh, Mrs Seed," said Chassa. "You still going to see her? I heard she'd retired to the Mumbles. Your private lessons probably paid for her bungalow."

Angeline flushed. I got the impression the reunion wasn't going the way she had planned.

"How are your family, Charlotte?" she enquired. "They must miss you. Especially as you left home so suddenly. Such a terrible time for you all."

"Nice to know you care," replied Chassa coolly. "Is that why you were going round the school asking people to find out more about what happened?"

Angeline's face turned even redder. A melodious tone sounded. Chassa pulled her mobile phone from her jeans pocket and strolled back into the kitchen. Angeline recovered her poise.

"Eat with me, Holly," she said. "Charlotte can serve us."

I didn't want to sit down with her. But it wasn't politic to offend a customer.

Unexpectedly, Patrice came to my rescue. "I will serve you myself," he announced. "*Assieds-toi,* Holly."

No getting out of it now. But then the café door swung open and Didier walked in.

"*Lapin!*" I yelped.

Angeline's graphite eyebrows rose.

"He's Chassa's best friend," I explained, grabbing Didier's sleeve and hurrying him into the kitchen, away from Angeline.

"What is it, that is so urgent?" asked the mystified rabbit, once released from my grip.

"*Rien*," I admitted, looking around for Chassa. But she was in the back yard, talking on her mobile. "I do not want to eat with that girl."

Before Didier could react, Patrice marched in, barking: "Holly! Get the Persil. And empty the dishwasher."

"But I'm not –" I began, then decided that if one of us had to serve Angeline her meal, I'd rather it was me than Chassa.

"*Monsieur Lapin*," growled Patrice. "You come here to gossip with my waitresses?"

"*Non, je prends un thé*," replied Didier. He glanced through the window at Chassa, then turned and headed back into the café.

"He wants tea," sniggered Patrice. "*Il devient anglais.*"

"*Gallois*," I corrected him, handing him the washing powder he had asked for.

"Not Persil! *Persil!*" screeched Patrice, yanking open the fridge door and snatching up a handful of parsley. I'd forgotten that, in French, *persil* meant the leafy green herb.

I sighed and went out to the yard. Chassa had finished her call.

"Chassa," I began. "I didn't know she was coming here."

"Don' worry," said Chassa. "Would you stand in for me tonight? I've got to nip out for a bit. I'll do your stint next Monday."

I'd led Angeline here, so I couldn't say no.

"Where've I left my keys?" wondered Chassa, hurrying back into the kitchen. "Oh, Hol, a parcel came for you."

"Parcel? Where?" I was surprised.

"Not here. At the post office." Chassa picked up her keys from the soap dish. "The postman brought a ticket – I put it by'yere, look. Take it to the *Poste* and they'll hand the parcel over."

I hoped Mam hadn't posted deep-frozen whinberries again. She'd once sent some to her cousins in Tenby. The cargo had defrosted in transit until the brown paper wrapping had dripped with deep red juice. The postman had been convinced it was a package from the Mafia.

"Didier's here," I remarked.

"Tell him I'll see him later, is it?" said Chassa. "Thanks, Hol."

She was out of the door and through the back gate in no time. I sat down heavily on the kitchen chair.

Laughter rang out in the café. I turned to see Didier sitting at the table with Angeline. She was looking at him as if he was the next item on *Le Menu Trois*.

I cringed. I could see it now. Angeline would turn the charm on Didier, just to get at Chassa.

Let her try, I thought. Chassa had more up her sleeve than her Pants tattoo.

14.

Contributory Negligence on the Dancefloor

"*Vous allez faire du sport, Mademoiselle,*" remarked the postal assistant as he pushed the package over the counter.

I took the box, flinching at its weight. The sender's address read *Davies*. Of course, Trevor and Yvonne. They'd sent Chassa's three bottles of wine. Sophie and Serge's Christmas box.

I hoisted my cargo. My poor arms. I'd have a job to lift the chalk in class the next day.

Back in the café, I undid the wrapping and stared at the contents. I couldn't speak for a moment. Then I found the card enclosed.

"Hi Holly," I read aloud. "Here's the first of your three dozen. Trev will post the next two tomorrow. He's thrilled about your order, been telling everyone the French want his wine. Can't wait to read about it in Kim's paper. *Bon Courage.* Yvonne."

"Three *dozen*?" I yelped. "I only ordered three. For Sophie and Serge."

"They *will* have a merry Christmas," cackled Chassa.

"But I can't afford three dozen bottles," I wailed.

"Patrice!" shouted Chassa. "Bargain of the year. Nine bottles of Welsh wine, goes grêt with *crêpes.*"

But that stubborn café owner was having none of it. "The clients will not order what they do not know," he stated.

I re-read Yvonne's card. "*Thrilled about your order...*"

I couldn't send the wine back. Trevor had had enough to cope with. "And he'll have posted the rest by now."

"They've packed it up nice, Hol," remarked Chassa, lifting out the bottles. "Oh, look!" She pulled a length of fabric out from underneath the bottles. Unfurled, it revealed itself to be a large Welsh flag.

"There's our new tablecloth," said Chassa, draping it over Table Three.

But I couldn't smile. *Three dozen bottles.*

"So I have thirty-three bottles of wine for sale," I explained.

Vicky laughed. The other teachers looked up from their *demi-tasses* of *café noir*.

"*Du vin gallois?*" Monsieur Giraud, the dark, bearded deputy headmaster, raised his bushy eyebrows. "*Original.*"

"I will bring a bottle to school. You can try some," I promised.

But the sheer munificence of the offer was too much for the teachers. They'd turned back to their ashtrays before I'd finished my sentence. (With a preceding direct object, and all. Wasted on the lot of them.)

"I would taste it, Holly," said the soft voice of Arielle, the lab assistant.

I thanked her, but was disappointed with the lack of interest. Perhaps it would be different when they saw a bottle of Château Trevor. I'd bring some in, next time.

The room had fallen suddenly silent. I looked up and saw that Monsieur Chevalier, the headmaster, was among us.

"*Mademoiselle,*" Monsieur Chevalier greeted me. "It is going better, with the TS1?"

"It is going better, thank you," I replied. My voice sounded small and clear. I wondered why the other staff were silent. Were they all terrified of him?

"I hope we will see you at the *bal de Noël,*" replied Monsieur Chevalier. He smiled, then turned his attention to his colleagues.

He had a nice smile. I wondered if there was a Madame Chevalier. No, Madame Vallentin had said she'd dined with him and his *compagne*. His girlfriend would probably be at the *bal*, looking glamorous. I sighed.

"What's wrong?" asked Vicky.

"It's this Christmas dance," I explained. "I haven't – er, I don't know what to wear."

"Oh, a little black dress will be fine," said Vicky. "You can keep your cardigan on!"

I glinted. The French expected British women to be as chic as chips. At the *bal*, I'd show them the Welsh standard. And now I knew how.

Chassa sprayed a mouthful of tea over the table. "Brilliant, Hol," she spluttered.

"I can't make it by myself," I said. "Can you help?"

"I can't sew," said Chassa. "Sophie can, though." She grinned in anticipation. "Fair play, Hol, you have grêt ideas. Patrice liked your logo for the café. You know, that roll of paper, the one you drew the words Bad Café on."

"He wants to have Bad Café painted on the windows?" I was startled.

"Yes, he thinks it's a cool name," said Chassa. "But the tight git won't hire a proper artist." She took another swig of tea. "You have a go."

"Me, paint the windows?" I panicked.

"If you can draw letters on paper you can paint them on glass," pointed out Chassa.

Another new job. And painted windows would make it harder for my pupils to stop and stare, whenever I sat at the window table opposite a man.

The thought of window-table couples nudged me.

"Seen Didier this week?" I asked casually. "I expect he's studying."

"Doubt it," said Chassa. "He was talking about meeting some girl, the other night. Don' look like that, Hol! We're just friends, remember? He can see whoever he likes. And I hope he stubs his toe," she added generously.

I laughed, although I had a nasty feeling that Didier and his new lady friend might be dining at the Mayor's tonight. Never mind the logo on the windows, I could see the writing on the wall.

"*Non,* you cannot sell wine to our pupils, Mademoiselle," shuddered Madame Lesourd. "But you will take it home with you at Christmas, *non*?"

"I'm not going home for Christmas," I replied, lifting my chin.

"But your poor parents, they will miss you," suggested Madame Lesourd, eyes wide.

I snorted. All my poor parents would miss would be someone to grumble at for Spending On Presents instead of Saving Your Money.

145

I'd mention in my next letter that I wasn't coming home for the holidays. And I'd include the return postage in whatever gift I sent Mam, so she could send it back, complaining that it wasn't her size/colour/style. She'd done this with every Christmas present I'd given her since 1993, including the M&S gift voucher.

"Gilles, do your parents grow vines on their farm?" I asked, as we drove to the school one afternoon.

"*Non*," replied Gilles. "We have cows, calves and chickens. You would like to do *les vendanges*?" He slowed to guide the car through the school gates.

I wondered what *les vendanges* were, but didn't like to ask. "I have a problem with wine," I began. Gilles listened as I related the story.

"*Pas de problème*," he replied. "We will buy the wine for the *bal de Noël*."

"You'll buy it?" I stared at him.

"The organising committee," explained Gilles. "It is we who buy the refreshments for the evening. The Welsh wine, that will make everybody sing." He smiled. "You are strong in singing, *les Gallois*."

I'd found a buyer. I gave Gilles a huge smile. And he even knew the Welsh were good singers.

"Even if, the men, they wear skirts," added Gilles, easing the car into a parking space.

Oh, dear. Wrong country. Still, that was a load off my mind, or three separate loads, if you went by Trevor and Yvonne's postal system.

We got out of the car. Walking across the car park with Gilles, I realised I was looking forward to this Christmas dance.

"The *bal de Noël*," I began. "Is it just for the teachers and the pupils, or for other people too?"

Séverine Stern looked up from the pile of papers she was filing. I liked spending time in the library, between lessons, with her.

"Some guests come from outside the *Lycée*," explained Séverine Stern. She paused. "Mademoiselle Chassa invited a young man last year."

Another thing I hadn't heard about. The library was the place to get information all right.

"Madame Stern," I said. "Why was Chassa sacked from the *Lycée*? She won't tell me. And I – uh, I do not wish to make the same mistake."

Séverine Stern raised her eyebrows. "Mademoiselle Chassa was not sacked." She paused. "Her contract was not renewed."

"Did she hit one of the pupils?" Sometimes it paid to be direct.

"The incident did not concern the pupils," replied Séverine Stern, her tone kind but firm. She returned to her filing.

So Chassa had laid into one of the staff? I marvelled at her nerve. I hardly dared speak to some of the teachers, let alone wallop them.

I'd learn the whole story one day, I told myself. But right now I had my own narrative to think about. I'd finally written an account of my life in France for The Fibs.

I was quite pleased with my turn of phrase. Some of my comments about Anne-Laure and her gang were a bit harsh, but they were never going to see the story in print, were they? And if they did, their English was nowhere near good enough to read it. Largely thanks to me.

"*Ca va.*" Sophie stepped back to survey her handiwork.

"*Génial, Sophie,*" said Chassa. "Holly thinks so too. Look at that grin, she could fit a baguette in sideways."

I giggled. I would be able to hold my head up at the *bal de Noël* after all. Sophie might be a bit slow, but she was sharp as a tack when it came to, well, tacking.

"That dress is too short," grunted Gran Chazelet, who was sitting watching us.

Even her crabbiness couldn't sour things. "Did you like dancing, when you were young, Madame?" I asked brightly.

Gran glared at me. "What is that to you? *Petite curieuse.*"

I recoiled. Chassa intervened. "Madame Chazelet," she called. "Tell us again what you said to the postman."

Gran launched into the story of how she'd put that uniformed miscreant in his place that morning. He'd had the nerve to approach the front door, with some wild tale about delivering a letter. I sighed. Chassa could connect with people. All I got was a sharp retort.

"Holl-ee," said Sophie. "Come drink a *sirop*. I will finish the dress this evening. You shall have it for the *bal*."

"*Merci, merci.*" I beamed. If only I'd thought of bringing Sophie a gift.

Once again, Chassa saved me. "*Tiens*, Sophie," she said, scrabbling in her handbag. "I saw these at the *marché* and thought of you." She drew out a small package. Sophie exclaimed in delight.

"Our Sophie is a liquorice fiend," explained Chassa, handing over the package.

I sipped my *sirop*. At least I didn't have to live with Gran Chazalet. She'd probably started life barging down the birth canal.

"Bend your knees, Lapin," instructed Chassa, as Didier lifted the wine boxes out of the car boot.

"The hall is at the back of the school, on the third floor," I explained. "We'll need to use the rear entrance."

"I know where the hall is, Hol," said Chassa, hoisting one of Didier's boxes. I bit my lip. Of course she knew her way around the school.

As we approached the building, someone pulled the door open and held it ajar for us to enter.

"*Merci*, Arielle," I smiled at her, as Didier and Chassa carried the boxes inside. "*Le Beaujolais nouveau est arrivé.*" I'd read this quote on posters around the town. Hoping Arielle was suitably impressed, I followed Chassa and Didier up the stairs.

"You may install yourself here, Mees Holly." Monsieur Giraud, the deputy headmaster, indicated a small table. Then he noticed who I was with. He stared as if a wild goat had just skittered into his hall.

"*Ça va*, Monsieur Giraud?" called Chassa. "I deliver the wine, that is all."

Monsieur Giraud looked relieved to hear this. I held up a bottle so he could see the Dewis label.

"*C'est votre enterprise export-import,* Mademoiselle Holly?" Séverine Stern was standing just behind me. I hadn't noticed her there.

148

Chassa had. She was moving towards Séverine, her face aglow. I watched, fascinated. Séverine Stern didn't seem demonstrative. But Chassa restricted herself to a firm handshake and a twinkle of the eye.

"Mees Holly!" I turned and saw Matthieu.

"We are excused from class this afternoon. We help prepare the ball," he explained. I looked over his shoulder and noticed Benoît and another boy dragging lamps even taller than they were into the hall.

"You have found a pretext to escape from your lessons," I teased.

"But never my lessons with you," said Matthieu, gallantry itself. "Ah! The famous Welsh wine?"

"Yes, although I cannot open the bottles," I admitted. "I'll have to ask someone to open them for me tonight."

"Mees Holly." Monsieur Giraud was back. "You will please displace your boxes. We need to put the lights up here."

I turned to the boxes. All those bottles of wine, plus the glasses we'd borrowed from the café. I looked around. Chassa was talking to Séverine Stern, and Didier had ambled over to the lighting crew.

Looked like it was workout time. I bent my knees, as recommended, and lifted one of the boxes.

"Hmm, it is not bad," said Matthieu, taking a sip from the glass in his hand.

"Matthieu!" I screeched, nearly dropping the box. "Leave those bottles alone!"

"You have said you needed someone to open them," replied Matthieu, all innocence. He showed me the Swiss Army knife in his other hand. "You will take a glass?"

I shook my head, sorely tempted to smack him.

"The drinks, they are for the evening, Mees Holly," called Monsieur Giraud, giving me a reproachful glance. I didn't trust myself to answer.

"How will you get to the *bal* tonight, Holly?" asked Didier, as we were trekking back to the car.

I hadn't even thought of this. "On the bus, I suppose."

"I can take you, if you want," continued Didier.

Chassa stopped in her tracks. "You're going to the *bal*, then?"

149

"*Ben, oui*," admitted Didier, striding along without looking at either of us.

Chassa caught up with him and seized his sleeve. Didier said nothing, but concentrated on wriggling his arm free. Chassa clung to his empty sleeve and shook it. "Ah! You are going with your new love."

Didier maintained a dignified silence.

"Is she a student at the *Lycée*?" Chassa pressed him. "Lapin, you are stealing them from the cradle."

"It would be very kind of you to take me to the *lycée* tonight," I told him. "Then I will be able to keep an eye on you."

Didier tried to smack my head, but I dodged him, giggling. Tonight was going to be fun. Even if Didier was with... no, *she'd* look down her nose at the very idea of a school dance.

"Holly!" Chassa's voice rang up the café stairs. "Didier's by'yere. You ready?"

I picked up my new evening bag, a little red one I'd seen in Talensac market, and walked down the stairs.

"*Voilà!*" announced Chassa as I stepped into the kitchen.

Patrice, Serge and Didier stared at me.

"Mees Holly," Serge said. "*Tu vas faire sensation.*"

"It is your wife who has made the dress for me," I explained, smoothing my hemline down under Patrice's gaze.

"Have fun, Hol," said Chassa. "You too, Laps."

I followed Didier outside to his car. Poor Chassa, stuck in the café while we were out enjoying ourselves. I'd bring her back a souvenir of the evening. Whatever *Lycées Agricoles* normally gave people for Christmas. Three French hens, probably.

All the smartly dressed people gathered near the entrance to the hall were of the older generation. Where were all the pupils? Perhaps they'd stayed home and sent their parents, with a note of excuses.

Inside the hall, I could make out groups of people talking while beams of light played on them. Some French pop song was *yé-yé*-ing in the background.

Monsieur Giraud was collecting tickets at the entrance. "Mees Holly," he greeted me. "You know your table?"

I smiled and nodded.

"Holly," said a soft voice behind me. I turned and stared. It was Arielle. I'd hardly recognised her with her hair up.

"Wow, Arielle, you look so much...." I stopped myself from saying *older*. "So nice," I finished firmly. "This is Didier."

"*Bonsoir, Monsieur*," said Arielle, looking up at him. "It is you who have brought the wine, *non?*"

Of course, she'd seen Didier with me that afternoon. I smiled. I'd helped organise part of the evening. We were all friends and colleagues together. And it was Christmas, or pretty near.

"You may leave your coats here." Arielle indicated the clothes rails lining the side of the corridor, behind us.

"*Ah, merci.*" I slipped off my Warm Coat and hung it up.

"*Ça, alors*," gasped Arielle, at the sight of my outfit. I grinned.

"*Oh, là*," Arielle breathed. "*Monsieur Giraud, vous avez vu ça?*"

Monsieur Giraud looked at me. His jaw nearly dropped right through his bow tie. Several guests turned to look at me.

"What is this?" asked a lady guest, bemused.

"*C'est le drapeau gallois, non?*" Monsieur Giraud asked me.

Exact. I nodded proudly. I wished Mam and Dad could see me, attending a ball, resplendent in Trevor's Welsh flag tablecloth. Sophie had stitched it into a mini-dress for me.

"Holly!" Vicky appeared, glamorous in a red creation. "Is this what people wear to go dancing in Wales?"

"Only when the sheep are wearing all the wool," I replied, smartly. I hadn't forgotten that cardigan jibe. To soften my retort, I smiled at her and the man beside her, presumably Monsieur Vicky.

"This is my friend Michel," said Vicky, as her escort shook my hand.

My turn to be surprised. Vicky explained: "My husband doesn't like dances." She turned to Didier. "Is this the cute pupil you always talk about?"

"No, no," I said quickly. "No, this is Didier. He's my friend's *lapin*." Let her work that one out.

"You have a most original dress," remarked Michel, studying my dragon with great interest.

"We'd better put the wine on the table." I tugged at Didier's sleeve, which, fortunately, contained his arm this time.

"Holly," said Didier. "There is someone I am to meet. See you later." He stepped away from me.

Ah, the girlfriend. I nodded. He walked off into the crowd.

Safe behind my table, I gazed around the hall. Lots of elegant people, but not many pupils, as far as I could see.

Michel and Vicky drifted over to my table. "Wine?" I asked Michel, holding up a glass. I searched through the boxes for the corkscrew.

"Your pupils, I think?" asked Vicky, as more guests approached us.

I glanced up. It was Thierry and Nadine, the clingy couple from my class.

"*Bonsoir*," I smiled at them as my fingers located the corkscrew. "*Du vin gallois?*"

Thierry and Nadine refused politely, looking revolted.

"Leave that for a minute, Holly," said Vicky. "There's champagne on the other table. Come and have a glass with us."

I edged out from behind the table. Thierry's eyes grew wide at the sight of my hemline, but Nadine dragged him away. Tossing my hair, I followed Vicky over to the free champagne.

"Here you go," said Vicky, handing me my champagne ("one glass per person, *s'il vous plaît*," the teacher in charge reminded us).

I felt light-headed. My dress was a hit. I smiled to see Benoît and Matthieu approaching, with some of their friends.

"Holly," said Benoît, kissing me on both cheeks. "You are sensational tonight."

His friends seemed to think so, too. It was nice to bask in a bit of male attention. I smiled and joked with the boys, each gulp of bubbly drowning any doubts I had about getting too friendly with the pupils.

"*Vous fêtez Noël en Angleterre, Madame?*" asked one of the boys, gazing at me.

Vicky snorted. "Of course they have Christmas in Britain. With turkey, goose and spiced wine. I spent Christmas in London once," she went on, dreamy with reminiscence. "In a typical English family home. I remember the name of the street. Garfield Mews."

"Well, he would, wouldn't he." I giggled at my own joke. Everyone else looked blank.

"If you ask her nicely, Miss Holly will bring you back a mince pie," teased Vicky.

"I'm not going back to Wales for Christmas," I explained.

"Not going back?" exclaimed Vicky. "Won't your parents miss you?"

"They won't mind," I said, taking another sip of champagne.

"My parents would never have forgiven me if I'd stayed away at Christmas," remarked Vicky.

"*Mademoiselle, votre robe est vraiment super*," remarked one excitable pupil. He lurched towards me. I promptly stepped back, out of his reach. One tug and the flag would be flying at half-mast.

"*Attention à mon pied*," warned a voice. I turned to see whose foot I'd crushed and nearly dropped my glass.

"What are you doing here?" I asked, forgetting to be polite.

Angeline turned and smiled at her escort.

I looked at him. Of course. It was Didier.

"Didier," I hissed as soon as Angeline had begun chatting to Vicky. "You've come here with *her*?"

"It is her friends at the *Mairie*," explained Didier. "They come here every year, it appears. She has invited me…" He shrugged.

I sighed and looked around for something to lift my spirits. And there it was, talking to Benoît and Matthieu.

"Gilles." I felt light-headed, not just from the champagne.

"Can you help me with my table?" I gabbled, gesturing towards the other side of the room. Gilles looked surprised, but followed me.

Thankfully, the corkscrew and bottles were where I'd left them. I handed Gilles the corkscrew: "Could you…?"

I watched him deftly removing the corks. What was the French for "tractable"?

"*Tu es très, euh, tracteur*…." I told him. Gilles raised his eyebrows. He probably thought I was mocking his agricultural background.

"*Non*, not that," I said hastily. "I mean, uhh…" I looked around for inspiration and got another surprise.

"*Bonsoir*, Holly," smiled Milou.

"I thought you had left the *lycée*," I said.

153

"I have come to the *bal* anyway," said Milou. "You spend the evening working? You should dance. *On y va?*"

She took my arm to lead me to the dance floor. I looked at Gilles. Time to use the old Welsh charm. A bit of cŵm hither.

"Do you like dancing, Gilles?" I lilted.

"*Allez-y, vous deux,*" rejoined Gilles, busying himself with the wine bottles.

Sighing, I allowed Milou to lead me away from the table.

"*Tiens, v'là* Monsieur Chevalier," remarked Milou.

I glanced back over my shoulder. Fair play, Monsieur Chevalier was a good-looking man. Was that his *compagne*, next to him? No, it was Séverine Stern, elegant in black. Arielle, standing near them, winked at me.

I sighed. I'd ruined things again with Gilles. But at least he hadn't turned up with another girl on his arm.

"This music is not cool," remarked Milou.

"Do you continue your singing lessons?" I asked politely.

"Yes," said Milou. "But there is nothing, here. It is to Paris that you need to go."

I felt sorry for Milou. How could she go and live it up in Paris, with the burden of a child? My glance strayed to her waistline. You wouldn't have known she was expecting.

"*Madame?*" I looked up to see none other than Thierry, Nadine's boyfriend, standing before me, an inviting smile on his face.

When Gilles saw me dancing with other boys, he'd realise what he was missing. I looked up at Thierry and instinctively smoothed down my evening flag.

"*Madame,* hold this." Thierry shoved a handbag into my arms. Taken by surprise, I clutched it. Thierry turned to Nadine - the owner of the handbag, presumably - and led her to the dance floor.

A burst of laughter came from the watching pupils. Vicky sniggered. Even Benoît and Matthieu were grinning. And, even after all these years, I still recognised the delighted peals coming from Angeline's direction.

"I must serve the wine," I announced to Milou, with what dignity I had left. I moved over to the champagne table and placed the bag on it. Then I walked back to my table, my face burning.

154

Gilles had gone, although he had filled several glasses with red Dewis wine. I was just thankful he hadn't witnessed the handbag scene.

My face still hadn't cooled down when Monsieur Chevalier, the headmaster, and his entourage approached my table.

"Mademoiselle," Monsieur Chevalier greeted me. "We may try your speciality?"

I gestured to the filled glasses with all the insouciance I could muster.

Monsieur Chevalier, Madame the secretary, Séverine Stern and Arielle all helped themselves to Dewis red. I half wished these French mockers would all get stomach aches and spend the rest of the night in the toilets.

A sudden exclamation made me look up. The secretary was bent over, holding her hand to her chest. For a moment I thought she'd cut her hand on the wineglass.

Monsieur Chevalier had a peculiar expression on his face.

"I am not sure your wine has matured, Mademoiselle," he told me.

Arielle lurched forward and grabbed the table, nearly knocking the bottles over. Her hand was clamped to her mouth.

"Arielle, what – " I began.

Arielle tried to speak but couldn't. Alarmed, I turned to Séverine Stern.

"Mademoiselle Holly," said Séverine, setting her glass on the table and breathing deeply, "your wine has a taste most bizarre."

What were they on about? I snatched up a glass and took a swig myself. I soon wished I hadn't.

Monsieur Giraud lumbered up to the table, picked up a glass of wine and sniffed the contents. To make matters worse, Gilles had reappeared nearby.

"Your wine is not good, Mademoiselle Holly," Monsieur Giraud informed me, his face grave. "You cannot serve it."

"But it is good, normally," I managed to reply, weakly.

Monsieur Giraud shrugged. The secretary was already telling people nearby how I'd nearly killed her with my foul wine. Séverine, her poise regained, was standing by, silently.

155

Only Arielle was game to try again. She reached for an unopened bottle of Dewis, picked up the corkscrew and pulled out the cork. Pale, but determined, she poured herself a glassful. In spite of my shock, I applauded the scientific mind. Arielle took a sip from the glass and almost retched.

I stared, horrified. I'd sampled Trevor's wine, that day we'd visited him. How come this batch was so bad?

"*Oh, là, là.*" Arielle was wiping her eyes.

"*Mademoiselle.*" Monsieur Chevalier was firm. "Evidently there is a problem. Your wine must be poured away."

"But it is fine, normally," I repeated hopelessly.

I turned away as Gilles helped Monsieur Giraud pack the bottles back into their cartons.

Monsieur Chevalier was escorting the secretary away. Arielle, unsteady on her heels, wobbled after them.

The best thing I could do now was pack up the café glasses. Bending over the packing box, I was dimly aware of the rest of the spectators drifting away. At least the evening couldn't get any worse.

Yes, it could.

"You've certainly made an impression tonight, Holly." Angeline was standing at the table, a glossy smile playing on her lips.

I glared at her. If only Chassa was around, to put her in her place.

"I just came to tell you, you'll have to arrange another lift back to your café." Angeline was savouring her words. "Didier and I are going on to meet friends."

So I'd have to find my own way home. That was nice of her.

"Well, have a good time," I replied. "See you back here on Sports Day? I'll look forward to seeing you and Francis in the three-legged race." I brushed past her and walked away.

Passing the dancefloor, I saw Benoît with a girl I didn't know. But Matthieu was still at the champagne table.

"Matthieu," I came straight to the point. "Will you take me home?"

"Ah." Matthieu set down his glass. "The problem, is that we have all arrived together in a taxi." He scanned the crowd. "But there is surely someone who will take you home."

He couldn't have heard about the wine then. I was about to tell him when, a calm voice spoke. "Mademoiselle Holly, I will take you home if you wish."

I turned. It was Séverine Stern.

"Thank you," I said, surprised. "But it will not inconvenience you?"

Séverine dismissed this suggestion with a wave of the hand.

The music was still pounding as I trudged away from the party, with nothing but a box of soiled wineglasses to show for the evening. Séverine had lifted the other box and was carrying it to the lift.

Her car was bigger than Gilles's, the purr of its engine the only sound as we drove back to town.

"The staff know you did not intend to poison them," said Séverine, breaking the silence.

I sighed. I wasn't sure if this constituted a sacking offence, although *"Put half the staff in the infirmary"* was probably not the best professional reference.

"I thought Benoit and Matthieu were my friends," I growled to Chassa, in the café the next day. "But they were laughing their heads off about that handbag."

"Don' take it personal, Hol." Chassa said. "It's the French way. They can't laugh at themselves, but they love seeing other people come to grief."

"And that wine." I shuddered.

"Hey, I hope those bottles I bought for Sophie and Serge are all right," said Chassa. "I've cŵtched them in the cellar. If the wine's bad, at least we can use it to get rid of the mice."

"It's not funny, Chassa," I growled.

"Why the gloomy face, Holly?" asked Patrice, walking in with an armful of baguettes. "Did they not like your dress?"

"Leave her alone," ordered Chassa. "She's had a bad time."

"Then this will please her," said Patrice. "Holly, this was in the letterbox."

He held out a small brown envelope addressed to me. Knowing my luck, it would be a summons from the Mauvoisins constabulary. I opened the envelope.

"Hol?" asked Chassa as I sat motionless.

I held out the contents of the envelope. A thin, typed message. "Dad ill come home Mother."

15.

Woof, Dr Pavlov

My hand shook as I lifted the receiver.

Mam's letters, mentioning Dad's headaches. And I'd paid no attention.

Mam's voice came on the line.

"Mam?" I croaked.

"Oh, hiya," said Mam. "I thought you was selling double glazing."

Double glazing? How could she talk about that at a time like this?

"Mam," I rasped. "How is Dad?"

There was a short silence. My heart nearly stopped beating.

"Your father's sat in his armchair, with his newspaper," said Mam.

"Is he out of danger?" I blurted. "What did the doctor say?"

"What doctor?" asked Mam, sounding confused. "Who's ill?"

"Dad is." I tried to break it to her gently. "I got your telegram. I'll be home as soon as I can."

It took a good few minutes before the tangle got straightened out. Dad wasn't ill, had never been ill, except for the odd headache, which Mam attributed to small newsprint and Radio 2. Mam had sent no telegram.

As she pointed out, if she'd wanted to get hold of me, she'd have rung the café. I nodded uselessly as she crackled down the line at me.

"Who sent you that telegram?" demanded Mam.

"How should I know?" Relief made me unfairly sharp. "Can't identify the handwriting, can I?"

"Oh, well, you'd better talk to your father, while he's still here," replied Mam, handing the phone to a bemused Dad.

Hanging up the receiver, I walked back into the café and ran through the conversation for Chassa and Patrice. Chassa sat silent, twitching the telegram between her fingers.

Patrice, in contrast, squealed with delight: *"C'est l'humour française!* You do not appreciate it!"

"I should have realised it was a fake," I admitted, taking the telegram from Chassa. "Look, it's signed 'Mother'. She'd have put 'Mam'."

Patrice took the paper from me. Not much good checking it for fingerprints now.

I jumped as the café door slammed. Serge's smile vanished as he saw our faces.

" *'S'qu'y a?* " he asked.

Chassa poured out the story.

"Ma petite Holly," said Serge. He put a comforting hand on my shoulder.

"And another thing," I said. "I have received some texts *bizarres.*" The three of them stared as I repeated some of the text messages I'd received.

"Holly, you should'a said." Chassa looked grim. "Have you kept those messages? We could go to the police."

Patrice snorted. "It is not a crime, to tell someone to go home. They will laugh in your face. And, Holly, you have effaced the messages, *non*?" (I nodded, unhappily.) *"Eh bien, tant pis."*

Too bad, indeed.

"Holly, you have an idea who sends you these messages?" asked Serge.

"There's a couple of pupils who don't like me," I admitted.

"Her mobile number's on those teaching-by-phone ads we put up in town," Chassa reminded us. "In the *'Oulangerie* window, in the school. Anyone could find it." She turned to me. "Next time you see these kids, Hol, drop a hint. Mention mobiles, or texting. See what reaction you get. Once they know you're on to them, they'll stop."

"Or you send a reply, even more bizarre," suggested Serge.

"That's an idea," said Chassa. "Years ago, my Granny Chappell used to get nuisance phone calls. So she got her Bible, and put it next to the phone. Next time the jokers rang, she started reading the Bible to them. They hung up pretty quick. Never bothered her again."

It was a smart tactic, but I couldn't see myself carting the New Testament around ready for the next time the Text Maniac flashed me a message.

"You only have to change your mobile number," suggested Patrice.

"Get a new mobile, for personal calls," suggested Chassa. "Let's go shopping on Saturday. Patrice, can I have an advance...? Just joking!"

That Saturday, after lunch, I cleared tables with new energy. An afternoon of shopping and laughs with Chassa. It was ages since we'd gone out anywhere together. She always seemed to be round at Didier's, or at her everlasting First Aid classes.

Patrice was in the kitchen. "You will buy Christmas presents for your family, Holly?"

I nodded.

"Chassa, she does not go home at Christmas," continued Patrice, one wary eye on the door. "Holly, why does she not like her family?"

"I don't know," I replied truthfully. "She never speaks of it to me."

"She does not go home, she does not call home," said Patrice. "I think they have sent her away. And she is bizarre about children," he went on. "She always says she does not want children. And she spends her life at those first aid classes." He lowered his voice. "Maybe she has seen someone die."

I glared at him. Going on about deaths in the family, when some creep had sent me that telegram.

But Chassa's face, so white, when I'd told her about Madame Silvain's suicide attempt. Her leaving school suddenly. What had Angeline said? *"Such a terrible time for you all."*

"Patrice, you are ridiculous." I told him. "I myself am not going home at Christmas. That does not mean I have killed my brother with a candlestick, in the library."

"Who's got a candlestick in the library?" inquired Chassa. I jumped. I hadn't heard her walk in.

"Oh, just saying about Christmas presents," I gabbled. "I might buy Cluedo for Griff."

"Will he want the French edition?" Chassa was surprised.

"It's all the rage, these days," I improvised wildly. "Once you've played a game in English, you try the foreign version. Shall we go?"

161

Mauvoisin's main department store, Fauret, was festooned with lights. I admired the fine wares on display. The *couverts à crustacés* - fish knives - gleamed in their presentation box. I couldn't see them gracing Mam's table every day, although Dad might find them handy for when his paint tin jammed.

I sighed. We'd looked at everything from candles to jewellery, and I hadn't found anything that would elicit a grudging "Not bad" from Mam.

"This stuff's a bit fancy, Hol," said Chassa, reading my thoughts. "Want to go across the road to the *salon de thé*? We can have a sit down and an *opéra*."

An opera? I rubbed my ears. The sit down sounded good, though.

The *opéra* in question turned out to be a luscious cake with chocolate filling.

"This is great," I said. "I'd send one home to Mam and Dad if it would survive the jiffy bag."

"There's always chocs," suggested Chassa. "Have you tried *Les Pyrénéens*? Smooth on the outside, cold on the inside. They call them 'The Chocolate Shiver'."

"They'll be calling Trevor's wine 'The Instant Retch'," I sighed. I hadn't been able to bring myself to e-mail Trevor and Yvonne the story of the Christmas dance.

"I've been thinking about that, Hol." Chassa set her cup back on its saucer. "Tell me again, when did you notice the wine was bad?"

"When Monsieur Chevalier and his friends were drinking it," I said, recalling the scene. "But I thought it was all right."

"Had you drunk any yourself?" asked Chassa.

"No." I ran through the sequence of events in my mind. The three of us arriving at the *lycée*. Unloading the wine, talking to Monsieur Giraud and the boys.

"Matthieu!" I exclaimed. "Matthieu drank some in the afternoon, when we were setting up the table. He opened a bottle on the quiet and poured himself a drink." I looked at her. "And he wasn't ill. Well, he was there that night, dancing."

"So when Matthieu opened that one bottle, the wine was OK," said Chassa. "How come one bottle was all right, and not the rest? Could someone have tampered with the wine?"

162

"How could they have opened the bottles, without me seeing?" I asked.

"Not the bottles," said Chassa. "The glasses. After you poured the wine. You weren't stood there watching the glasses all the time? You were off dancing, right? Was anyone minding the table?"

"Gilles opened the bottles," I admitted reluctantly. "Then I went off to dance. By the time I came back, he'd filled the glasses and gone."

"So the wine glasses were just standing there," said Chassa.

"Anybody could have touched them," I added.

"So everyone had the opportunity," said Chassa. "Who had the motive?"

We looked at each other. Not for long.

"Angeline," I grumbled. "She was gloating over it."

"But she was with Rabbit," pointed out Chassa. "He'd have noticed if she'd touched the wine. Although she could have left him for five minutes." She took another swig of tea. "Bet she had some perfume in her handbag. A squirt of that in each glass, that would have done it."

"Thierry and Nadine," I said, at the mention of handbags. "They don't like me. Although they were dancing, too. But they could have got their mates to do it."

I looked up to see Chassa smiling at something over my shoulder. Turning, I saw a familiar face.

"*Salut*, Milou," Chassa greeted her friend. "Come and join us."

"*Ca va?*" Milou greeted Chassa with a *bise*, then turned to me. I put on a smile. Not that I disliked Milou, but she did seem to hang around a lot.

"We were just talking about the *bal de Noël*," said Chassa. "We think someone sabotaged Holly's wine, that evening."

I winced. Detective Sergeant Brake seemed to have forgotten that she was talking to one of the suspects. Knowing the delightful French sense of humour, it wasn't impossible that Milou had spiked the wine, for a "joke".

Another thought struck me.

"You're wrong, Chassa," I told her. "The wine must have been bad in the bottle, before it was poured."

"But you said it was all right, that afternoon," said Chassa.

"The bottle Matthieu opened was OK," I said. "But, when people started complaining about the taste, Arielle, the lab assistant, opened a new bottle. She drank some and nearly vomited." I sighed. "So, you see, the wine in the bottles was bad. Matthieu must have a strong stomach."

Much as I'd have liked to put the fault on Angeline or Thierry, I had to face the truth. Trevor's wine hadn't travelled well. And, sooner or later, I was going to have to tell him so.

After the *opéra* interlude, back to shopping. Milou proved a useful source of local knowledge. She took us to a clothes shop where I picked out a red jumper for Dad. For Mam, an equally radical departure, a pair of low-waisted trousers. "They hide your stomach," advised Milou, who clearly knew what she was talking about. Not that I was counting the weeks, but surely she wouldn't be able to fit into those jeans for much longer.

Mam didn't usually wear trousers outside the house, but once she saw that "Parisienne" label, you could venter she'd be parading them down Ponty High Street while shoppers tried in vain to look away.

"I've got to get back to the café now in a minute, Hol," said Chassa. "Have to mop the floor before we open. But you've got time to get something for Griff."

She had a good memory for names. "OK," I nodded. "I'll try the record shop."

Chassa and Milou walked off, and I turned and headed for Top Discs, the Mauvoisins record emporium.

So many French singers I'd never heard of, I marvelled, picking up a CD from the display rack. But which of them were any good? Would Griff like their songs? So many times I'd heard him dismiss bands as "harmless".

"It is to learn French?" The voice woke me out of my musings. I turned and nearly dropped the CD. Gilles was standing beside me.

"You learn French by the songs?" asked Gilles.

"*Ah*," I replied, intelligently. Even after the fiasco at the dance, he didn't seem embarrassed to be talking to me.

"It is by songs that I have learned my first words of English," continued Gilles, as if I'd given him a sensible answer. "When we were young, we have seen some English tourists, in Mauvoisins one summer. I spoke to them in English, but when they answered, I ran away."

I giggled.

"You should make a CD of your lessons," remarked Gilles. "Everyone has bought the cassette."

I laughed. "I do not think – Cassette? What cassette?"

"The cassette you have made with Matthieu," said Gilles. "He has sold copies to all the class, so they can pass their *examen oral anglais* at the end of the year."

Once I'd got my breath back, I told Gilles that, *non*, I had not known about Matthieu's enterprise, I had not said he could copy the tape, and I did not approve of his venture.

"Myself, I did not buy one," Gilles said.

Oh. Didn't he want to hear my voice?

"Matthieu will be in detention for three years," I announced. "And after that, I will make him tidy the stationery cupboard."

"He will be glad to escape to the army," smiled Gilles.

"He's joining the army?" I couldn't see Matthieu marching to orders.

"It is for one year only," explained Gilles. "The French boys, they do a year in the army, normally after they leave school."

Ah, national service. "And you?" I asked, noticing the slight wave in Gilles' brown hair. Be a shame if he had to have it cut short.

"*Bof*," replied Gilles. "First the exams, and then we will see."

I nodded. Except that, once he'd sat his exams, I'd have gone back to Pontycynon.

"And there is the race, this summer," added Gilles.

I hadn't sponsored him yet. I was about to explain that my Christmas shopping had left me short of cash when he remarked: "If you like, we can go running one evening. You like to run?"

"Uh, when I was at school, I ran quite often," I told him. It was true that, most mornings, I'd had to put a spurt on to reach the bus stop in time.

"One evening, we will go running around the lake," suggested Gilles. "After the *fêtes, bien sûr*."

"*Bien sûr*," I agreed. That would give me time to go back to that shop for some running clothes that would hide my lumpy bits.

165

"I look forward to Christmas in France," I told him. "I will enjoy eating the oysters and drinking the champagne, on Christmas Day."

Gilles smiled. "Then you will be eating the leftovers. In France, we eat the Christmas meal the night before."

"Oh." Yet again I looked stupid in front of him. But yet again, he had been more than kind. In spite of my dodgy wine.

Lucky Gilles had told me about the *réveillon*, the Christmas meal eaten on Christmas Eve, I reflected, as we sat at Serge's table. My tum rumbled in anticipation.

"*Du vin*, Holly?" asked Serge, pouring me a glass of *rouge*. I smiled, looking around the table at everyone. Just the Chazalets, Chassa and me. Although I was glad I wasn't sitting next to Gran. You wouldn't spill her *pinot*.

"Leave a bit of room, Hol," advised Chassa, as I polished off yet another of the little toasts spread with *pâté*. "There's another six courses to go yet."

"You like the *vin rouge*, Holly?" asked Serge.

"It is much nicer than the Welsh wine I bought," I admitted.

Serge and Chassa burst out laughing. Gran and Patrice paused in their conversation and looked up.

"Hol, this is the Welsh wine you bought," explained Chassa. "I gave those three bottles to Serge and Sophie today, so we could drink it tonight."

"But it's nice," I said weakly.

"See," said Chassa. "Told you someone had messed with the wine at the dance."

"Nasty thing to do," I grumbled.

"What is so nasty?" asked Gran. Serge launched into the story of the wine and the dance. He described it in such detail that for a moment, I thought he must have been there himself.

"*En plus*, Holly receives *des messages bizarres*," finished Serge.

Gran shrugged with such indifference, her cardigan fell off her shoulders. Warm with the spirit of Christmas, I got up, walked over to her chair and placed the woolly garment around her.

"*Merci, ma petite*," said Gran, unexpectedly mellow. I nearly fell over, but managed to weave my way back to my chair.

166

"Hear her," I murmured to Chassa. "She'll be offering me a Werther's Original next."

"She has her moments," said Chassa. "And old Patrice isn't so bad. Hol, there's something I've been meaning to talk to you about."

A strange idea struck me. Chassa and Patrice? Surely not. They were always bickering.

"Chassa!" interrupted Serge. "Go give a hand to Sophie."

"*J'arrive,*" called Chassa, jumping from her chair and running to the kitchen. Serge smacked the back of her head affectionately as she passed him. I tried to blank out the image of Dad, Mam and Griff, all sitting at this year's festive table, gazing at the plateful of uneaten mince pies.

Chassa had been right. By the time coffee was served, I could hardly move.

"All right, Hol?" asked Chassa, sitting back down next to me.

"I don't want to eat for another two weeks," I breathed.

"We'll give the presents now in a minute," said Chassa. "I've got something for you."

"What was the thing you had to tell me?" I asked. "Something romantic? About Patrice?"

"Him?" Chassa chuckled. "Heck, no. He likes them tall and cool, like Kim Wilde. Anyway, he's a grumpy beggar." She took a gulp of coffee. "I always fancied that racing driver, Gilles Villeneuve."

"Gilles who?" I asked.

Chassa chortled. "Got you, Hol. You didn't even notice when I said the name Kim, did you? But mention a Gilles, and your ears prick up."

"Woof, Dr Pavlov," I replied with great dignity. Fortunately, Serge called for everyone's attention.

"*Jeux de société,*" he announced. "Which one will it be?"

"A *jeu de société* is a board game, Hol," explained Chassa. "Did you buy Cluedo for Griff, in the end?"

"Er, no," I mumbled.

Patrice, scorning the board game suggestion, plonked himself down on the sofa, in front of the late-night film. I glanced at the screen credits, introducing "*Le Père Noël Est Une Ordure.*"

167

"It's a classic French comedy," explained Chassa. "They show it every year."

"Where's your Lapin tonight?" I asked.

"Gone to his Mam and Dad's farm, in the Sarthe," said Chassa.

I hesitated: "Doesn't it bother you, Didier going out with Angeline?"

"Oh, that's finished now," said Chassa. "After the dance, Angeline made a few cracks about you and your wine, and Didier wasn't pleased."

"He finished with her because of me?" I was amazed.

"Well, that was what started the row," said Chassa. "But they didn't have much in common. Poor dab. Her, not him."

"You feel sorry for her?" I asked.

Chassa poured herself more Château Trevor. "Well, with her, it's all about appearances. She only does things so she can tell people she's done 'em. Only buys stuff to show people she's got it." She took another swig. "And only picks friends who give her status. Think she'd bother with the Mayor if he worked in the 'Upermarché?"

Chassa was becoming more confidential by the glass. I wondered if I should bring the conversation around to home and family, but Serge interrupted again. It was present-giving time.

"Happy Christmas, Chassa." I presented the package with a flourish.

"Ooh." Chassa tore the wrapping paper. I smiled at Sophie and Gran, both watching with interest.

"Wow, Hol." Chassa took the earrings out of their box and deftly attached them to her ears, the turquoise and blue stones catching the light.

"They'll go with your eyes," I told Chassa. At last I'd been able to afford the present I'd wanted to give her. With help from Madame Silvain, that is. I was pretty sure she didn't allow all her customers to pay in instalments.

"Here's yours, Hol," said Chassa, handing me a small, square jiffy bag. I squealed as I opened it to find the Whinberries CD I'd wanted.

168

"Wherever did you get it?" I asked. "They're not well known over here."

"I got Sion on the case," said Chassa. "Useful man to know."

"Well, thank him for me," I said. "Send him a really rubbish postcard."

"The worst I can find," promised Chassa.

"So what was that thing you were going to tell me?" I asked, while the Chazalets unwrapped their gifts.

"Oh, yeah," said Chassa. "Have you seen Serge's garden?"

"Only through the back window," I said, puzzled.

"He's got a bungalow at the bottom of his garden," explained Chassa. "When Patrice has friends to stay, they sleep over in there."

"Ah." I wondered what she was getting at.

"And you know Milou's got a baby coming," continued Chassa. "Well, her mother's tamping about it. Ordered her out of the house. Milou's got nowhere to go."

"Oh." Light was dawning. "You want me to help you clean this bungalow so that Milou can live there?"

"Not exactly," said Chassa. "I said she could come and stay with me, in the café, and I asked Sophie and Serge if you could move into their bungalow. You won't mind living in the garden, will you, Hol?"

16.

Bad News Takes The TGV

I stared at Chassa. She was throwing me out of my room because some teenage loser wanted it.

"*'T'ain't your room*," pointed out the voice in my head.

True. Chassa had taken me in when I'd needed a home. Now she was doing the same for Milou. Chassa wasn't throwing me out, just arranging for me to stay somewhere else.

"The bungalow's nice, you'll see," said Chassa.

"Why can't Milou move in there?" I asked.

"Gran Chazalet don' approve," said Chassa.

At least Gran wouldn't be able to carp that I led a wild life. At this thought, my spirits sank even lower.

I forced myself to cheer up. "I have made something for you all," I announced, reaching for my handbag.

"Not those cakes again?" groaned Patrice, who always wolfed down my home-made treats.

"*Non.*" I handed sealed envelopes to everyone, even Gran.

"Holly, *c'est adorable*," exclaimed Sophie, opening her envelope and admiring the contents.

"You have made these, Holly?" asked Serge. "You have talent, you know."

"How stupid she is," sniggered Patrice.

I looked up, startled. I'd drawn my Christmas cards, a depiction of the Nativity. True, my donkey slightly resembled a wolf, but overall I didn't think I'd done that bad a job.

"We give cards at New Year," Patrice smirked. "Not Christmas."

"You could have told me, Chassa," I grumbled. "That's a couple of things you've forgotten to tell me lately."

"Oh, Hol." Chassa looked as sheepish as my Nativity ox. "Let's go and see the bungalow. Serge?"

Minutes later, I was inching down the garden path behind Chassa, while Serge's torch flashed over the ground.

"Here." Serge stopped. The torchlight played on the windows of a building. Serge creaked open the door, stepped inside and switched on the light.

I was pleasantly surprised to see a small room with clean white walls and a tiled floor. A solitary chair was in a corner, near a table piled with magazines. Next to it, a kitchen, with cupboards below the sink. This wasn't the corrugated iron shelter I'd imagined.

"Here's the bedroom." Chassa pushed open a door and switched on the light.

I looked from one camp bed to the other, the cupboard and the curtains. The room was almost as big as my bedroom at home.

"It's great," I breathed. "Can I really move in here?"

"*Bien sûr*," said Serge. "I shall install an ironing board, and bring my shirts for my au pair girl to iron."

I giggled. Of course, I'd told the police I lived at his house. Now it would be true.

The three of us moved back into the living room. Chassa headed into the kitchen and drew back a curtain to reveal a basic, but serviceable, shower unit.

"There is hot water," explained Serge, opening the shower unit door. "But if you leave it flow too long, the shower leaks."

I smiled at him. I was going to have my own castle, what did I care about the occasional moat?

"And the neighbours are quiet," joked Serge. Chassa laughed, took the torch from him, opened the front door and shone the light over the wall at the foot of Serge's garden.

"Next door's the cemetery," she explained. I took a step backwards, then shook myself.

"I can bring your letters round," offered Chassa, as we walked back up to Serge's house. "Save you paying the Post Office to send them on."

"My letters? Oh, yeah." I hadn't thought of that. "Mam and Dad will want to know."

"You want to call them now?" Serge asked. "It is what time in Wales? One hour behind France? Will they still be up?"

"Oh, hiya," came Mam's voice down the line. "I was gonna phone you this afternoon, only I didn't."

Happy Christmas, Holly. "Have you had your parcel?" I asked.

"Aye," replied Mam. "Lovely, it was. And I've warned your father not to wear that jumper outside the house. Have you had *your* parcel?"

"No," I said, trying to sound as if I hadn't noticed.

"I sent it last week," grumbled Mam. "Them French postmen want to pedal faster."

"Tell Emlyn to take the TGV," I joked.

"He don't drive a lorry," sniffed Mam. "Oh, I saw Mr Wheeler up the Tower, yesterday. He said to tell you they'll be coming over, Easter."

Of course, the townsfolk's annual trip to Mauvoisins. "You and Dad could come," I suggested. "And Lin."

"You'll have Owen and all, then," said Mam knowingly. "And his mother. Right, I better go, the kettle's boiling. Tara."

I put down the receiver with a sigh. My Christmas parcel, still *en route*. And any signs that they were missing me? *Jacques merde.*

"17 rue Jacques Cartier," I spelled out to the *Lycée* secretary.

"*C'est noté.*" The secretary smiled at me. "*Vous êtes bien installée?*"

She was friendlier than usual. Word must have got around about my poisoning half the staff. They were being nice to me before I found the way to the school canteen.

"*Oui,*" I replied. "I have fallen on my feet."

The secretary's eyes opened wide. "But you speak French well."

I smiled graciously, without explaining that we used the same expression in English, then left the office. My smile lasted until the end of the corridor, when I opened the heavy swing door and saw a familiar face.

"Mees Holly!" Matthieu was properly respectful in school.

"Matthieu," I scolded him. "You have sold those tapes of me reading lessons, to your classmates."

"*Ah, oui,*" enthused Matthieu. "They all want to hear you speaking English."

"They all want to cheat in their exam," I grumbled.

172

"It is not cheating," argued Matthieu. "They wish to practise."

"And you wish to make money," I pointed out. "Please stop selling those cassettes."

"*D'accord*," agreed Matthieu. "In any case, all the class has already bought them."

"Except Gilles LeBrun," I couldn't resist adding.

"Gilles LeBrun, he did not buy one," agreed Matthieu. "But we all understand why not. He spends a lot of time with you. We have all noticed that he brings you to the *lycée* in his car."

"So now they all think I'm seeing Gilles," I remarked to Chassa that evening as we packed my stuff.

"Oh, there's always gossip, in schools," said Chassa. "What's this roll of paper, Hol?"

Pink-faced, I took the scroll from her. I'd been too embarrassed to stick my poster of Neil Morgan, the Whinberries' guitarist, on the wall of Chassa's room. But if I was going to be on my own down the bottom of the garden, it would be quite nice to have Neil to look at, of an evening.

"How's First Aid going?" I lifted a cardboard box and squeezed through the door. "Got your certificate yet?"

"Practical's next week," said Chassa, edging down the stairs after me. "Last week we did a practice run, a sort of dress-the-wounds rehearsal. I bandaged this bloke, put him in the recovery position, called the ambulance, and sat back. The trouble was, I'd left him on the floor with his head under the radiator. If he'd sat up a bit sharpish..."

I giggled and nearly dropped the box.

"So I better get it right on the day," said Chassa, as we reached the foot of the stairs. "Or I'll have the firemen after me."

"The firemen?" I asked.

"The fire station's where we do First Aid," explained Chassa. "In Britain, it's the St John's Ambulance people that train you, but here, it's the firemen."

"Ah," I nodded. Another thing the school books didn't tell you.

"If something goes wrong during your test, will the firemen let you resit?" I asked.

"They'll probably throw me out of the building," said Chassa. "And then run outdoors with the net before I hit the ground. Got the door? Right, here we go."

The café door jangled as we stepped into the street.

New year, new lodgings, new start, I reflected, trudging along the *rue* to Serge's house. Once I'd moved in, I wouldn't be able to speak English to anyone else on the premises of 17 rue Jacques Cartier.

Chassa rummaged for the matches and lit the gas stove Serge had rigged up for me in the little kitchen.

"Got the teabags?" she asked, taking a saucepan from under the sink. "And those biscuits?"

"In the pillow case," I directed her.

"You could invite your Kim over," suggested Chassa, scrabbling in one of the boxes for the teabags. "Won't mind sharing a bedroom, will he?"

"I might well hear from him soon," I replied. "A couple of weeks ago, I posted The Fibs that story I wrote about working in France."

"Grêt!" exclaimed Chassa. "Hey, when they print it, you should send them a follow-up. Get a regular column."

"Well," I said. "There's loads of stuff I didn't have room to put in - how letter boxes here have two slots, your region and the Rest of the World - and why bus drivers tell you to *compost* your ticket -"

"When they send you the paper, with your story in it, get it scanned and e-mail it to your university," suggested Chassa. "

"I'll ask my new friend the school secretary," I joked.

"Newspaper columnist, that would look good on your CV," noted Chassa.

"Yeah," I laughed. "And then it'll become a best-selling book, and I'll be on the talk shows. People will go through my bins, and sell my rubbish on eBay."

"Wouldn't want to buy celebrity rubbish," remarked Chassa. "All those worn-out mirrors." She began doing an impression of a vulpine actress advertising her empty lipstick containers to a camera. I had to sit down for giggling.

"They should do a telly show like that," I remarked, as Chassa poured the hot water into the tea mugs.

Chassa looked at me. Her eyes lit up. I panicked.

"Hol," said Chassa, handing me my mug of tea. "Me and Lapin were watching Canal 36 the other day. It's a local cable channel. Only broadcasts to about three streets. Lapin's friend from college went on there one night to talk about *film noir*."

"So now you're going to go on telly and advertise your rubbish?" I was intrigued.

Chassa said no more, but drank her tea with a gleam in her eye. I decided not to inquire further. After all, it wasn't as if I'd be getting involved in her latest scheme.

I glanced up at the priest. To think that people actually bought this stuff. Unbelievable.

The priest gazed over my head, apparently waiting for a sign. I fidgeted.

"*Bonjour*," began the priest. "Today my special guest is Aurélie Tourette, who will be showing us the rubbish she has thrown out this week. Welcome, Aurélie."

"*Merci, mon père*," replied Chassa, with such a vacant smile that Serge, standing behind me, choked back a laugh. I frowned. Now Didier would bark "*Coupez*" again and we'd have to do another take.

But, no, it seemed this was going to go OK. Chassa, as Aurélie, showed the viewers a musical bread-knife, a Burberry shower curtain, and an aromatherapy kit. From where I squatted, out of shot, I handed each item to Chassa, whereupon she minced through a speech about how heartrending it had been to bin the thing. By the time she got to her faux-ostrich handbag, a gift from the talented, younger co-star of her latest movie, Serge and Patrice were chuckling openly.

"*Bon, ça va*," said Didier, forgetting his professional role, and instead waving his hand to indicate that filming was over.

"*À vous le festival de Cannes*," said Serge, handing glasses of *sirop* to the cast and crew. "Chassa, you have talent."

"It's my leading man who shines," said Chassa, nodding at the priest. "Patrick, this will be your breakthrough role."

Patrick – for it was he – twitched his moustache pleasantly and fidgeted with his dog collar. Chassa had charmed him into performing in Didier's film.

"But why is he disguised as a priest?" asked Sophie, who had joined us in the backyard of the café, today billed as "the set".

"It is because of the title of the film, *Maman*," explained Patrice. "They have chosen a stupid title."

"You laughed when you heard it," said Chassa. "And so will Didier's teachers. And we're going to offer it Canal 36. They'll love *Le Père Noël Et Ses Ordures*. Won't they, Hol?"

Everyone turned to look at me.

"Father Noel and His Rubbish," I said. "Won't the Catholics object to us making fun of priests?"

"We are making fun of the guest and the rubbish, not the church," pointed out Patrick.

The back gate suddenly banged shut. We all turned to look, but no one came into the yard.

"It is the breeze," remarked Patrice. He frowned at his father. "For weeks, you have told me you will repair that gate. Anyone could walk in."

"You are expecting someone, Holly?" asked Serge.

I flushed. *"Non, non,"* I replied unconvincingly. I hadn't told anyone that Gilles was taking me running that afternoon. I'd arranged to meet him by the lake at 4pm. Although I'd rather hoped he might come and pick me up here.

I shook myself. Gilles wouldn't come to meet me at the café, in front of everyone. For one thing, he wouldn't want everyone gossiping about him and his teacher. And for another, he probably thought I could do with the walk.

"It does you good to run, in the evenings," said Gilles, slowing to a walk after completing his circuit of the lake.

I bent down to hide my burning face. That last lap had nearly killed me.

"Out of breath?" asked Gilles. And they said the British were the masters of understatement.

"A little," I panted, straightening up.

"It will come, with practice," Gilles assured me. "To keep fit, you could get a bike and ride it to school."

But then I wouldn't be able to get a lift with you, I thought.

Aloud I said: "You want to get fit before you will join the army?"

"No, I prefer to do the *co-opération*," explained Gilles. "If they accept me. It is two years, but you can do something interesting, abroad. One of my friends has worked on an irrigation project in Togo. That would suit me."

Africa. He wanted to go to Africa. Great.

"You will find lots of trees there," I said. "For jumping in."

Gilles looked astonished. I went even redder. I hadn't meant to imply he was one step up from a monkey.

"*Le Parkours*," I explained weakly.

Fortunately, Gilles laughed. And then offered me a lift home. He was incredibly kind to someone who managed to insult him every time she met him.

We drew up in front of Serge's garage. "My new home," I said proudly. "Well, I live at the bottom of the garden. Would you like to come in for a coffee?"

Then I noticed Sophie and Gran standing on the Chazalet doorstep. Sophie waved to me. She gazed at Gilles with great interest.

"*Je préfère pas*," said Gilles, looking uncomfortable.

Oh, well. I told Gilles I'd see him in class the following week, then got out of the car.

Sophie was still watching as Gilles drove away, although, thankfully, Gran had upped stick and gone back inside the house.

"Who is that nice boy?" asked Sophie at once.

"My pupil," I explained. "We go running together."

"You should introduce him to Chassa," said Sophie. "It will do Chassa good, to meet a nice young man."

I looked at her, slightly surprised.

"You are going to the *soirée* tonight?" asked Sophie. "At the actor's home. Chassa has said they are going to *tirer le roi*, for the New Year."

So Patrick was having a New Year party, and Chassa was invited.

"*Tirer le roi*, that means they will each cut a slice of the *tarte*." Sophie was delighted to explain something. "And the person who finds the token inside his slice, he is the king for the evening."

"So Chassa will wear the crown." I'd seen these New Year *tartes*, encircled by gold cardboard crowns, in the *Oulangerie* window.

"Or her Rabbit," nodded Sophie. "Or the young girl, she who expects the baby."

So Didier and Milou were going to this party too.

"You do not go with them?" said Sophie, finally deciphering my expression. "This evening, Serge and I, we will visit friends. If you want, you come with us."

"*Non, merci*," I said promptly. I wasn't going to be the sad case, only invited to places out of pity.

I took my leave of Sophie, opened the garage door, walked past Serge's car and down the garden path to my new lodgings. Looked like I'd be spending the evening here alone, while the others were having fun.

My mobile beeped in my handbag. A text message. Perhaps they were asking me to the party after all.

I fished out the mobile. My heart sank. The Fickle Finger of Hate was at it again.

I erased the message, feeling slightly sick. This was one aspect of my stay in France that I wouldn't be mentioning in my next story for the Fibs.

The Fibs. I stopped in my tracks.

I fumbled in my handbag again, this time for my address book. If Chassa and the others didn't want me around, I'd forge a path for myself. They could leave me out, but they wouldn't leave me behind.

"*Y Llais*," sang the voice down the phone.

"Hello," I said. "Could I speak to Kim Meredith, please?"

"He's no'yere," said the voice.

"Could I leave a message?" I said. "Holly Gethin called -"

"He don' work 'yere no more," explained Voice. "He left about a month ago. He've gone to London."

Get this sorted, Holly. You can collapse later.

"I'm calling from France," I said. "I sent you a story about Mauvoisins, Pontycynon's twin town. I wrote about my job there, teaching in a school. I haven't heard back from you, if you liked the story, if you wanted to print it, I mean –".

"Oh, right," said Voice. "No, we won't be using that. Not our sort of thing."

"Right," I managed.

There wasn't much to say. I mumbled goodbye, put down the receiver and retrieved my phone card. I stood for a moment, staring at the card. Then I rammed it back into its slot, snatched up the receiver and punched another number in.

"Yes, I heard," came Lin's voice. "Mrs Whipple met his Mam at Save The Rhino. He's working on a motoring magazine in London. Anyway, it's time you moved on from him. All this time you've been in France, he hasn't even e-mailed you."

"He might have lost my address," I said weakly.

"Stop making excuses," scolded Lin. "Find someone else."

"You've never told Owen to do that," I snapped.

"Holly," said Lin. "Owen and I have been going out for two months."

"I thought you didn't want him," I said, bewildered.

"People change," said the new mature Lin.

I gritted my teeth. "Well, there's lovely. You'll be able to double-date with Mansel and Shireen. Right, can you look up a phone number for me?"

"It's not Kim's magazine, is it, Hol?" asked Lin. "You're not going to ring him up at his new job?"

"No, I'm not," I snapped. Dammit, she gave me less credit than the phone card. "Get a pen and I'll explain."

Back in my new living room, I sat alone. I'd thought I'd settled in here. I'd thought these people liked me, but I wasn't part of their circle. And now my friends back home had moved on. I'd tried to live in two worlds and ended up in limbo between them.

As for Kim, I'd always known he'd never want me. He was much too popular and ambitious to look at a pudgy Valleys girl. Taking me to the vineyard, making plans for my time in France. And all he'd cared about was his next byline. I cursed the time I'd wasted on thoughts of him.

"Lin," I typed. "Sorry if I was short on the phone yesterday. I was a bit shellshocked about Kim. And then hearing about you and Owen was a surprise. But I hope it's going well, and that you like working with your mother-in-law.

179

"Mam says the twinning committee are planning their Easter trip to Mauvoisins. Do you and Owen fancy coming over? Mam and Dad might.

"The Fibs didn't want my story, so I phoned the *Western Mail* after you looked up their editorial desk number for me. They asked me to e-mail them my article!"

I pressed the *Send* button. Of course I wanted Lin to be happy, although I couldn't understand how she was suddenly so keen on Owen. Could people change that much in just a few months? What if, next week, I started nuzzling Patrice's pinny? A thought to chill the bones.

As for Patrick, he hardly knew me. No reason why he should have invited me to his party. And Chassa had kept quiet about it so as not to hurt my feelings.

"Your *amoureux* has left you?" Madame Silvain sympathised.

"He was not my *amoureux*," I admitted, setting down my cup of coffee. "But I was hoping that his newspaper would print my story."

"Your story." Madame Silvain was intrigued. "You have written about your bad French pupils?"

"*Pas vous*," I reassured her. "About the girls who are learning to be secretaries. They complain that the lessons are difficult, but they do not want to work."

"They have not your determination," smiled Madame Silvain.

I lifted my chin. She didn't know the half of it.

"I sent my story to another newspaper, a national newspaper." I couldn't suppress a grin. "And then I rang to ask if they liked it. They did, and they are going to print it."

"*Mais c'est merveilleux*," Madame Silvain's eyes shone. "You deserve it."

I tried to look modest, but failed miserably.

"And your parents, when they visit at Easter, they will be welcome to stay in our home," added Madame Silvain.

I caught my breath. "Oh, *merci!*" This was the perfect solution. Mam and Dad wouldn't have enjoyed sleeping on camp beds in a garden bungalow, even with Neil Morgan looking on benignly from the bedroom wall.

"It is nothing," smiled Madame Silvain. "After all you have done for me and my family."

I thought she was exaggerating, but it was nice that she appreciated her English lessons.

I finished my coffee and took my leave of Madame Silvain. Imagine, Wales' leading newspaper was going to print my story. I'd send Mrs Whipple a copy. Then she could show it to Kim's Mam at Ban The Whale, or whatever cause they were into these days. This thought cheered me on my way to the *Ecole Vallentin*.

"You look happy, *mademoiselle*," remarked Lydie Lesourd, as she opened the door to let me in.

I rummaged in my bag, where, amazingly, I happened to have a copy of my story. I'd printed it out at Mauvoisins library. "For you, *Madame*." I knew Lydie was keen to improve her English. She often asked me questions that arose from her study of the *Méthode Vallentin*.

Lydie clasped the story as if it were her New Year present. If only the pupils were so delighted with my texts, I thought. Right, time to make the future secretaries take notes.

The lesson wasn't too bad. Either I was getting used to the Méthode, or the girls had decided that English had its uses after all. Some of them even wished me *au revoir* as they left the classroom.

I smiled. Life was good, on the whole. OK, things would be different now that my best friend had suddenly become half of a couple, but she was happy. As for me, I had other projects.

I smiled again as I saw Lydie in the corridor, my printed pages in her hand. But Lydie looked as if she were about to cry.

"*Mademoiselle*," she said. The pages trembled in her hands. "Madame Vallentin wants you to leave. She has asked me to show you out of the building. And, *mademoiselle* – " she took a deep breath - "she says you are no longer employed at this school."

17.

When One Door Closes, Paint The Windows

This brick landed square on my forehead.

"Madame Vallentin does not like your article, in the newspaper," whispered Lydie. "You write about the Méthode Vallentin. She does not wish people outside the school to know the Méthode."

I moved towards the office door. I'd talk to Madame V myself.

"*Non, Mademoiselle*," hissed Lydie. "You must leave now. And you must give me your copy of the Méthode, before you go."

In a daze, I allowed her to escort me down the stairs. I'd come back the next day and sort this out with Madame V.

"Hiya, Hol," said Chassa, wiping glasses behind the bar. "Let the kids out early?"

Serge appeared from the kitchen. He seemed to spend more time at the cafe than he did at home or work. He greeted me, then noticed my expression.

"Another nasty text?" he asked. "These pupils, they are *idiots*."

Chassa saw the look on my face, dropped her cloth and hurried over to me. She and Serge listened, wide-eyed, as I explained what had happened.

"But you have written nothing defamatory about the school?" asked Serge, as Chassa took the story from me and skimmed through it.

"Nothing," I insisted. "I have only explained how the girls learn by repeating dialogues from the Méthode."

"Telephone the newspaper," advised Serge. "Tell them that the school does not wish its name to appear in the story."

As I considered this, Patrice appeared from the kitchen, followed by Milou. Of course, Milou lived here now. She'd be in on everything we did.

"Holly has had a shock." Chassa ran through my story in swift French. Milou responded with her all-purpose "*Merde*".

"So now you will be free to paint my windows, Holly," said Patrice.

"Patrice!" exclaimed Chassa. "Holly is upset. Your windows, they can wait."

"You can paint, Holly?" asked Milou. "You are very gifted."

She wasn't a bad kid. I nodded at Milou's jewellery: "Pretty bracelets."

"They are from your friend," said Milou.

I froze. The screen in my mind filled with a close-up of Gilles fastening the bracelets around Milou's wrists. I'd never even asked who the baby's father was.

"Your friend who owns the jewellery shop," added Milou.

I smiled, relieved. Of course, Milou had met Madame Silvain at the *crêperie*'s opening night.

"At least I still have my job teaching Madame Silvain," I remarked.

"The mother of Eric Silvain?" asked Patrice.

"Yes, her son is called Eric," I said. "He is in Australia. You know him?"

"Oh, we all knew Eric Silvain." Patrice smirked. "I thought he was in San Francisco, with all the other *folles*."

Milou giggled. Patrice smirked at me. I rolled my eyes. Did he think I'd never heard of gay people? Us Valleys girls grew up in the real world of iron and steel. We weren't innocent lambs. (Mind, in some parts of the Valleys, neither were the lambs.)

"Teach his mother to say '*My son-in-law*'," sniggered Patrice.

Serge intervened. "I have found some white paint for the windows, Holly," he announced. "You could paint the name *Bad Café* on the front door glass pane. You will need a ladder."

"I'll get the stepladder," said Chassa. "It's down below." She hurried behind the bar. I heard the creak of the cellar hatch. I was glad of a task to distract me from my troubles. At least some people wanted my services.

I climbed on to the bottom rung of the stepladder. It wobbled slightly. With one hand on the café window and the other on my paint can, I ventured higher.

"This is OK. I can reach the top of the windows," I called down to Serge.

"I will find the white spirit," replied Serge. He went back inside the café. I clambered back down the ladder.

"*C'est de la peinture, Madame?*" The voice came from behind me. I turned to see a small boy looking at me through round spectacles.

I smiled. He was obviously intrigued by the sight of an artist at work.

"The pot is not big," I told my young spectator. "But the paint should suffice for my task."

Whether or not the pot contained enough paint to suffice for my task was destined to remain a mystery. The little boy grabbed the pot, flung the contents over me and ran off down the street. I stood, dripping with paint, numb with disbelief.

Serge arrived, stopped in the doorway and stared at me.

"Holly!" Patrice was behind him. "I have told you to paint the windows, not yourself!"

Milou appeared next to them, giggling. Chassa hurried out of the café, saw me, and started laughing.

Some friends they were. I pushed past them into the café. Too bad if I left a trail of white footprints across the café floor. I seized my handbag, marched through the kitchen, into the back yard and through the back gate.

The French, I seethed, stomping back to my garden bungalow. Couldn't see a joke unless it was on someone else. Usually me.

I might as well pack up and go home. Chassa might have taken to France like a duck to *l'orange*, but I never would. And France didn't seem to have taken to me, either. Hysterical employers, rude pupils, friends who laughed at my problems, wayward little brats. And horrible texts from someone who clearly loathed me.

A few hours later, my mood had lightened. Amazing what a shower, a change of clothing and a tin of Quality Street could do.

184

This last being a gift, brought to me by Chassa. She'd persuaded Milou to wait at table that evening so she could come and see me.

"Sorry I laughed, Hol," said Chassa. "It just looked funny at the time."

"That little boy looked so tidy," I sighed, helping myself to another green triangle. Kids today. Going around acting respectfully, and addressing people politely. What were things coming to?

"Wasn't your day today, was it?" asked Chassa, plonking her mug of tea on the floor. "But tomorrow will be better. You'll sort things out with that Vallentin woman. And don' let that little rodney put you off doing the windows."

A sudden crash resounded. Something had smashed against the front door. Chassa was on her feet and out through the door before I could put my mug down.

I heard a scuffle outside. Then a shout from Chassa. What had she found in the garden, free-runner beans?

I opened the door. As my eyes adjusted to the dark, I made out the figure of Chassa at the bottom of the garden. She was climbing over the wall that separated Serge's garden from the cemetery.

I slammed the bungalow door behind me and ran after her. Whatever Chassa had tracked down, I wasn't going to leave her to wrestle with it alone in a graveyard at night.

I clambered over the wall. In the distance, Chassa was grappling with something that shrieked. I ran towards her, tripped over a stone and fell to the ground, pain stabbing my knee. I got up and staggered to where Chassa was holding on to something wriggly and squeaking. Did they have raccoons in France?

"Gottim, Hol," growled Chassa. She switched to French. "*Hé.* What were you doing in the garden?"

"I did not want to hurt the lady," wailed the raccoon. "It was they who have told me to do it."

The raccoon's face was small and round. His spectacles had been pushed askew.

"Chassa!" I said. "This is the little boy who threw the paint!"

The raccoon burst into tears. Chassa let go of him.

"*Calme-toi,*" she said. "But what were you doing in the garden?"

"I have brought you some flowers, Madame," sobbed our prowler. "*Pour m'excuser.*"

Five minutes later the three of us were sitting in my bungalow, drinking hot tea. The raccoon was sitting in my chair, blowing his nose into my kitchen tissue, while Chassa and I looked at each other, bemused.

"Why did you throw the paint at me?" I asked. "To amuse yourself?"

Roch – that was his name – shook his head.

"It is the others who have told me to throw the paint over you," he blurted. "They gave me some money."

"Someone paid you to do that to Holly?" said Chassa. "Who?"

"*Le couple*," wailed Roch. "In the car. They have told me an English lady is on the ladder outside the café, they have given me 20 euros to throw the paint over you. They have said they will watch from far off."

This was the first time I'd seen Chassa speechless. I patted Roch's shoulder awkwardly. He didn't seem like a bad boy. And it was true he'd brought me flowers. The crash we'd heard had been him tripping up and meeting my front door head-on while trying to deposit the bouquet.

"*Prends un chocolat*," I urged him, offering him the tin of Quality Street.

"And tell us about this couple," urged Chassa.

Through his caramel, Roch told us the man in the car had been dark-haired. ("Narrows it down a bit," said Chassa.) The lady had been chestnut-haired. She was "quite old – about your age, Madame". The car seemed to have made much more of an impression. Roch described it as a dark green Peugeot, number plate showing that it came from this *département*.

"This is incredible." I shook my head.

"I know," said Chassa. "The nerve of 'em. Calling you English."

"It's not funny," I growled. "Someone hates me so much, they paid a little boy to attack me in public."

"They probably meant it as a joke," soothed Chassa. "They probably didn't even know you. Maybe they were students, messing around."

"Or pupils." I hadn't forgotten Thierry and Nadine's behaviour at the dance.

"Roch, how did you know that Holly lived here?" Chassa asked.

"I have gone to the café this evening," explained Roch. "The lady in the café, she has told me where to find you."

"Does your mother know where you are?" asked Chassa. "It's getting late."

"You'd better go home, your mother will worry," I said. "Chassa will accompany you home."

And then I got my third surprise of the day.

"No," said Chassa. "I can't walk home with him, not this time of night. Suppose there was an accident, when we crossed the road? We'll get Serge to drive him home."

Soon we were standing on the pavement outside Serge's house, waving goodbye as Serge drove Roch away. I looked sideways at Chassa. She'd chase a prowler through a graveyard at night, but she wouldn't escort a little boy across a road.

"There's some drama you've had today, Hol," said Chassa, as we parted. "Still, better than staying in by yourself with no-one but Neil Morgan to talk to."

"S'pose so." I yawned. Suddenly the thought of bed was very appealing. Neil would be lucky if he got a quick goodnight, instead of the usual review of my day.

But when I was in bed, sleep refused to come. I couldn't help listening for mysterious prowlers scuffling outside my front door. Worse still was knowing that someone had paid a passer-by to attack me.

Chassa was probably right, I told myself. They'd just been passing, and had thought it would be fun. Although I wished they'd stuck to the traditional pastime of slowing the car down and hurling insults at me. A drive-by shouting.

The thought of Chassa brought something else to mind. I sat up in bed and peered at my wall, in the dark. How had Chassa known...?

I yawned. I'd ask her about it in the morning.

Pressing the buzzer, I heard its sound echoing inside the entrance hall.

She always opened the school by 8.30am. I pressed again, for longer.

Then I realised what was happening. Madame Vallentin had seen me from her window. She was refusing to open the door to me.

I walked away. Once I'd turned the corner, I rummaged in my bag. Once inside the *cabine*, I jammed the phone card into the slot, dialled the number and waited.

"*Ecole Privée de Secrétariat*," crisped the voice.

"Madame Vallentin?" I began. "*Ici* Mademoiselle Gethin. *Je vous appelle –*"

Click. The line went dead.

I tried again, but the phone told me in no uncertain tones that it was busy.

So that was her game. Well, I could play too.

"Do I begin '*Chère Madame*' or just '*Madame*'?" I was keen to get my business letter right.

Sophie stopped dusting and came over to the table. "I think the both are acceptable," she said.

I'd come up to the house to borrow the Chazalet family's Larousse dictionary. Now I was sitting at their kitchen table, writing to Madame Vallentin. In my letter I assured Madame that I would make the newspaper remove the name of the school from my story before the relevant edition went to press.

"*Voilà*." I set down my pen. "And while I wait for her reply, I'll finish the café windows."

"Your parents will admire them," said Sophie.

Of course, the Pontycynon gang would be over here in a few weeks' time. I'd have to arrange some outings. Mauvoisins wasn't that far from the coast. And I'd have to get in a few sacks of potatoes. (Dad would insist on his staple diet of roast, boiled and mashed).

"If I lose my job, at least I'll have more time to spend with my parents," I remarked.

"One lost, ten found," Sophie nodded sagely.

I studied Sophie for a moment. She'd left Poland, come to a foreign country. Shop assistants sniggering while she stared at her change. Gran Chazalet at her elbow, finding fault with how she made beds and cooked dinners. Raising a son who sneered at every mistake.

188

"*Uh*, Sophie," I asked. "What does it mean, one lost, ten found?"

Sophie smiled. "*Un de perdu, dix de retrouvé.* It means, you have lost one thing, but you have found something better."

"In my case, I lose one kilo and I gain ten," I joked.

"*Mais non*," said Sophie. She pushed her hands closer together to indicate shrinkage. "*Mademoiselle Toute-Mince.*"

I felt about as *mince* as a Christmas pie. Although my trousers weren't pressing me quite as tightly as usual. But my bum still felt like a sack of potatoes. Dad would be scrubbing it and putting it on to boil the minute he plonked his suitcases down.

Outside the *Poste* I found the yellow postbox on the wall. Next to it, the row of *cabines*. Shoving my letter into the 'local' slot, I dashed into a cabine.

"Oh, hiya," said Mam. "I've only just sat down. Nice film on s'afternoon," she added pointedly.

"Mam," I said. "I've got it all sorted out. This lady I teach has got a spare room for you and Dad. And I'll do all the cooking."

"What are you on about?" demanded Mam.

"When you come out here," I said. "With the Twin Town trip."

"Don't be so soft," said Mam. "We're not coming over there."

"But you said – " I began.

"You know your father won't want to be bothered going all that way for a couple of days," said Mam. "And he'd miss the Six Nations."

"France is one of the – " I argued, but Mam swept on. "And we can't be travelling abroad at our age."

"Mrs Hathaway's going," I argued. "And Mr Wheeler."

Mam sniffed. "Do you think we want to go away with them? They're years older than us." She changed tack. "And you'll be home in a couple of months, anyway. And don't go pestering people about spare rooms."

"But you said you wanted to visit," I barked.

"Don't you raise your voice to me!" bellowed Mam. "I don't know who you take after."

There wasn't much else to say. I hung up the receiver.

"All the trouble I went to," I snarled, thinking of the outings I hadn't planned, the bungalow left dusty and the potatoes unpeeled.

"Your other friends'll be coming over though, won't they?" asked Chassa, turning to the kitchen sink to rinse her rubber gloves.

"No good inviting Lin to stay with me," I was thinking aloud. "She'll want to be with Owen." Then the solution hit me.

"Griff," I nodded. "I'll ask Griff over."

"Oh, you don't want to ask him, Hol." Chassa swung round to face me. "He won't want to go on the coach with the pensioners. And you said he don' speak French."

"He did a bit in school," I said. "He'd come here if I asked him."

"That's my point, Hol." Chassa twisted the gloves between her fingers. "He might feel he had to come over, just to please you. Wouldn't he rather be with his mates?"

She was right. I was being selfish.

"He's never mentioned coming over in his letters," I reflected. "And he can't bear to impose on people. If there's one sausage left at the barbecue, he'll pretend he's just gone vegetarian."

"Aye, you're right," agreed Chassa, scrunching up the rubber gloves. "I mean, you'd know him."

She seemed troubled. Perhaps this talk about home was getting to her.

"Chassa," I ventured. "When Sion writes for your Granny, don't they want to see you?"

Chassa gave a long sigh. I was taken aback. Chassa didn't do wistful. It was like seeing a tiger up a tree, mewing plaintively at you to fetch a ladder.

"Sion came over, once, when I lived in Brittany," Chassa said. "But Granny Chappell wasn't up to the journey." She was about to speak again when Milou burst into the kitchen.

"Chassa, this has come for you this morning," she shrilled, waving an envelope. "*Salut*, Holly."

Chassa dumped the rubber gloves and tore open the envelope.

"Holly!" she yelped. "We're gonna be rich and famous!"

Milou and I stared.

"It's from Canal 36," explained Chassa, waving the letter. "They want me and Lapin to come and talk to them about *Le Père Noël*!"

190

Chassa and Patrick would be on telly. Didier would be hired as a director. Patrick would get his big break. Chassa would be offered other acting jobs. I broke into a huge smile. Milou was grinning from earring to earring.

I gazed at Chassa. My friend, the actress. And she finally seemed to trust me enough to talk about her family. One day I'd learn why she hadn't been home in all those years.

"Ready, Hol?" Chassa lobbed a packet at me. I lunged for it and nearly lost my balance.

"Look out," said Chassa. "It's a long way down there."

I clutched the railings and stood up carefully. You never saw gardening programmes like this. The expert crouching on a city balcony, telling people how to plant their seedlings, while his colleagues, the cameraman, and most of the viewers were waiting for him to fall off.

"You've had enough accidents on that pavement already," joked Chassa. "We don't want them painting an outline around you next."

"Don't keep on about that," I grumbled.

"Sorry, Hol," said Chassa. "I'll keep a lid on it. 'Course, that's what you should have done..."

She ducked just in time. My clod of earth whizzed past her head, over the balcony railings. If there was any justice, a dark-haired, Peugeot-driving Frenchman with a fondness for practical jokes would be passing below at that very moment. But life didn't seem to work like that.

The postman handed me a large envelope. I recognised Mam's handwriting. It was nice to hear from home, especially after our telephone spat. But what I'd really been waiting for was a reply from Madame Vallentin. I'd been to the school a couple of times, rung the bell but got no answer.

I thanked the postman and clutched the envelope. Wait till Chassa saw this.

I rushed over to the café and flung open the door. "Here it is, Chassa," I announced, as she emerged from the kitchen. Grinning, I reached into the envelope and drew out a copy of the *Western Mail*.

Leafing through the newspaper, I stopped and held it up with pride. "Look, I got nearly half a page."

"Wow, Hol," said Chassa, taking the newspaper from me to get a better look.

I grinned. "Do you think I should post a photocopy to Madame Vallentin?"

No answer. I glanced up. Chassa had gone pale. She dropped the *Western Mail* and ran to the kitchen. I started to follow her, but paused to pick up the newspaper. Then I heard the back door slam.

"Chassa?" I called.

A crash. And a shriek.

I rushed out to the back yard, the *Western Mail* still in my hand. Chassa was nowhere to be seen. Instead, in the yard, was a pram turned on its side.

And something smelled horrible.

I took the pram by its handle and righted it. And then recoiled at the smell.

Inside the pram was a slab of rotting meat.

18.

What's Welsh For Not Paying Your Debts?

I ran to the back gate, which was still open. "Chassa!"

Behind me came Patrice's voice. "What is this? Get rid of it for me, Holly."

I almost rubbed my ears. "It's nothing to do with me!"

"*Bof.*" Patrice wrinkled his nose and turned to go back inside, but I grabbed his arm.

"Patrice. First the paint, and now this. Someone does not like this café."

For once, Patrice stood and listened.

"Do you have a rival?" I asked. "Who would dump this in your back yard?"

"It is the latest escapade of you and Mees Chassa?" asked Patrice. "Another of your films?"

"*Non,*" I snapped. "We found it here." I thought of Chassa's white face, her sudden flight.

"Patrice, Chassa ran out of the café like she had seen a ghost," I told him.

I held up the *Western Mail* newspaper, with my story in it.

"She was reading this," I told Patrice. "Then she ran away."

Patrice took the newspaper. "Ah, it is your story? The one for which your employer threw you out?"

"Chassa read it and her face went white," I told him.

"*Les femmes,* it happens every month," sniggered Patrice, tossing the *Western Mail* back to me. "I will get rid of this mess. Mees Chassa will be back by lunchtime."

Lunchtime duly arrived.

"*Uhh,* Holly." Patrice approached the table where I sat. "Chassa has not come back. You will help me serve?"

I raised my eyebrows. Then relented. He did look worried.

"*D'accord.*" I got to my feet.

"I need another box of eggs, from the cellar," Patrice directed me. He sighed. "Holly. I cannot manage without my right hand."

He must really value Chassa. "Don't worry," I said. "She'll be back soon."

"Not *her*." Patrice snorted. "My right hand." He held up his bandaged index finger. "I have cut myself, loading that metal pram into the bin. And now it pains me to hold the spatula." He stomped away, muttering.

The back gate didn't have a bolt. Anyone could have got into the yard. I shuddered, knowing that someone had deliberately left us that ugly cargo.

I had to spend all afternoon at the *Lycée Agricole*. When my last lesson ended, I rushed out of the classroom before the pupils did. I needed advice and I knew where to get it.

"Mademoiselle Holly, you look tired," remarked Séverine, as I hurried into the library.

I nearly told her about Chassa, but decided against it.

"I have lost my job at the private school," I explained.

Séverine raised an eyebrow. Before she got too worked up, I explained the situation.

"What is the law?" I asked. "Can they just sack me?"

"They must follow the procedure," said Séverine. "They must first give you a warning, or you may take the matter before the *Prud'hommes*."

"The *Prud'hommes*?" It sounded like a Molière play. Séverine explained that the *Prud'hommes* was a small claims court that dealt with business and contractual disputes. "The school has paid you your salary?"

"They owe me almost three weeks' worth," I admitted.

"Then you must seize the work inspector," Séverine told me.

"No! No violence," I said, horrified.

Séverine smiled. "No, to seize the work inspector, that means that you report the employer's behaviour to him, or to her."

"Who is this work inspector?" I pictured a shady figure with a notebook, sidling around factory floors.

"Each area has a work inspector," explained Séverine. "If an employee has a problem, he reports it, and the work inspector advises if the case may go to the tribunal."

A court case? This was serious.

"But, we say in France, better a bad agreement than a trial," continued Séverine. "You must write to your employer and say that you will take legal action, if she does not pay you what she owes you. Then she will prefer to settle the affair amiably."

"I've written to her." I lifted my chin. I wasn't a helpless foreigner.

"*Par lettre recommendée?*" asked Séverine.

My chin sagged. I hadn't thought to send my letter by recorded delivery.

"You will write another letter." Séverine was brisk. "I will explain what you need to say. And I will find for you the address of the work inspector for this district."

It was good to have someone around who knew the law. But I wasn't sure about taking the *Ecole Vallentin* to court. Given my luck, they'd win the case and I'd end up in the Bastille.

At the café that evening, Patrice looked like a thunderstorm in a pinny.

"Chassa came back this afternoon," said Sophie, who was wiping tables.

Relief surged through me. "Where is she?"

"She has gone again," said Sophie. "I saw her leaving the café, with a bag. I called to her from across the street, but she did not answer me. Patrice, he has shouted after her. But it was not Patrice she came to see." She moved to the next table and began scrubbing it vigorously.

I ached with guilt. Chassa had come looking for me, and I hadn't been there.

"Patrice has asked Milou to help in the café tonight," added Sophie. "But she says she has a singing lesson. She has often the singing lessons. Especially when there is work to do."

Not much debate about how I would be spending my evening. I went into the kitchen. I might not have Chassa's sparky charm, but I could land a plate on a customer's table. With most of the contents intact.

That evening, Sophie, Patrice and I greeted customers, took orders, served pancakes, and loaded the dishwasher as a trio. An equal division of labour that would have delighted Emlyn Kremlin, but did nothing for Patrice's temper.

"That Chassa," he spat, once we'd closed the door behind the last customer. He stormed around the café, slamming chairs under tables. The *Fermé* sign on the door rattled against the glass plane.

"Women's problems!" he grumbled.

"*Non,*" I insisted. "One minute, she was reading – look, Sophie, she was reading my story." I unfolded the *Western Mail* and spread it on the table in front of Sophie.

Sophie nodded gravely, perusing the story exactly as if she were reading it. She pointed at a photograph on the page.

"It is your national costume?" she asked.

"What?" I looked at the photograph. It showed a group of children, faces painted in stripes, wearing pointy ears, posing with their mothers on a pavement in front of a row of houses. The children were beaming, but the placards in the mothers' hands read: "Kerb Death" and "Save Our Children".

I skimmed through the story. Parents in Croesy were demanding a zebra crossing across a busy road near Kemys Street Primary. The children had dressed up as zebras to publicise the campaign. Sadly, the photographer hadn't positioned the group well. The zebras had railings sticking out of their heads, and one placard was overshadowed by the For Sale sign on the house behind it.

That paper needed Mr Wheeler as photojournalist, I thought. I turned back to the story. *Croesy.* Chassa's home town. A busy road. Traffic accidents. Children crossing.

"Sophie," I said. "Patrice. This is why Chassa has gone." I pointed to the picture of the demonstration.

"*Ah,*" Sophie's eyes lit up with understanding. "She is afraid there will be an accident?"

"*Non.*" I tried again. "I think there has already been an accident. And that Chassa was involved in it."

"I have always said it." Patrice was triumphant. "She has run over a child, in her car, on this road." He jabbed at the newspaper. "And then she has run away to France, because of the young life she has snuffed out."

"Don't say that!" I exclaimed. "It's horrible."

"*I don't drive,*" Chassa had said. But she had a driver's licence. She'd mentioned it, the day we'd gone to get my residence permit. And she hadn't wanted to walk Roch home in case he crossed a road and got hit by a car. Patrice might well have put his finger on more than a shard of metal.

The rest of the week went by with no sign of Chassa.

"That deserter," Patrice would snarl, as I came in to do an evening shift.

"It must have been an emergency," I would reason. "She would not just run away."

"She ran away from her home," Patrice would grumble. And I had yet to come up with an answer to that.

Of course I'd thought of Didier. If Chassa had confided in anyone, it would have been him. But none of us had seen him since she'd left. Milou didn't know his phone number, and none of us knew his surname. He was unlikely to be listed in the *annuaire* as Lapin, Monsieur.

"I just need to know she's all right," I fretted to Madame Silvain, after our lesson. "If she's really gone back to Wales." The irony. Chassa taking off for Wales, when in a couple of weeks' time, half of Pontycynon would be descending on Mauvoisins.

"And your job?" asked Madame Silvain.

"I have been to see the work inspector," I told her. "They are going to contact the school about my case."

"It is a pity that your parents will not be here to support you," remarked Madame Silvain. "But we still have room for two of your friends."

I smiled. Lin could stay with Madame Silvain. Owen too. He might well be inspired by Eliane's evening dresses.

"How is your daughter, Madame?" I asked.

Madame Silvain sighed and looked into her coffee. "Still in Paris. She finds Paris more amusing than Mauvoisins." She paused. "When I was young, we thought of marriage and children. But today, the young girls think only of enjoying themselves."

I wondered why she was so keen on seeing her daughter married, with children. Then I remembered what Patrice had said about her son.

"And your parents, they are not concerned for you?" asked Madame Silvain.

"Well, they worry," I said. "But not so much that they want to come and see me." I smiled to disguise the resentment I still felt about the visit-that-wasn't.

"They are not concerned that you will marry a Frenchman?" asked Madame Silvain. "You say they do not speak French. How will they talk to their grandchildren?"

Dear me. I'd only come out here for a year and already she had me married with a family.

I shrugged. "We shall see. It is kind of you to offer your room to my friends."

Madame Silvain brightened. "But it is nothing, after all you have done for my family." She beamed. "And your friend, she will surely contact you. True friends, they help each other."

I hadn't been much help to Chassa, I reflected, as I walked back to the bungalow. Showing her upsetting stories from home, not being around when she needed to confide in me. She'd probably phoned Sion and told him what a useless freeloader I was.

Sion. I stopped in my tracks. I'd ring Griff and get him to find out if Sion had heard from Chassa. At last I'd got the answer.

But one other matter still nagged me. I didn't have a contract, or any pay slips, to certify that I'd been employed by the Ecole Vallentin.

Madame l'inspecteur had raised her eyebrows in a perfect imitation of Séverine. "You have no proof of employment?"

"I have my bank statements," I'd offered. They would show that I'd paid a certain sum of money into my account every month. "And witnesses who could affirm that I worked at the school."

I probably wouldn't be able to persuade Lydie Lesourd to testify against her employer in court. But surely the school would cough up what they owed me when they heard from *Madame l'inspecteur*. They wouldn't want to go through a legal rigmarole over a measly three weeks of a modest salary. With *Madame l'inspecteur*'s calculator, we'd worked out exactly how little I was owed.

If this went to court, I'd just ask some of the pupils to confirm that I'd taught them. Like Corinne and Viv, my guests at the *crêperie* after they'd won the Speaking English challenge. I'd make sure they gave good answers again.

"Mop the kitchen floor," Patrice announced with his usual charm, as I walked into the café. "Your friend is still not back."

I went into the kitchen. Through the window, I saw Serge in the yard, wrestling with the gate. So he'd finally got around to fixing it.

I opened the back door and greeted him. "I replace Chassa, tonight," I explained. "She is still not back."

Serge nodded, apparently unmoved. I was surprised. He'd always seemed to get on well with Chassa.

"I am worried she may be in trouble," I added. Surely the fatherly Serge would be concerned.

"Oh, Chassa will always get herself out of trouble," said Serge, turning back to the gate.

Was I the only one who cared? I'd phone Griff at his workplace tomorrow. Sion would know where Chassa was.

I took the mop out of its cupboard. I didn't mind doing Chassa's work for her. Without her, I wouldn't have come to the café, wouldn't have met Serge, Sophie and their bungalow, wouldn't have started teaching Madame Silvain. And when I'd got that mysterious note about the job vacancy at the *Lycée Agricole*, Chassa had encouraged to me go there. Otherwise, I would never have met Gilles.

I held the mop close as we tangoed around the kitchen floor. There were some debts you couldn't add up with a calculator.

19.

Wish You Were By'Yere

I shifted from one foot to the other. The coach had been due half an hour ago. How many traffic lights could have turned red in between here and Upper Waun Street?

Lucky I was here to welcome the visitors, and translate everything for them. These days, I was so immersed in French culture, I'd even lapsed into French when I'd phoned Griff to tell him to ask Sion if he'd heard from Chassa.

"Sion's in Scotland. On a rugby tour," Griff had grunted.

Of course. On that postcard to Chassa, Sion had scrawled that he was taking his Pants to Scotland in the spring. Had Chassa joined him there?

A blast from a car horn made me jump. I leaped out of the coach's way. So much for being acclimatised. I'd been looking to my left.

"Bonjour, mademoiselle." I rolled my 'r' until it nearly bounced off down the road.

"Oh, Hol." Lin gave me a cwtch. "There's French you are. Isn't she, Owen?"

More passengers stepped down from the coach. I spotted a familiar moustache. "Mr Wheeler! How are you?"

Mr Wheeler, staggering under a pile of matching luggage, smiled a greeting.

"Put 'em by'yere, Jeff," directed Mrs Whipple, teetering behind him. "Holly! You're looking well. You've lost weight."

I beamed. It was good to see old friends.

"Are you hungry?" I asked. "The café isn't far." I turned to Lin. "Or I can take you and Owen to your lodgings first."

"Well, we're meeting the Mayor at four o'clock," said Lin. "We'd better not go wandering off. Here's someone now."

A young woman in a navy suit was approaching us. I straightened up. Now I'd be needed as interpreter.

"Welcome to Mauvoisins," began the young woman in impeccable English. "We have arranged a reception for you."

The Ponty visitors picked up their luggage and followed Mademoiselle. Looked like I wasn't needed.

"Holly." Mrs Hathaway had alighted from the coach. I straightened up. *Now's your chance.*

I smiled. "Welcome to Mauvoisins, Mrs Hathaway."

Mrs Hathaway eyed me. I kept smiling.

"Let me take your bag," I offered, seizing her holdall. We followed the rest of the Ponty visitors to the Town Hall, where we were ushered into a side room.

"The Mayor will join us shortly," announced the tailored young woman.

"Holly!" hissed Mrs Whipple. "Where's the Ladies? I need to do my hair."

I led her to the lobby, Lin following. We found the ladies' room and congregated around the washbasins.

"I've scagged my hold-ups," sighed Mrs Whipple. "Holly, nip out and get me a pair of tights, will you? Here's some euros." She might have been sending me down the Cwarp for her gin and a packet of firelighters.

"No-one will notice," I told her. "Pull your mini-skirt down a bit. Where are you staying? Lin said you'd made your own arrangements."

"Jeff – er, Mr Wheeler – sorted it all out," said Mrs Whipple. "We're staying with this couple he knows."

"Monsieur and Madame Le Floch?" I went cold all over.

"No, some Spanish name," said Mrs Whipple. I breathed a sigh of relief.

"I saw you with Mrs Hathaway, Hol," said Lin. "Are you friends, now?"

"Oh, you've got to reach out to people," I said. This particular connection could be the most useful feat of engineering since the Newport Transporter Bridge.

201

Back at the reception, Mr Wheeler was deep in hand gestures with a French couple. He turned to me. "Holly, these people are asking if Pontycynon is bigger than Mauvoisins."

"Only if you add the mountain," I replied in swift French. The couple laughed and introduced themselves as Vincent and Isabelle Carrasco. I explained that I wasn't a visitor, I was working in Mauvoisins for a year.

The tailored young woman joined us. Her name badge read *Laurence Guilbaud*.

"You are here for one year?" she enquired, clearly not pleased to meet someone who might correct her English.

"I arrived last September," I explained. "My first day, I went to the supermarket to buy some chocolate. Spent half an hour looking round the *Confection* aisle before I realised it meant 'clothes'."

Vincent and Isabelle laughed, but Laurence Guilbaud didn't.

"You think our signs should be in English also?" she snapped.

"In your country, are the signs bilingual?"

"Yes, actually, they are," I said. Mr Wheeler cackled. Perhaps he was thinking of the Ponty thoroughfare helpfully named Gorse Meadow Bank Road/Stryd Gorse Meadow Bank. Just then, the Mayor walked in, putting an end to further linguistic debate.

Fair play for Francis The Mayor, he made his speech of welcome in English. Must have been studying Sis's Méthode. As we applauded, Laurence hurried over to him. I sidled close enough to listen.

"This young lady knows all about Mauvoisins," announced Laurence, indicating me.

"Holly?" Mrs Hathaway laughed. "She washes up in a café."

"Holly does journalism." Mrs Whipple defended me. "She's been writing for a newspaper about life over here."

"You must follow current affairs," said Laurence smartly. "What is making the headlines in Britain today?"

I froze. These days, I never saw the British papers, or watched telly.

"Holly?" Mrs Hathaway was glinting. A familiar sight to all Ponty pupils who'd ever struggled with their nine times table.

I lifted my chin. "In London, they're thinking of banning Tube travel," I said.

"Banning Tube travel?" Laurence stared.

"Yes," I said. "But they're worried that'll drive it underground."
I turned back to Mrs Whipple, Mr Wheeler and the Carrascos.

"This is our host family," said Mrs Whipple, smiling at Vincent and Isabelle. "Jeff asked if they could put the two of us up."

The two of us, indeed. I tried to catch Lin's eye, but she was gazing fondly at Owen. Looked like the whole of Pontycynon had paired off, the minute I'd left.

"We'll see you later, is it, Holly?" asked Mr Wheeler.

"Yes," I said. "You must come and eat in the café."

"Ooh, the café," said Lin. "I've got to meet Patrice. See if he's as bad as you say."

"You won't be disappointed," I promised. "I'll walk you to Madame Silvain's house. *On y va?*"

Since the Ponty visitors didn't need me to show them around, I could go to work at the *Lycée* as usual. As for the court case, I'd had a letter from the *Prud'hommes*, setting the date of my initial hearing.

"At the first hearing, they will ask you to confirm your name and address," Séverine had explained. "And your claim that you worked in the school on these dates. The school may send a representative to confirm that they contest your claims."

I nodded, but my main concern these days was Chassa.

"She has not telephoned?" I asked Sophie one evening, before opening time.

"Not to our house," replied Sophie, her lips thin.

I couldn't understand it. Chassa must know we'd be worried.
I applied mop to café floor with renewed determination. The French mustn't think we Welsh went round letting people down.

They wouldn't think we went around letting our hemlines down, I thought, as Mrs Whipple shook hands with Patrice.

"This is Lin," said Mrs Whipple loudly. "She works with me. Up the Tower."

Patrice looked at Lin. His face lit up. Someone would be getting extra Chantilly on her banana split tonight.

"Holly, she is cute, your friend," Patrice exclaimed. "You did not tell me you had pretty girls, in Wales. I thought they were all like you."

I was too busy picking up menus to answer him back.

"Go sit with your friends," said Patrice. "I will serve you."

He just wanted an excuse to hang around Lin. Still, it let me off an evening's work.

"Madame Silvain not coming?" I asked Lin. I hadn't seen Madame since she'd welcomed Lin and Owen.

"She went to visit someone," explained Lin. "She keeps saying how good you've been to her family."

I smiled. Madame Silvain must really be enjoying her English lessons.

"She's got this painter in," added Lin. "Doing up one of the bedrooms."

"Candy pink," put in Owen. You could tell he'd been to art school.

"Owen helped her too," said Lin. "She's knitting this white lacy thing, and he wound her wool for her." She smiled at her beloved.

The café door swung open to admit Mrs Hathaway. "So this is the crêperie," she remarked. "I thought it would be bigger."

"Over here, Mrs Hathaway," I carolled, rushing to the corner table and drawing back a chair.

Mrs Hathaway was gracious enough to join me. Serge approached our table with two kir-cassis and a wink for me.

"Doesn't a Croesy girl work here as a waitress?" enquired Mrs Hathaway, opening her menu. "Angeline knew her at school. Said she wouldn't go far."

I clutched my glass. "Chassa was head girl at that school. And she speaks French like a native." I turned to Serge. "Serge, Chassa parle français parfaitement, n'est-ce pas?"

"I not understand," teased Serge.

Mrs Hathaway laughed. I should have known better. Still, his joke had put her in a good mood. Which would help my plan.

"Your French obviously hasn't improved since you've been here, Holly," said Mrs Hathaway, with a satisfied smile.

"I'll never speak French as well as Angeline," I sighed.

Mrs Hathaway sipped her *kir-cassis*. "Angeline used to teach English in France, during her summer holidays."

"I thought Angeline didn't do teacher-training?" I asked.

"She didn't," said Mrs Hathaway. "But she'd had a good example. She had an excellent French teacher, at school."

I remembered Chassa and Angeline's meeting in the café. Chassa mentioning that Angeline had spent a fortune on private lessons.

"Mrs Seed wrote books on language teaching," added Mrs Hathaway. "Angeline and I heard her lecture on the subject, in Swansea."

"Is Angeline still in touch with Mrs Seed?" I asked.

"I don't think so," said Mrs Hathaway.

"No more private lessons, then," I said. Mrs Hathaway frowned.

"I mean, Angeline doesn't need lessons," I babbled.

Mrs Hathaway studied the menu. I looked at Lin and the others. Chassa would have thought of some great places to take them to. I scribbled a mental postcard to her. *Wish you were by'yere.*

"Dessert all right, Lin?" I asked.

"Lovely," Lin said. "A lot of cream, too. It's great here, Holly. Owen can't get over the French architecture."

"Neither can my free-running pupils," I said.

Lin laughed. "Matthieu and Benoît?"

"Well remembered!" I was surprised.

Lin smiled. "I've shown a couple of your e-mails to the regulars, at the Tower."

"I like writing," I admitted. Perhaps I'd have another story printed, one day.

"Where's the eighth wonder?" asked Lin. "Giles, isn't it? I notice he's taken over from Kim."

"Gilles hasn't been in class lately," I said, trying to sound as if this didn't matter.

"Holly," called Mrs Whipple. "When are we coming to see your house? Jeff – er, Mr Wheeler - promised your Mam she'd take a picture of it."

"Come round tomorrow afternoon," I said. "We'll have tea and cakes. Lin," I lowered my voice. "There's something I want you to do for me, when you get back to Ponty. I'll write it down for you. But keep it to yourself."

"*Fromage!*" I smiled at the digital camera.

"Lovely, Holly," said Mr Wheeler, stepping back.

"There's nice to have your own little house, Holly," sighed Mrs Whipple. She moved closer to the bungalow to admire Serge's handiwork.

"She'll be doing up the coalhouse, now," murmured Lin.

"It'll be somewhere for you and Owen to start married life," I told her. "More *opéra*, Mr Wheeler?"

"I'll be looking like the fat lady who sings," joked Mr Wheeler. "Do much gardening, Holly?"

"Not really," I said, cutting him a slice of cake. "But my friend Chassa grows some plants." I remembered those balcony gardening sessions. Clods of earth whizzing around. Chassa shouting: "*Hé*, Mr Garden, don't get your ears caught in the railings."

Mr Garden.

"'Scuse me." I tipped the cake on to Mr Wheeler's plate and raced up to Serge's house.

Sophie didn't ask questions, just directed me to the telephone book. My fingers scrabbled for the page.

"*Jardin, Didier.*" An address in Mauvoisins.

I dialled and heard the ringing tone. Then a voice.

"Didier?" I hazarded. "*Ici Holly. Du* Bad Café."

"*Ah! Salut, Holly.*" I recognised Didier's pleasant tones.

"Have you seen Chassa?" Anxiety made me brusque. "Has she phoned you?"

"*Non*," replied Didier.

"Chassa has disappeared," I almost shouted. "No one has seen her for two weeks."

"Oh, she will be OK," replied Didier. "How are you? And the Bad Café?"

Was that all he had to say? "I'm well," I replied. "But I must go the *Prud'hommes* on April 1st."

"It is perhaps a fish," Didier laughed.

He'd really lost it. "Fish?" I asked.

"On April 1ˢᵗ, people play jokes," explained Didier. "When someone wants to play a joke on you, he sticks a paper fish on your back. *Un poisson d'avril*."

"Ah." I resolved to stay indoors for as much of April 1ˢᵗ as possible, avoiding citizens intent on affixing cardboard images of marine life to each other. There wasn't much else to talk about, so I said goodbye.

No news of Chassa, but at least I'd found Didier. A pity I hadn't been able to introduce him to my guests. And, as Lin had remarked, they'd missed Gilles too. But not as much as I had.

"Leaving already," I sighed. "Don't seem two minutes since you arrived."

"Hol, who's that waving at you?" asked Lin.

I turned to see a small boy standing nearby, watching us. I went over to him.

"*Bonjour, Madame*," said Roch. "Is that your sister?"

My heart sank. There was Angeline, talking to her aunt.

"Not my sister," I grumbled. "Roch, have you seen that lady again? The lady who asked you to throw paint over me?"

"*Non, Madame*," said Roch. "I have not seen her. *Mais elle avait une blouse blanche*," he added.

He meant well, but searching Mauvoisins for women in white blouses wouldn't get me far.

"*Voilà votre bus, Madame*," said Roch.

I hurried back to Lin. "You've got that note I wrote?"

"It's here," said Lin, patting her pocket. "No, it's in my passport, I think. I know I've got it somewhere."

To think she was in charge of the library filing system. Cwtches all round, then I was waving them goodbye.

Angeline was still standing there when the bus had disappeared from view.

"Angeline," I nodded to her.

"Holly." She might have been saying: "*Cockroach*." "Still here? I thought you'd have crawled home now you've lost your job."

"I have a job," I replied. "At the agricultural school. And I'm taking Madame Vallentin to court for unfair dismissal."

207

Angeline laughed. "You were never employed at the Ecole Vallentin."

"Of course I was," I said. "You met me there, remember?"

Angeline's smile said it all. My mind raced. No contract, no pay slips. No proof that I'd worked at the school.

"I have witnesses," I said.

Angeline's smile widened. "Do you think those pupils will risk expulsion, for you?"

"So Madame Vallentin has threatened to kick the pupils out if they admit I taught them," I said, keeping my voice steady. "What exactly did I do wrong?"

"You've been indiscreet, Holly," said Angeline. "Foolish."

"She'll look foolish in court," I bluffed. "My friends can testify that I worked at the school."

Angeline laughed. "The court won't listen to Charlotte after what happened."

"The accident, in Croesy?" I said. "I know all about it."

Angeline looked at me, then laughed.

"No, you don't," she said.

And walked away.

20.

And Anything But The Truth

"You are going to defend yourself in court?" Gilles whistled.

We were sitting on the grass beside the lake.

I smiled at Gilles' admiring glance. I decided not to tell him I had no papers proving I'd worked at the school. Then he wouldn't think I was completely hopeless. He'd know I was.

"Your Welsh friend will go with you?" asked Gilles.

"She's gone away." I found myself telling Gilles about Chassa's disappearance and the pram in the back yard, with its putrid cargo.

"That's not all," I added, and launched into the story of the mystery woman paying Roch to throw paint over me.

"Umm... would you come to the court with me?" I asked Gilles. "My case will be heard on the afternoon of April 1st."

"I have lessons that afternoon," replied Gilles.

"No matter," I breezed. "But I shall panic, in front of all those judges in their robes."

"It is only their *blouse de travail*," smiled Gilles. "I will give you my mobile number. You can call me and tell me how the judgement went."

I managed to get through the morning of April 1st with nothing untoward on my back. Unless you counted Patrice, grumbling as usual.

"Be here on time this evening, Holly," he ordered me.

"That will depend on the *Prud'hommes*," I told him.

"Well, if they lock you up, you call me, to let me know," replied Patrice.

Just then my mobile rang, so I went into the back yard to get a better signal.

"*Allô?*" A man's voice. "*Ça va?*"

"Who is this?" I asked.

"*Holl-ee? Ici* Serge." Serge sounded confused.

209

"Serge, I'm just leaving the café," I explained. "To go to the *Prud'hommes.*"

"*Ah! Bonne chance!*" said Serge. "You will tell us about it tonight?"

That was nice of Serge, phoning to wish me luck. I thanked him and promised to tell them the details.

It was only like going to the doctor's, I told myself, as the imposing wooden doors closed behind me. Some dignified personages were walking through the lobby, resplendent in their courtroom attire. I took a deep breath. This would be like Dr Vaughan's evening surgery, only with fewer wigs.

I looked at my official letter for the hundredth time. Where was Chamber 6?

A lady in a suit was nearby. Perhaps she'd know.

"*Madame,*" I ventured. She turned to face me. I gasped.

It was Annick Le Floch.

"Holly," said Annick, eyes wide. "You have come back to Mauvoisins?"

"I have never left Mauvoisins," I blurted out.

"I know you left France," said Annick. "Christian told me you were homesick."

I nearly yelped. That liar.

"Annick, I didn't leave Mauvoisins," I explained. "Didn't you get my message? I wrote you a note to explain why I was going away. I hid it in the bathroom."

"In the bathroom?" Annick stared.

"I didn't want Christian to read it," I explained. "So I hid it in your packet of, er, …" Dammit, what was the word for sanitary towels? "*Serviettes hygiéniques.*"

The light dawned in Annick's eyes. "*Ah,* Holly." She placed her hands on her rounded stomach.

No wonder she hadn't found my note. She was expecting again. She hadn't needed to open that particular packet.

"I am sorry, Annick," I said. "But I could not stay in your house. Your husband was putting his hands on me." I braced myself for the explosion.

But Annick just looked pained. Then I understood.

It had happened before.

Annick sighed. "I knew well he had a bad conscience, when he said those things."

"What things?" I asked.

"He said you were following him everywhere," said Annick. "He said you kept putting your arms around him, and he had to push you away."

This time I did yelp.

"I asked him why he has not told me this before," said Annick. "He shrugged and walked away. I have not believed his story," she reassured me. "But if I tell him that, he will say we are finished."

I gawped. "He'd rather lose you than admit what he did?"

"Oh, yes," said Annick, sounding almost proud of her husband. My turn to sigh.

"I am sorry this has spoiled your sojourn in France, Holly," said Annick.

"It didn't, really," I said. "I found a job in a school -" I broke off. I'd remembered something.

"Annick," I began. "You have studied French law." I ran briefly through the reasons why I had turned to the *Prud'hommes*.

"Could you come with me?" I asked. "Help me present my case?" Annick shook her head.

"I am sorry, Holly," she said. "But I do not want Christian to find out that I have helped you."

So loyal to her husband. Her husband, who had made advances to me in their home, then told her a family-sized pack of lies about it.

"*Bonne chance*, Holly," said Annick. She nodded at me, then walked out of the building.

I watched her go. I could have done without that shock. But at least now she knew why I'd left.

Inside the chamber a small platform looked down on rows of empty seats. I sat down in the second row, facing the platform.

If only Annick had been with me. What if the judge asked me some complicated legal question?

People began arriving. I looked at my official letter yet again. This hearing was billed as the stage of *conciliation*, a chance for both

211

parties to settle out of court. No chance Madame Vallentin would agree to that.

Seven people were taking their places at the table on the platform. Were they all judges? Perhaps some were stenographers. None of them were wearing gowns and wigs.

The man in the centre of the panel appeared to be the chairman. He began to read out names and addresses. I gathered that he was listing everyone whose cases were being heard that afternoon.

I heard him pronounce my name (approximately) and that of Madame Vallentin, Nicole, *directrice* of the *Ecole Vallentin*.

I glanced around the room. Plenty of people here now, but no Madame Vallentin. If the opposition was a no-show, did I get awarded the win?

The chairman read out the first two names on his list, then waited for the people concerned to approach the panel. I hoped the chairman was a Gallic version of that judge in the TV drama, John Deed (*Jean Fait Accompli?*). Championing the underdog, out to discover the truth.

Name after name was called. I glanced round. Still no Madame Vallentin. Perhaps the hearing would be postponed if she didn't turn up. She knew I'd be going back to Wales at the end of the school year. With delaying tactics, she could string the case out until I'd left the country. Then she wouldn't need to settle her debt.

"*Mademoiselle Gay-tan, Holl-ee,*" announced the chairman. "*Madame Vallentin, Nicole.*" I got up, walked forwards and stood before him.

The chairman glanced over to my right. I turned and froze. A tall man in a grey suit and a briefcase was approaching.

"*Mademoiselle.*" The chairman addressed me. "You maintain that you worked in the school in question on these dates." He scrutinised his papers.

"*Oui,*" I said, eyeing Monsieur Briefcase.

"*Monsieur, vous êtes...?*" The chairman turned to Monsieur Briefcase.

"Monsieur Vallentin, Dominique," responded that gentleman. "*Directeur-associé de l'Ecole Vallentin.*"

So this was Madame's husband.

212

"As you see, Mademoiselle does not recognise me," said Monsieur Vallentin, Dominique.

"Although she claims she has worked at the school which I run jointly with my wife." He handed the chairman a selection of documents, presumably proof of his identity and position at the school.

"*Excusez-moi*," I blurted out. "I have worked with Madame Vallentin, not Monsieur. And Madame Lesourd, too." There, I knew the staff.

"Mademoiselle has no doubt seen our establishment," remarked Monsieur Vallentin, ignoring my mention of Lydie Lesourd. "She is trying to profit from the fact that we teach English."

"*Non*," I said. "I have taught English at this school, using the *Méthode Vallentin*."

"We advertise our teaching method widely," said Monsieur Vallentin, still addressing the chairman, without so much as a glance at me. "Mademoiselle has seen the advertisements for the *Méthode Vallentin*."

"Your *contrat de travail*, Mademoiselle?" asked the chairman. "Your pay slips?" He looked through his papers again.

"The school did not give me any pay slips." I spoke clearly. Let the whole panel hear how unprofessional the Vallentins were. "But I can prove that I know the *Méthode Vallentin*. I can repeat the first few lessons by heart."

"The *Méthode* is sold as a correspondence course," responded Monsieur Vallentin. "Mademoiselle will have memorised parts of it."

I wasn't beaten yet. "I taught final year students at the school," I announced. "Viviane Lefèvre and Corinne Bourot can confirm that I was their teacher."

Jean Fait Accompli shook his head. "It is for you to produce evidence, Mademoiselle."

"But they won't testify against their *directrice*." I kept my voice steady.

A new thought nagged me. Could the Vallentins have sent me those nasty text messages? Telling me to go home, so I'd drop the case? Could they have been the couple in the car who had bribed young Roch?

"If you have no evidence of your employment at the school, Mademoiselle," said Jean Fait Accompli, "you cannot proceed with your case."

Monsieur Vallentin looked at me.

"Mademoiselle has never been employed by my school," he repeated. "To my knowledge, she has never set foot in the establishment."

"*Monsieur*," rang out a voice from behind me.

I turned to see Chassa, dressed in a black suit, standing behind me. She had a large folder tucked under her arm.

"I am here on behalf of Mademoiselle Gethin," said Chassa. She turned to Monsieur Vallentin. "You say, Monsieur, that Mademoiselle Gethin has never set foot in your school?" She turned to the panel. "*Messieurs-dames*, I can disprove that assertion immediately."

Monsieur Vallentin began to speak, but Jean Fait Accompli held up a hand, motioning to Chassa to continue.

Chassa opened her folder, took out an exercise book, and handed it to me.

"Mademoiselle Gethin," said Chassa. "You will please draw a detailed plan of the interior of the Ecole Vallentin." She passed me a pencil.

I opened the exercise book. My hand shook slightly as I drew rectangles representing the classrooms and Madame Vallentin's office. Better add the stairs. I even put in small oblongs for the cupboards and the typewriters.

In the square representing the main classroom, I drew four rows of desks. Suddenly I was back there, manual in hand, facing the girls again. I scrawled the names of the front row pupils – Corinne, Viviane, Sylvie, Isabelle and Christine. Not forgetting sulky Anne-Laure and Maryline, at the back.

Chassa took the book from me and handed it to Jean Fait Accompli. "Mademoiselle Gethin. One question. What is the name of the pet that Madame Vallentin keeps in her office?"

"Cousteau," I responded promptly. "The only goldfish left in her aquarium."

I only wished I'd had time to do a drawing of Monsieur Vallentin's face. His expression was one I'd remember for a long time.

"*Intéressant,*" noted Jean Fait Accompli. "And yet, Monsieur, you claim that Mademoiselle has never set foot in your school."

"We are prepared to settle out of court," Chassa told him. She guided me back to my seat.

Suddenly it was all over and we were leaving the building.

"Chassa," I breathed. "Where have you been? We've been worried sick."

"At Rabbit's, where'd you think?" replied Chassa, striding along.

"He told me he hadn't seen you," I grumbled.

"No, he told you I hadn't phoned him," said Chassa. "Which I hadn't. I went straight round there. He told me your hearing was today. Did you see that bloke's face? They'll appeal. But they'll have a job to explain how you could do that."

"I'm on to them," I growled. "My friend Lin's going to find out -" I paused.

"Chassa," I said. "I know what happened in Croesy, with the child. I worked it out, when we read the newspaper."

Chassa said nothing, but kept walking.

"Don't worry about the café," I reassured her. "Me and Sophie filled in for you."

"Yeah, Milou told me," said Chassa.

So she'd kept in touch with Milou. Didn't the rest of us matter?

I pushed the café door open.

"Patrice! Serge!" I exclaimed. "I've won my case! Well, I'm going to win, thanks to Chassa."

"*Au diable* your case," snapped Patrice. "Someone has stolen money from the café. And you!" He pointed at Chassa. "I should fire you. You abandon your work, you leave me to do everything – "

"*D'accord*, Patrice," replied Chassa. "I will go and pack my bags." She didn't even greet Serge, just walked past him into the kitchen.

As Chassa's footsteps sounded on the stairs, Serge turned to me.

"Holly," he said. "This afternoon, we have noticed that a lot of money is missing from the till."

They both looked at me. My face felt hot.

"You checked the till last night, Patrice," I said. "And Chassa was at the *Prud'hommes* with me. She was brilliant. She proved to them that I'd worked at that school."

"In her new clothes?" demanded Patrice. "Where did she get the money to buy them?"

"We will sit down and talk about this." Serge was the voice of reason. "All of us, together."

I opened the stairs door and called: "Chassa?"

No answer.

Serge joined me.

"She will really leave?" he asked.

"I don't know," I said. "Chassa!"

Still no answer.

I went up the stairs, Serge following.

Chassa's door was ajar. I pushed it open and walked into a mess. Clothes and shoes strewn everywhere. Books and papers covered the floor. Chassa's black bin bags had been torn open and the contents were scattered all over the room.

Chassa was sitting on the bed, clutching a cushion.

"Chassa?" I asked. "What have you...?"

"It is not Chassa who has done this," rasped Serge.

And then I knew.

"*Merde*," I said.

21.

Stabbed In The Backyard

"Milou," I breathed.

Serge sat down on the bed beside Chassa. Chassa said nothing, but held up a piece of paper. Serge took it and unfolded it.

"Chassa," he read. "I have gone to Paris to be a singer. I lost the baby before I came to live with you. I did not tell you this, as I did not want to return *chez Maman*. Milou."

Serge pulled Chassa close to him. "Now we know where the money from the till has gone."

Chassa was gripping the cushion. A small, silky cushion that I hadn't noticed in her room before.

"I think that cushion has spent the last few months up Mademoiselle Milou's pullover," remarked Serge.

Chassa burst into tears. Chassa, who tackled life head-on, who left everyone else standing.

Serge stroked Chassa's face, stopping her tears with his fingertips. I turned away, embarrassed. Good thing Sophie wasn't present.

"I will talk to Patrice," said Serge, getting up. "Holly, you will verify if anything more has been stolen." He looked uncomfortable. As well he might.

Serge closed the door behind him, calling to Patrice as he headed downstairs.

Chassa raised her eyes to meet mine.

"I hope that wasn't what it looked like," I joked, trying to lighten the moment.

"It was," said Chassa.

"Serge?" I breathed. "But he's old! He's somebody's dad!"

"Don' look at me like that," said Chassa. "Neither of us meant anything to happen. We just got on really well." She found a tissue and blew her nose. "It sort of went from there."

"I wondered what was keeping you in this job," I said.

"You nearly caught us, once," said Chassa. "Up here, on opening night."

My mind raced back to the evening of the *crêperie*'s launch. The pupils taunting me through the window, Gilles and I on the doorstep, Chassa's bucket of water cascading over us. Chassa running out, Serge behind her with the towels. Chassa ushering Gilles and me up to this room, *smoothing down the bedcover*.

"I thought you were Sophie's friend," I said.

Chassa looked away. "Why do you think I kept giving her sweets?" she growled.

And I'd thought she was so considerate. It had all been out of guilt.

"I did wonder if she'd guessed, when I started First Aid," admitted Chassa. "They give the lessons at the fire station. That's where Serge does his maintenance work. I needed a way to see him, well clear of the café." She gripped Milou's unborn cushion.

I sat down beside her.

"You were a mother hen to Milou," I said. "Had she threatened to tell Sophie about you and Serge?"

"No," said Chassa. "Milou was talking about getting rid of her baby. I couldn't let another one die."

"Another baby?" More revelations. "You mean, you'd had one?"

"Not me," said Chassa, with a dry laugh.

"Chassa," I said. "What happened in Croesy? Did you run over a child?"

Chassa looked up, startled.

"The photo in the newspaper." I gabbled. "The children, demonstrating about the zebra crossing. You said you didn't drive, but then you told me about the bad photo on your driving licence."

"Oh, Hol," Chassa sighed. "I've never run anything over. And yes, I passed my test, years ago, but I don't drive over here. For a start, they're all nutters on the road, and for seconds, I'd be bound to forget, and drive on the left."

"You wouldn't walk Roch home, that night, in case he got run over," I grumbled.

"True," said Chassa. "I didn't want people putting the fault on me, if anything happened to him, and I was the last one to see him alive."

"So why did you leave home?" There, I'd asked it.

Chassa made an odd noise.

"I was still at school, just done A-levels," she said. "My brother and his awful girlfriend had had a baby. They went out one Saturday night and left me babysitting. I'd invited someone around, and we were having a drink, getting to know each other. I went to check on the baby, and she wasn't moving."

I kept quiet. Chassa continued. "We tried to wake her up. I rang Russell, and he went mad, shouting that I should have minded the baby, instead of messing with boys. And that Gaynor screamed the place down. She'd never liked me anyway. Hol, it was a nightmare."

"But it wasn't your fault," I said.

"It was a cot death," said Chassa. "But if I'd checked on the baby every five minutes, I might have realised something was wrong. My Dad sided with Russ. Went beserk."

So Chassa had a brother and a dad.

"And your Granny Chappell?" I asked.

"She was the only one who stood up for me," said Chassa. "But I wasn't going to stay and be treated like a leper. I packed my bags and pushed off to France. I'd always fancied going there. Sion was the only one who knew the full story, outside the family, but there were rumours going round."

"Angeline dropped hints," I admitted.

Chassa nodded. "I thought you might have read about it at the time, in *Y Llais*. You said you used to read it, to see if your Kim's name was in there. I thought you might have read about the funeral. Well, someone in your family might have - " She broke off and put her head in her hands.

I clasped her shoulder. She'd been carrying that burden all this time.

Chassa's voice was muffled. "That photo in the paper was the last straw."

"The kids in Croesy, dressed as zebras?" I asked. "Did you recognise them?"

"No," said Chassa, raising her head. "But I recognised one of the houses behind them. The one with a For Sale sign. It was Granny Chappell's house. She's always sworn she'll only leave her home feet first. Hol, she must have died, and nobody's told me. I've been trying to ring Sion, but he's not answering."

"He's in Scotland, on his rugby tour," I said.

Chassa nodded. In her torment, she didn't think to ask me how I knew.

"Have you rung your family?" I asked.

Chassa shook her head. "Too late now. Seven years, it's been. And if they'd wanted to, they could have found me. I've kept sending Granny Chappell postcards. Sion goes round and reads them to her. Least, he used to." Her face tightened again.

"I went away 'cos I needed time to come to terms with it," she added. "I knew old Rabbit wouldn't let on where I was."

I remembered my phone call to Didier. And then remembered another phone call.

"Chassa, Serge phoned me this morning," I said. "Said he'd rung to wish me luck. Did you know about that?"

Chassa sighed. "Oh, Hol. He'd dialled the wrong number, that's all. He was trying to call me. Think about it. Your mobile phone, the one you're using, it was my mobile before I gave it you, remember?"

"So it was." Light dawned. "No wonder he was surprised when I answered."

Chassa nodded. "I'd kept in touch with him all along. He knew I was OK."

That explained why Serge hadn't been concerned about Chassa's disappearance. The jigsaw pieces in my head were fitting together at top speed.

"Chassa, cot death happens." I racked my brains for anything I'd ever read on the subject. "If they knew how to prevent it, no baby would die like that again. And no babysitter checks on a child every five minutes. Not even the mother would do that."

Chassa half-laughed. "Don't get me started on the mother. That was another reason I kept my eye on Milou. Didn't want her sneaking off for cigarettes, like that Gaynor used to."

We sat in silence for a moment.

"I wish you'd told me all this before," I said. "Instead of bottling it all up."

Chassa sighed. "Not much you could have done, Hol."

"But I let you down," I argued. "The day you ran off, Sophie said you came back to see me. And I wasn't there."

"It was Serge I came to see," admitted Chassa. "I couldn't face Sophie just then. I pretended I didn't see her waving at me."

I remembered Sophie's sharp voice, as we'd cleaned the café tables together, that night: *"It was not me she came to see."*

"Chassa," I said. "I think Sophie does know about you and Serge. She may not have said it, but she does have an idea there's something going on."

Chassa stared at the wall. I decided I was in no position to judge her. I'd wasted enough time and affection on a bloke who couldn't have cared less about me.

Part of me still couldn't believe what I'd heard. To think I hadn't twigged before. And I'd thought Sophie was slow.

"Chassa," I said. "Remember that night when Roch came round to the bungalow, to say sorry? You said that for once I hadn't had only Neil Morgan to talk to. How did you know that I had a pin-up of Neil Morgan on my bedroom wall? You've never been in my bedroom."

Chassa went pink.

"Don't tell me," I groaned. "You used to meet Serge in my bungalow."

"Only once or twice, Hol," Chassa admitted. "He's got a key, and you were out teaching."

"How could you?" I demanded. "Sneaking into my house."

"Well, Serge does own it, Hol," pointed out Chassa.

"I know," I growled. "But I don't like to think of you and him.... in my room."

"Don' worry," said Chassa. "I only went in there with a bucket, when Serge was fixing your radiator." She managed a smile. "I know he won't leave Sophie. I'd never ask him to."

"But as long as you're working here, you'll be around him," I said. "How long are you going to keep that up?"

Chassa sighed. "Right mess I've made of things. A career waiting tables, a bloke who's already attached, and a friend who's turned out to be a liar and a thief."

"But you're brilliant," I exclaimed. "Look what you did today in court." I stood up. "I'll make some tea. There's a couple of other things I want to talk to you about. The *Lycée*, for one."

Chassa smiled properly. "OK, Hol." She got up with something like her old energy.

I nodded. Now to start the clearing up.

22.

Mrs White, In The Ballroom, With Enough Rope

"Well, well." Vicky Tessier poured herself more coffee. "Maryline Guilbaud, running off to Paris to be a singer."

We were sitting in the staffroom at lunchtime. I wasn't teaching that week, as my pupils had exams, but I'd come to the *Lycée* anyway.

"Patrice called the police," I said. "But Chassa reckons that, even if they find her, he won't get his takings back."

"Is Chassa back working in the café?" asked Vicky.

"Yes," I began. Just then little Arielle, the lab assistant, walked in.

"I have not stopped all morning," sighed Arielle. She sat down and grasped the coffee flask. "And still I have to tidy the laboratory."

"I can help you," I offered. "I have no lessons today." I hadn't even heard from Madame Silvain that week. Normally she called without fail each Sunday to arrange a time for her English lesson, later in the week.

"*Tu es gentille*, Holl-ee," said Arielle, gulping down her coffee.

I'd never been in the laboratory. It looked smarter than our old science lab at school. Although I'd hated science lessons, so I'd largely blocked the memories out of my mind. (There was probably a scientific term for this sort of psychological barrier, but I hadn't hung around long enough to learn it.)

"It is kind of you to help me, Holly," said Arielle, closing the door behind us.

"Well, I've been meaning to talk to you," I said. "About why you paid the little boy to throw paint over me."

Arielle stared at me.

"I know it was you," I said. "The little boy, Roch, came to see me afterwards, to say sorry. He said the lady who paid him was wearing a *blouse blanche*. At the time, I didn't know a *blouse blanche* was a

223

lab coat. It was only when my friend Gilles explained that a *blouse de travail* was overalls, or working clothes, that I found out what a *blouse blanche* was."

I looked at Arielle. "But I was not your target, was I? It was Chassa you were out to get. You saw Chassa putting up the ladder outside the café. You told Roch to throw paint at the girl from the café. He got me instead of Chassa."

Arielle turned away, but I hadn't finished.

"You sent me those nasty text messages. But they weren't intended for me. They were for Chassa. You'd found Chassa's mobile phone number in the school records. But you didn't know she'd given her old mobile to me." I stared at Arielle. "And you seemed so nice, at first."

"You are sick, Holl-ee," said Arielle.

I caught her by the sleeve of her *blouse blanche*. "You have hated Chassa ever since she slapped you, in front of your colleagues."

Arielle's face flushed.

"She had only to mind her own business," she spat.

"Chassa liked the headmaster's wife," I said. "So when you began bragging about your affair with the headmaster, Chassa shut you up. And then your boyfriend sacked her."

Arielle narrowed her eyes.

"At the Christmas dance," I added. "Monsieur Chevalier had no *compagne* on his arm. But you were hanging around him all evening. At the time, I did not know that you were his mistress."

There, I'd said it. I'd felt a bit of a muckraker, grilling Vicky and Chassa about the headmaster's affair and subsequent separation from his wife, but I'd found out the truth.

"Tell me," I said. "Does Monsieur Chevalier know that it was you who spoiled the wine?"

Arielle snorted.

"You were standing near the table when I went off to dance," I said. "You put something in the wine. With one of those little droppers that you use in the lab."

Arielle rolled her eyes. "Frankly, Holly, you are ridiculous."

"Frankly, Arielle, that wine was good before it was poured into the glasses," I said. "My pupil Matthieu drank some that afternoon, before the dance. And when the guests complained about the taste of

the wine, it was you who opened a fresh bottle and nearly vomited."
My turn to roll my eyes. "Nice acting, Arielle. You deserve a *César*.
You thought it was Chassa's wine, didn't you? You saw her carrying
the boxes into the school. I wondered why Chassa didn't speak to
you, at the time."

I felt like a detective at the end of a mystery novel. All I needed
was the drawing-room audience admiring the use of my little grey
cells.

"I have heard enough of your wild accusations," said Arielle.

"Only two more," I said. "The rotten meat in the pram. That was
nasty. How did you know about Chassa and the baby that died?"

Arielle's mask slipped for a second.

"Angeline," I said. "Your boyfriend, the headmaster, has taken
you to dine with the Mayor, and his sister, Madame Vallentin. You
will have met Angeline there. And she repeated the rumour about
Chassa killing the baby."

"You make some serious allegations," said Arielle, dangerously
calm.

I laughed. "Why did you send me that telegram, telling me my
father was dying?"

"I did not send a telegram," said Arielle.

"Enough," I said. "Or Chassa and I will go to the police. Your
pupils and their parents, they will all read about it in the newspaper."
(I wasn't sure such a thing was legally possible, but enjoyed saying it
anyway.)

Arielle pushed past me and marched out of the lab. She'd go
straight to her boyfriend. Well, let him sack me if he liked. The
school year would be ending in a few weeks' time, so I'd be leaving
anyway.

The next morning, I slipped into the *Lycée* via a side entrance,
rather than risk an awkward meeting with the headmaster. There was
a phone in the library. I'd get Séverine to show me how to dial an
outside line, then I'd be laughing. (Although not loudly, of course.)

I left the library, unable to keep the grin off my face.

"Holly." A deep voice addressed me. I stopped in my tracks and
looked up to see Gilles.

225

"You have won your court case?" asked Gilles.

I went pink. I'd forgotten to phone him.

"I have finished my last exam," said Gilles. "You would like a lift home?"

Great idea. Soon we were in Gilles' boxy little car, heading to town.

"So you went to the tribunal," prompted Gilles.

"Yes, but it was complicated," I said. "I had to reveal the name of a secret goldfish."

It felt good to hear Gilles laugh. He must be light-headed after finishing his exams.

"Gilles, would you like to come to the café?" I said. "We can have an ice cream. Chassa will be there. I have good news for her."

"*D'accord*," responded Gilles.

He'd said yes. I'd have done a dance if I hadn't been wearing a seatbelt.

"No place to park," observed Gilles, as we neared the café. "Step out here, Holly. I will park the car, then I will join you for the ice cream."

An ice cream together. Just him and me. I beamed, nodded, opened the car door and stepped out.

I rushed into the cafe. "Chassa!" I called. Wait till she heard what I'd found out.

No answer. But the front door had been open. Chassa must be upstairs.

"Chassa!" I shouted, racing up the stairs. I could hear her moving about, in her room.

"Chassa," I said, pushing open the door. "You'll never guess."

I just had time to leap out of the way as something came flying towards me. I yelped as Chassa's heavy wooden table crash-landed, inches from me.

What was going on? I stared across the room at the woman facing me.

It wasn't Chassa. It wasn't Milou, either.

And it wasn't Arielle.

23.

Jack Hughes

It was Madame Silvain. Her face was flushed.

"Did we arrange a lesson for today, Madame?" I was bewildered.

"Lesson?" shrieked Madame Silvain, seizing Chassa's radio. I jumped out of the way as it flew past my head.

"Madame?" I was astonished. "Is it your homework?"

Madame Silvain's face contorted. "The homework!" she shouted. "All we wanted was a grandchild."

Either my hearing was going, or my brain was. I stared at her.

"We invite you to our home," howled Madame Silvain. "We welcome your friends. And you have ruined my life."

"Madame." I fought to keep calm. "What is this story of a grandchild?"

"Your friend," shrieked Madame Silvain, her face crumpling. "She has promised us that we can have her baby."

My mouth fell open. *Milou.*

"She told us of your idea," Madame Silvain shouted. "She said you had suggested that we could bring up her baby. We kept it secret, as you wished. We did not even go to the hospital with her, but you went with her every time, so we knew all was well –"

"What?" My turn to shriek. "I never went to the hospital with Milou."

"She told us about it," insisted Madame Silvain. "How you went with her and you told her to ask us for money in advance –"

"Milou lied to you," I seethed. "In any case –" I looked straight at Madame Silvain – "to sell a baby, it is illegal." The phrase rolled off my tongue, clear, fluent, and spectacularly the wrong thing to have said.

"You seek to blame me?" Madame Silvain was shaking so much, her chandelier earrings were wobbling.

"Madame," I said, moving towards her, "come downstairs. We will talk."

227

But Madame Silvain pushed me away and clambered on to Chassa's balcony.

"Madame!" I shouted, rushing to the window. "*Rentrez.*"

Madame Silvain was looking down at the traffic. Oh, no, please, no.

I edged on to the balcony behind her. She didn't move.

I reached out and put my hand on her shoulder.

Madame Silvain whirled round, grabbed me and pushed me back against the balcony railings. I tried to wriggle out of her grip, but she held me with surprising force.

"Madame." I had to keep a clear head. Not easy when someone is bending you backwards over a balcony, with a street full of traffic below.

The railings bit into my back.

"Madame," I said, breathing hard. "Let's go inside. We can find Milou in Paris and get your money back."

"Money!" howled Madame Silvain. "You think it is all about money?" She gripped me tighter.

From the street, I heard a shout. I twisted my head and glimpsed figures moving in the street below. Oh, praise be. People had seen us. Somebody would come up here and help me.

I turned my head as far as it could go. People were standing in the street, looking up at us. And doing nothing about it.

Right, said my inner voice. *If no-one will help you, help yourself.*

I glanced at Madame Silvain, then looked back down at the street.

"Eliane!" I shouted to the onlookers.

Madame Silvain loosened her grip. It was all I needed.

I broke free, then grabbed Madame. Bearing down hard, I pushed her head through the railings. She gasped and struggled, her large earrings clanking against the metal.

I stepped back, my legs shaking.

"Holly?" The voice came from inside Chassa's room.

I turned and ran into Gilles' arms. I was still there when the police arrived.

"*Oui*," Gilles nodded at the policemen. "It was I who called you."

"But I was the one who pushed Madame's head between the railings," I added, anxious that there should be no misunderstanding. "Will you call the fire brigade?"

"*Non, mademoiselle*," replied the policeman. His colleague had removed Madame Silvain's earrings and was coaxing her head out of its restraints. Both *agents* seemed more amused than shocked. I wasn't looking at a long stretch after all. Unlike Madame Silvain's neck.

Madame Silvain wept as the policemen escorted her down the stairs. I half wanted to comfort her, but held back. Getting involved in the Silvains' family problems had landed me in this trouble in the first place.

"It was self-defence, Hol," said Chassa, pouring me more tea. "The woman nearly pushed you off the balcony. You've got witnesses."

"Including Patrice." I nodded at that gentleman. The warm tea and the huddle of Gilles, Chassa, Didier, Serge and Patrice around a café table had revived me. "I bet you were down there, taking bets on who'd fall first."

"I saw you, Holly," said Patrice. "I came outside to see what the people were looking at. But I did not intervene, in case she pushed you off the balcony."

"Oh, you thought you'd wait until she'd done it?" I snapped. "I could be lying splattered on the road, now."

"*Mais, non, Holly*," said Patrice. "The dustmen would have swept you up."

Chassa went into the kitchen and returned with a container of ice-cream and a bowl.

"Have some of this, Hol," she said, plonking the *sorbet-citron* down in front of me.

"Listen to the First Aider," teased Serge.

I glanced at him, then at Patrice. Had Patrice ever wondered why his father spent so much time at the café?

"She'll get help, Hol," said Chassa, handing me a spoon. "They'll send her for treatment, most likely."

"She kept saying how grateful she was to me for all I'd done," I said, not even touching the ice cream. "I thought she meant the English lessons. Lin and Owen told me she was doing white lacy knitting. She was getting ready for the baby."

"I should have been up there with you," said Chassa. "Together, we could have squared her."

"Chassa, no," I said. "You can't stay in your room all day, in case a nutter turns up to attack me." I wasn't having Chassa heaping yet more guilt on herself for turning her back at the wrong moment.

The telephone rang. Chassa jumped up and went to answer it.

"Are you going to eat that ice cream, Holly?" The wistful note in Didier's voice gave me the first laugh I'd had that afternoon.

"Holly," called Chassa. "*Elle arrive,*" she told the telephone receiver. I took it, wondering who this could be.

"Mademoiselle Holly." I could hear the agitation in Monsieur Silvain's voice. Sharp words formed on my tongue, but I swallowed them.

Monsieur Silvain poured out his story. His wife, disappointed by her two children, who had no desire to settle down and give her grandchildren. Then this young girl, pregnant, but willing to give away her child.

"My wife only thought of the baby," Monsieur Silvain assured me. "She was persuaded that we could give the child a better life than she would have had, otherwise."

She. Milou must have told them the cushion up her jumper was female. Owen had mentioned the pink bedroom.

"My wife would not have hurt you," Monsieur Silvain assured me.

Easy for him to say. He hadn't been the one holding on to the railings for his life.

The café door jangled open. I quickly told Monsieur Silvain I had a customer to serve. Hanging up, I saw that the 'customer' was none other than Vicky Tessier.

"Miss Holly," teased Vicky. "What have you done this time? Chassa says the police have been here today."

"Long story," I said, glancing at Gilles.

"Séverine Stern asked me to pass this on to you," said Vicky, handing me a large brown envelope. I couldn't suppress a grin as I realised what the contents must be.

"Holly was really brave," Chassa told Vicky. She ran through the story. I exchanged smiles with Gilles.

"You have had some strange times here, Holly," remarked Vicky. "You will go home with a very bad impression of the French."

"Not all bad," I said, risking another smile at Gilles.

"That Milou," growled Chassa. "And Arielle. Did you hear about that, Vicky? Arielle was the one who put stuff in Holly's wine, at the dance. And she paid this kid to throw paint over Holly."

"And she sent me nasty text messages," I added. "Except they were meant for Chassa. And all because Arielle was fooling around with the headmaster. I wondered why you all used to go quiet, when he came in the staffroom."

Vicky laughed. "We could hardly say, Monsieur Chevalier has come to see his mistress. You might have slapped her, like Miss Chassa."

"Give over," said Chassa. "She kept bragging about the jewellery he'd bought her. I thought she had some nerve."

"You knew his wife, didn't you?" inquired Vicky.

Chassa nodded. "Met her at the *Lycée*. She always made the effort to talk to me."

"The only thing I can't work out is that telegram," I mused. "Arielle wouldn't say why she'd sent it."

"Telegram?" asked Gilles.

"The day after the Christmas dance, I got a telegram," I explained. "It said my dad was ill, so I was to come home at once. Only it was a hoax."

"Oh, I sent you that," laughed Vicky. "I thought you ought to spend Christmas with your family. Well, I must be off. Don't eat too many *crêpes*, you won't fit into your flag." She breezed out.

"Can you believe it?" I raged.

"She meant it for a joke," said Chassa. "French people have a strange sense of humour. The times I've gone to the cashpoint, and some French person standing nearby has told me it isn't working, when it is. And if you ask two shop assistants which one's the manager, they'll point at each other."

231

"But telling me my father was dying," I growled.

"The telegram only said he was ill," said Chassa. "She must have meant you to phone home straight away, and then feel so relieved, you'd go back and visit them."

"It is not only the French who have a strange sense of humour," remarked Didier. "I remember once, when I cooked dinner, someone offered to wash up. I became suspicious, knowing them quite well. And when I followed them into the kitchen, they were hiding the dirty plates in my fridge."

"I only did it once," argued Chassa. "Stay for a *crêpe* and I'll let you hide all our dirty plates in the dishwasher. You will stay too, Gilles? And Holly?"

"Yes," I said. "Back in a minute."

While Chassa was handing menus to the boys, I slipped out to the back yard with my mobile phone.

"Mam?" I said. "Bit of drama today. This woman went mad and blamed her problems on me. It was real *J'accuse* stuff."

"Well, write us a letter about it," said Mam. "Don't waste your money on phone calls."

"I'll write," I promised.

"Aye," encouraged Mam. "And tell us about this Welsh feller."

"What Welsh feller?" I was mystified.

"This Jack Hughes you were saying about," said Mam. "Right, enough of your chopsing. Get and write that letter."

I rang off, smiling.

Back at the table with the boys, I asked Chassa for a *Crêpe Paysanne*. "But without mushrooms, Holly," Didier advised me. "You have had enough excitement already, today."

I munched away as the boys chatted about leaving school and doing military service. Gilles talked about his plans to do the two-year equivalent to military service – *la co-opération*.

"Maybe they will send me to Africa," he said.

"That will not be fun," averred Didier. "Ask for the Caribbean."

I thought Gilles would be ideally suited to manoeuvres on the mountains of South Wales. With frequent leaves of absence, to be spent drinking tea and going for long walks with a local student.

"So what's in this envelope from Séverine, Hol?" asked Chassa, after the boys had left.

"Look at this," I told her. "You won't believe it."

Chassa took the papers and studied them. I watched, gleeful, as the light dawned on her face.

"Hol!" exclaimed Chassa. "So this is why – "

I nodded.

"This stuff is Semtex in Times New Roman," said Chassa, poring over the documents.

"We'll go round there tomorrow and sort it out," I said. "I checked the address with Didier, now just."

"Will he answer the door himself?" I murmured to Chassa as we stood at the gates, the intercom buzzing.

"Probably got servants for that," replied Chassa. "With a bit of luck, he'll be out running the town, and we'll get *Mademoiselle* to ourselves."

The intercom crackled into life.

I made my request, trying to sound pathetic. That would get her.

Sure enough, the glossy white front door open and out stepped Angeline, in a white T-shirt with a sweater flung over her shoulders.

"*Tiens.*" She raised her eyebrows. "Holly and Charlotte. You wish to speak to me about teaching?"

"If you have a moment, Angeline." I injected a note of pleading into my voice. Angeline smiled. Now she'd have a chance to put one over on me, in front of her old school adversary.

"I can't promise to help you, Holly," she drawled. "Not after the way you betrayed Madame Vallentin's trust."

Beside me, Chassa stiffened. I shot her a glance. *Not yet.*

"You'd better come in," said Angeline. "We can sit out on the patio."

"Grêt, Angeline," said Chassa, breathless with sincerity. "Is that a backyard, only without the coalhouse?"

I shook my head at her. We didn't want to get thrown out. Not until we'd done the job.

Angeline led us through the Mayor's home, pausing so we could admire the furnishings.

"Vitalina, *du sirop, s'il vous plaît,*" Angeline called to the dark-haired woman who was dusting in the conservatory. I grinned at Chassa. She'd been right about the servants.

Fair play, Francis' garden was fantastic. A lawn the size of a park, trees in blossom, bushes and flowers. I fought the impulse to go and explore it. We had business to take care of.

"You want my advice on teaching?" asked Angeline, inviting us to sit at a white table. "Well, you could begin by not revealing the school's confidential business. And, in your case, Charlotte, behaving like a civilised human being, if possible."

"This is nice, Angeline," said Chassa, looking around. "Madame Vallentin got a nice garden as well? Those CDs of her teaching *Méthode* must bring in a few euros."

"Madame Vallentin's finances are none of your concern," said Angeline, coldly.

"Perhaps not," said Chassa. "But they do concern Mrs Barbara Seed. Remember her, Angeline? Our old French teacher, from school. Used to give you private lessons on weekends, so you could keep up with the rest of the class. Is that where you learned the *Méthode*, Angeline? And copied it, to use on your own pupils?"

"What are you talking about?" Angeline stared.

"That's why Madame Vallentin sacked me, wasn't it?" I asked. "Because I mentioned the *Méthode* in my story for the Western Mail. It wasn't because she was worried that other people might read about her teaching method, and copy it. It was because she'd copied it from someone else."

"From Mrs Seed, to be exact," added Chassa. "Mrs Seed showed you the first drafts of the book she was writing, on teaching English to the French. You must have been a good pupil. Learned the method off by heart, didn't you?"

"I don't –" began Angeline, then lowered her voice as the smiling housemaid brought a jug of water, a bottle of sirop and three glasses to the table. Chassa and I chorused our *mercis*.

"Your Aunt Maggie told me the lot," I said. "About the summers you spent in France, teaching English to French students. She boasted that you hadn't needed to do teacher training, because you'd had a good teacher at school."

"A teacher who'd devised a good method," said Chassa. "Holly and I wondered why that *Méthode* had so many references to places in Wales. You don't get many English language textbooks teaching French kids how to travel to Brecon. Usually they talk about Buckingham Palace and the Tower of London."

"Ridiculous assumptions, Charlotte," said Angeline, pouring *sirop* into her glass and adding water. I thought her hand shook a little.

"We can always contact the schools where you used to teach," I pointed out. "Your Aunt Maggie told me their names. And Mrs Seed will confirm that you used to help her teach the foreign students who were visiting Wales."

"Yeah, I'm looking forward to talking to Mrs Seed again," said Chassa. "These school reunions can be fun, can't they, Windowlene - er, Angeline?"

"As for proof," I opened the brown envelope and drew out some photocopied documents. "My friend Lin works in a library. I asked her to check for details of language teaching publications written by Mrs Barbara Seed. And Séverine, the librarian from the *Lycée*, double-checked from over here." I passed the documents across the table to Angeline.

"Séverine is going to order a copy of Mrs Seed's teaching manual, for the *Lycée* library," I said. "I'm paying for it. My parting gift to the *Lycée*. The French courts will be interested in the strong similarities between Mrs Seed's method and the Vallentin one."

"Think of all those CDs the Vallentin school has sold," pointed out Chassa. "Mrs Seed will be able to claim a fair percentage of the profits, once we've proved that she's the real inventor of the *Méthode*."

"This won't do the Mayor any good, either, when the story comes out," I added. "His sister, a plagiarist and a thief. The press will have a field day with that, before the next election."

Angeline sat silent for a moment.

"What is it you want?" she asked in a tight voice.

"Madame Vallentin pays Holly what she owes her," said Chassa. "And that *Prud'hommes* case gets settled out of court. Otherwise, Mrs Seed gets a package in the post and the name of a good solicitor."

"Blackmail?" Angeline tried to look scornful but couldn't quite manage it.

"Just a warning," said Chassa. "Oh, and your name would come up in court as well. Then you really would have to worry about who read the *Western Mail*. Suppose someone sent your boss a copy?"

"I think you should leave," said Angeline, icily.

"Mmm," I agreed. "We've got to go to the bank. Put a certain envelope in a safe place."

"Oh, and Angeline," said Chassa. "If Madame Vallentin wants to stay in business, tell her to make some changes to that teaching method. Like all the content. Coming, Holly?" She led the way back through the conservatory, through the Mayor's lounge, to the front door and down the drive, without looking back at Angeline. I followed, hurrying to keep up with Chassa.

"Should we put the envelope in the bank?" I murmured to Chassa, as we closed the Mayor's gate behind us.

"Probably wise," said Chassa. "At least, 'til that Vallentin woman coughs up what she owes you. I can't go today, though, I said I'd clean the cafe this afternoon."

"Chassa," I hesitated. "Have you told Serge that I know about him and you?"

"I went to see him yesterday," admitted Chassa. "Told him it was over. Don't worry, Hol, we didn't go in your bungalow. We stood in the garden, with Gran Chazalet watching, through the window."

"Didn't Gran ever suspect anything?" I hadn't thought of this.

"I don' think so," replied Chassa. "I don' reckon she thinks of Serge as a human being. He's just there to fetch her *eau de vie*, and move her chair out of the draught. See you later, Hol."

As I walked down Serge's garden path towards the bungalow, my mobile rang.

"*Allô?*" I murmured. Please, not the Silvains again.

"Chassa!" bellowed a voice. "Been tryin' to get 'old of you this long time."

"I'm sorry, this isn't Chassa's number," I said.

"Oh, sorry," said the voice. "Hey, tha'ss not Holly, is it?"

"Yes," I said, surprised. "Who is this?"

"Dunno if you remember me," said the voice. "I came round your house once, for New Year. This is Sion."

24.

The Past Is Another Postcode

"Chassa!" I shouted, bursting into the café.

Chassa turned. "Can't talk now, Hol, the rush has started." She smiled at the lone customer. I held myself back until she'd taken the order, then followed her into the kitchen.

"One *Paysanne* for Table 3, Patrice," said Chassa, tearing the slip from her order pad and handing it to him. "What's up, Hol? That Vallentin woman been bothering you? Tell her we've got a photo of Brecon bus station."

I took a deep breath. "Chassa, Sion just rang me. When you were away, I thought you'd gone to see him. So I phoned Griff and asked him to get Sion to ring me."

"Your brother Griff?" Chassa looked at me.

"He works with Sion, remember?" I told her. "Griff said Sion was away in Scotland. But he's back now. And, Chassa, he said, last night, he had a cup of tea with Granny Chappell!"

"Wouldn't surprise me," said Chassa, rinsing her hands under the sink tap. "He's always going up the cemetery with a flask. He says it helps him think up team tactics -"

"No!" I shouted. "Not up the cemetery. In her house! Granny Chappell isn't dead!"

Chassa swung round.

"That *For Sale* sign you saw on Granny Chappell's house," I gabbled. "She's selling the top floor. She's had it converted into a flat, cos she can't manage the stairs any more. She's going to live downstairs, and sell the top half of her house."

"She's not dead?" Chassa said.

"No," I said. "Sion says she's asking why you haven't written. She says if you've been out till ten o'clock eating chicken sandwiches again, there'll be trouble – "

Chassa leapt at me, grabbed my head with her wet hands, and screamed so loudly, Patrice dropped his spatula.

"*Merde!*" he began, but Chassa had let go of me and jumped on him. I couldn't help giggling at the sight of Patrice fighting off a delirious Welsh octopus.

"Oh!" Chassa let go of Patrice and wiped her face with her hands.

"Let me serve that *crêpe*," I told her. "You'll frighten the customer." It felt good to be the bearer of good news. Although Patrice's pinny might never recover from the experience.

"When are you going to phone her?" I asked Chassa, once our customer had left.

"Well, she has a sleep after dinner," explained Chassa. "And in the evening, there's always summat on at chapel. Chicken sandwiches indeed, she goes out more than I do."

"Chassa," I said. "You don't want to ring her."

Chassa looked at her daps.

"My dad goes round there sometimes," she said. "Once, on the phone, she said he was there, so I hung up."

I stared. "I thought they never got in touch with you?"

"They ask Sion about me," admitted Chassa. "I've told him he's allowed to say I'm OK and working, but that's all."

"Chassa." I was stern. "You said they hadn't been in touch."

"They haven't written," admitted Chassa. "But I've had the odd message filter through. Usually bad news, like when Andy crashed his motorbike."

"Andy?" I asked.

"My little brother," said Chassa. "See him on two wheels and you'll know why they need zebra crossings by there. But I get the good news, too. That Gaynor left Russell, a couple of years ago."

"You're missing out on their lives," I exclaimed. I pictured myself staying in France, getting snippets of news from Lin. Hearing about Griff's wedding or Dad's retirement. Just thinking about it, my throat tightened.

"Chassa, ring your Granny." I wasn't having any arguments. "Now. And tell her you'll call back tonight, when your Dad and your brothers can be there."

I thought Chassa was going to turn on me, but she smiled, still shining with the news.

"Got it all worked out, haven't you?" she said. "The touching reunion. Tears flowing down the phone. I don' think so."

"I'm not taking their side," I said. "But your Granny won't be around forever. Families." I sighed. "Mine have been a pain before, and they will be again. But I've realised they'll never change. We're never going to agree on everything. The main thing is to make the most of what we do agree on."

"Easy to say now," grinched Chassa. "Wait till you get home."

"If it was easy, everyone would do it," I said. "But you wouldn't have to live with them, if you went back home."

Chassa eyed me. "Go back to Wales?"

"You're wasted in this job, Chassa," I said. "You should be acting, communicating."

Chassa's eyes were suddenly wary.

"Tell me," she said. "What if your Kim had been minding a child that died?"

"He's not my Kim," I said firmly. "I had second thoughts about him. And since then, I haven't given him, er, well, a second thought."

"Gilles, then," said Chassa. "Imagine you've gone to see Gilles one evening, and next thing you know, an ambulance is screeching down the road and *papa-maman* are yelling that it's his fault for taking his eyes off the baby, and yours for distracting him. Would you still be friends with him?"

"Yes," I said.

Chassa was silent. Of course, she'd had a friend with her on the night she'd been babysitting. A male friend.

"You mean Sion," I said. "But he's still friends with you."

Chassa didn't seem to have heard this.

"And your family," she asked. "They think like you, do they?"

I started to say that they were reasonable people, but decided it was better to tell the truth.

"Praise be, it's never happened in my family," I admitted. "But if it did, I think they'd realise there was no sense in blaming the babysitter."

"And your brother?" asked Chassa.

"Griff?" I was surprised. "Oh, he's the sensible one. No, Mam and Dad can't complain about Griff."

"Would he stick by his friends?" asked Chassa. "If something like that happened?"

I blinked. Strange question.

"Of course he would," I said.

"Funny," said Chassa. "I never heard from him after that night."

My jaw almost hit the floor.

Griff? But he hardly knew Chassa.

Or did he? My mind raced back to when Griff had first mentioned Chassa. *"She went to school with Sion. A lot of Sion's friends used to watch him play rugby."*

"Griff was at your house that night?" My mind buzzed.

Chassa sighed. "Yes. His first visit. I used to see him at the rugby, when Sion played. He was really funny. Told me about his family. That's how I recognised you, when I first met you – you look like Griff."

I remembered it now. That first meeting with Chassa and Didier, after the cinema. Chassa looking at me: *"Yep, you're Holly all right."*

"Why didn't you say you knew Griff?" I demanded.

"You'd have asked too many awkward questions," said Chassa.

"So what happened that night?" I had to know.

"We were talking, having a drink," said Chassa. "Least, I was. Griff didn't want alcohol. Said he always fell asleep on the settee after the work Christmas party."

"You brought that up, once." It was coming back to me. "When we came home after the wedding reception. You talked about me falling asleep after parties, but then you said it wasn't me. I thought you were just rambling drunkenly."

Chassa sighed. "Well, anyway, we were talking, and then I nipped upstairs to check on the baby. And then... it was Griff who rang the ambulance. Russell and that woman came home, and went beserk. I told Griff to go home, and asked him to ring me another time. But he didn't ring. And then I went to France."

"Should I tell Griff you've told me this?" I asked. "I'll keep quiet about it if you want me to."

"I dunno." Chassa sounded tired. "No point raking up the past."

"You'll ring your Granny then?" I urged.

241

"Tonight," promised Chassa. "Although she might be at choir practice."

"She goes to choir?" I was impressed.

"She's always sung," said Chassa. "When she was younger, her teacher wanted her to have her voice trained, but she didn't want to. She used to joke that she couldn't sing on stage, with a name like hers."

"What was wrong with her name?" I asked.

"Her first name's the same as mine," said Chassa. "She thought it was awful old-fashioned, though. Said you couldn't be a singer, with a name like Charlotte Chappell."

"You look happy, Mademoiselle Holly," the school secretary greeted me as I entered her office.

"The exam results are out today," I explained. "I have come to see if some of my pupils have passed their exams."

"Ah." *Madame la secrétaire* nodded. "Gilles LeBrun? Yes, he has his diploma."

"*Merci*," I said, going pink. Even the staff were gossiping about me and Gilles.

The *secrétaire* looked amused. Before she could add anything, the headmaster's office door opened. I flinched. Arielle was bound to have gone running to Monsieur Chevalier after I'd confronted her. Now he'd rip into me.

But it was not the headmaster who emerged from the office. Instead, a tall, dark-haired lady appeared, and closed the door behind her.

"*Vous avez besoin d'autre chose, Madame?*" The secretary was obsequious.

The lady had noticed me.

"*Mademoiselle Holly?*" she said.

"*Oui*," I said, wondering if she was one of the teachers. She looked vaguely familiar.

"Teaching at the *Lycée*, that pleases you?" asked the lady.

"*Beaucoup, merci*," I said, digging around in my memory. Had I poisoned her at the Christmas dance?

"Madame Chevalier," begged the secretary. "May I take your new address?"

242

The lady took the pen from the secretary and began writing on a card.

Madame Chevalier, I thought. The headmaster's wife. I didn't remember meeting her. Yet she seemed to know me.

Madame Chevalier set down the pen. "Please note that the postcode has changed," she told the secretary.

"Oui, Madame." The secretary couldn't do enough for her.

Madame Chevalier thanked her, and to my surprise, beckoned to me. Intrigued, I followed her out of the office, into the corridor.

Madame Chevalier closed the office door behind us.

"I have wondered how you were progressing at the *Lycée*," she said. "You were looking so hard for a job. I knew you would do well here."

I still couldn't work out who she was.

"You have met me when you arrived in Mauvoisins," said Madame Chevalier. "But I see you do not recognise me."

My mind raced back to my early days in Mauvoisins. Trudging round schools, looking for work. Going back to the women's refuge.

I stared. "You are Valérie. The lady from the refuge."

"My marriage was ending," said Valérie. "I needed a place to stay. Mademoiselle, I would be grateful to you if – " She nodded towards the office.

"I will say nothing about meeting you in that place," I promised. I couldn't stop gazing at her. With her glossy dark hair and glowing skin, she looked completely different from the careworn mother I'd met in the refuge.

Valérie smiled. "You have many qualities, you Welsh girls. I knew your predecessor, Mademoiselle Chassa. Very loyal to her friends."

"You have found a home, now, Madame?" I asked.

"With the children, we are installed in our own house," said Valérie. "My divorce is on the point of being finalised. And you, you still live at the café?"

I blinked. "How did you know I lived at the café?"

"You have told this to the lady in charge of the refuge, before you moved out," said Valérie. "That is how I contacted you, to inform you of the job vacancy here at the *Lycée*."

"It was *you?*" I was doing a fine impression of Cousteau the goldfish.

Valérie nodded. "Mademoiselle Chassa lost her place here for defending me. It seemed right that I should direct another Welsh girl to this job."

I didn't know what to say. Valérie smiled at me.

"*Bonne continuation, Mademoiselle Holly.*" She turned and walked through the *Lycée* front doors, out to the car park. I watched her go, eyes wide. That headmaster. Choosing the malicious Arielle over someone like that.

"If Gilles LeBrun has passed his exams, then he is no longer a pupil at this *Lycée*," pointed out Séverine. "You know what that means."

I sighed. "It means I will not see him any more."

"*Non,*" Séverine corrected me. "It means you are no longer his teacher."

I hurried to the window. The library overlooked the *Lycée* car park.

"Gilles," I called, rushing up to the car.

Gilles turned, his car keys in his hand.

"Umm, I congratulate you on your diploma," I said.

Gilles smiled, equable as ever.

"Have you plans for the summer?" I asked him.

"I will help my parents on the farm," said Gilles. "And do the *vendanges* in the summer, as every year." He grinned. "They do them in Wales, too? With the ambulance men present in the field?"

"Welsh wine is good," I retorted. "You know who poisoned it." I stopped short. This could be the last time I'd ever see Gilles, and I was scolding him.

"Holly!" A shout went up from behind me.

I turned. Normally, I was pleased to see Benoît and Matthieu. Now was not one of those times.

"Holly," said Matthieu. "You have not gone back to Wales yet?"

"You are in a hurry to be rid of me?" I managed a smile.

"You must come to see our race," said Matthieu. "We will do a Parkours, around the town, in July. We will help people in wheelchairs to get around."

"People in wheelchairs?" I was astonished. "How will they get from roof to roof?"

"*Non*," said Benoît. "They will not run with us. But we have learned that there are not enough ramps in the town centre to help people in wheelchairs to get into to buildings. We have contacted the authorities about this. We will put posters everywhere. Everyone will know why we are running."

"And then they will construct ramps for the handicapped people," explained Matthieu.

"Great idea," I said. "But how did you know about the lack of ramps?"

Benoît nodded at Gilles.

I turned back to Gilles. "You thought of it."

"*Bof*, it is the clinic," explained Gilles. "Where my nephew gets treatment. When you see the problems people have, getting around in a wheelchair..."

I looked at him fondly.

"*Bien*, we must go," said Benoît. "We will be late."

"Late for what -?" began Matthieu. Benoît nudged him and ushered him away.

I turned back to Gilles. No time for maidenly reticence. Soon he'd be gone.

"Here is my address," I said, tearing paper from my diary. I scribbled Mam and Dad's address on the paper and handed it to Gilles. He smiled and put it into his jeans pocket.

I turned my head away. He wouldn't write. He'd meet a young country girl. Something gripped me inside as I pictured them spending long summer evenings chasing an ox around a field.

"...our barn, but we have converted it for visitors," Gilles was saying.

"*Uhh, pardon?*" I asked.

"We have room for visitors," said Gilles. "On our farm. If you come back to see the Parkours race, come and lodge with my family. Call me, and I will come and fetch you from Mauvoisins station."

I just had enough breath to thank him. Gilles got into the car and reversed out of his parking space. I watched as he drove away.

When Séverine appeared, eyebrows raised in question, I couldn't speak for smiling.

25.

And They All Lived

"Your *apéritif*, Madame." I walked out of the kitchen into the backyard sunshine.

"Thanks, Hol," said Chassa, taking the mug of tea. I sank into the deckchair beside hers, moving my handbag so I could stretch out my legs. A moment to bask in. Warmth, sunlight, the scent of pancakes wafting from the kitchen.

"Fair play, Hol," said Chassa. "Without you, things wouldn't have turned out like this."

"That's right, put the fault on me," I teased. "Are you and your family friends now?"

"We're talking," said Chassa. "Dad's mellowed a bit, and the boys have been OK. Sion says he don' know what to do with himself, now no-one needs him to carry messages."

"Tell him to join the Post Office," I said. "Everyone's fed up with Emlyn. They reckon he's filling in the postal votes himself, these days. Don't tell Angeline, that's another method she'll export."

"Have you heard from the Vallentins again?" asked Chassa.

"Not since I got the cheque for what they owed me," I said. "All helps with the student loan. It'll be weird, being a student again."

"It will be for me, and all," remarked Chassa.

"Essays and tutorials and – " I broke off. "For you?"

Chassa grinned. "A couple of months ago I applied to a drama course in Cardiff. Attached a clip of *Père Noël*. They interviewed me over the phone. I kept quiet about it, cos I didn't have much hope. But they've offered me a place, starting in October."

"Chassa!" I exclaimed. "That's brilliant. But won't you miss France?"

"I'll go back in the holidays," said Chassa. "Rabbit'll keep a mattress on his floor."

"He can come and visit you," I suggested.

"He can afford to, now the cable TV station's bought *Père Noël*," said Chassa. "I won't be in it, I'll be in Cardiff. But Patrick will play Father Noël. He's wondering how he'll cope with fame. You'll have to interview him. That'll show your Kim."

"He's not my Kim," I grumbled. "You know, I think that was why I liked Kim in the first place. Because he'd done it, he was writing for the papers, and that was what I wanted to do. Only I didn't know it. Does that make sense?"

"None at all," Chassa assured me. "But what do I know, I fell for my boss' dad. And when I ended things with him, he was all right about it. Didn't even grab my throat and swear that if he couldn't have me, then nobody could. Men! Hopeless."

She paused to drink her tea. "And your Gilles. Driving off into the sunset without you."

"At least he didn't say *adieu*," I defended my absent Frenchman.

"Enough of that old French, now," said Mam, appearing at the kitchen door. "I'm putting the tea. Pancakes, now my girl is home." She beamed. "Griff'll be back from work, now in a minute."

"Oh?" Chassa sat up. "I'll help you set the table, Mrs Gethin." She jumped up and rushed past Mam, into the kitchen.

"There's a nice girl," approved Mam. "Lucky you had her with you, over there. Helped you out when you got yourself into a mess."

I smiled. No point in getting annoyed.

"Now we can all get back to normal," said Mam. "You've been to that old France, and seen it. And now you're home."

I got up. And reached for my bag, with the ticket inside it.

"Grêt," I said.

- The End -

248

Printed in Great Britain
by Amazon

81013333R00145